"Nick?" she whispered, terrified and thrilled at the same time

Jordan reached out one finger to touch his soft bottom lip. Yep. He was still there, tangible and 3-D. "Wow."

"Do I know you?" he asked.

He narrowed his eyes, boldly surveying her from top to bottom, making her feel warm under his intent gaze. And more turned on than ever. She didn't feel free and saucy anymore in her miniskirt and camisole. Instead with her skirt scrunched up and covering almost nothing, Jordan felt indecent, naked, exposed.

"I thought——" He broke off and then started again, pulling his eyes away from her body to focus on her face. "You seem very familiar to me. But surely I'd remember if we'd met before."

"Only in my dreams," she said without thinking. The vivid memory of the lovemaking in those dreams was making her heart beat fast. She smiled. "You don't know how glad I am to finally meet you, Nick."

Closing her eyes, she tangled her arms around his neck. She held on tight, enjoying the feel of his arousal, so amazingly *right*. She'd been with him many times in her fantasies. All the things she associated with Nick came flooding back. Comfort, belonging, destiny…

And sex. *Oh, yeah.*

Blaze™

Dear Reader,

When I was asked to be part of the PERFECT TIMING miniseries for the Harlequin Blaze line, I was eager to jump in. I have always loved time travel. There's something romantic and exciting about characters leaving their old world behind and leaping into somewhere dangerous and different.

It didn't take me long to choose turn-of-the-century Chicago, with the lovely White City of the 1893 Columbian Exposition and World's Fair as a backdrop.

Like my heroine Jordan, I studied history, with "Scandalous Women" such as Catherine the Great and Marie Antoinette showing up in my favorite classes. I love the idea of someone like Jordan—perfectly normal in her own time, longing to rock a few more boats than she really does— hitting Victorian times with a bang!

I tossed Jordan into the White City alongside Nick Tempest, who is himself chafing to break free of the restrictions of wealth and privilege of his time, and upped the ante by sticking them both under a shockingly beautiful marble arch carved with sexually charged images. For Nick and Jordan, the arch's erotic powers are impossible to resist.

Scandal, sex, art and romance… Sounds like the stuff history is made of!

Happy reading!

Julie Kistler

SCANDAL
Julie Kistler

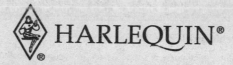

HARLEQUIN®

TORONTO • NEW YORK • LONDON
AMSTERDAM • PARIS • SYDNEY • HAMBURG
STOCKHOLM • ATHENS • TOKYO • MILAN • MADRID
PRAGUE • WARSAW • BUDAPEST • AUCKLAND

ISBN-13: 978-0-373-79272-6
ISBN-10:   0-373-79272-7

SCANDAL

ABOUT THE AUTHOR

Julie Kistler is well-known for her fast-paced romantic comedies for the Harlequin Temptation and Harlequin Duets lines. Now she's excited to be writing for Harlequin Blaze—and flirting with the past in *Scandal,* part of the PERFECT TIMING time-travel miniseries. "I love a challenge," this former RITA® Award nominee exclaims with a grin. Julie and her husband live in Illinois. Check out Julie's Web site at www.juliekistler.com.

1

How to Be a Scandalous Woman, Rule 1:
Throw out the rules.

JORDAN ALBRIGHT'S OFFICE DOOR creaked open. "Professor Albright? Can I ask you something?"

Without even looking up from her laptop, Jordan said automatically, "No, Catherine the Great did not have sex with a horse. And, no, Marie Antoinette was not a 'major ho-bag,' as somebody put it last week." She smiled as she glanced at the young woman hovering in the doorway. "Anything else you want to know, you'll have to come to class. And I'm not Professor Albright. Just Jordan, okay?"

But the student lingered, shifting her weight to her other platform sandal. "How did you know what I was going to ask?"

Jordan tried to be patient. "It's not hard. I'm only teaching one class this semester. Scandalous Women 101. Everybody wants to know the same thing."

"And you're sure Catherine the Great never, you know, *did it* with a horse?" the girl persisted.

"Yes, I'm sure." With that, Jordan turned her attention back to the display on her computer screen, trying not to be frustrated by this latest in a series of interruptions.

"Thanks, Professor Albright." The student ducked into the hallway, already moving on.

"Come to class, okay?" Jordan called out after her. This time she didn't bother to correct the "professor" thing. At twenty-six she was only a few years older than some of her students, so she kind of enjoyed being called "professor" every now and again, even if she hadn't really achieved that status yet. Nope. Just a lowly grad student. A lowly grad student working desperately to get her PhD sooner rather than later.

Jordan heard footsteps patter down the wood floor of the hallway as the student departed.

Thank goodness. Now if only she could concentrate long enough to figure out a decent ending to the damn dissertation that had been plaguing her for the better part of four years.

Ending. Right. She wiggled in her wooden chair, twisted her long, dark hair into a loose knot, stared down into her laptop screen, and tried to focus. Focus.

Methodically, she scanned the outline that formed the spine of her project, which centered on one particular scandalous woman. She'd begun with her subject's childhood and family life, moved on to her education and an important trip to Europe, and then dealt with her artistic influences and the effects of wealth and privilege on her development.

She had everything in order, everything perfect, step by step, up to the point that Isabella Tempest, notorious sculptress and the subject of this blasted, never-ending dissertation, had vanished from the pages of history. It was what made Isabella so fascinating and yet so frustrating, all at the same time.

Jordan frowned. The story of a talented artist who'd

created the work of a lifetime—a magnificent marble arch brimming with erotic nudes—and then up and disappeared should've been the perfect topic for someone involved in the study of scandalous women. It should've been a piece of cake. But how could she fully analyze Isabella's place in history without knowing what had happened to her after the big whoop-de-doo that ended her career in June of 1893?

There had to be something she'd overlooked. Jordan tried to put herself in the right frame of mind to puzzle it out. "Okay, so it's June 1893," she mused. She pulled up a picture on her laptop, a wide shot of the Columbian Exposition and World's Fair in Chicago. "The White City is open for business."

It was called the White City because of the magnificent, bright white buildings built just for the fair, all gleaming under a dazzling display of electric lights. Famous politicians, dukes and princesses, the cream of society, artists, writers and inventors, citizens from far-off lands including belly dancers, gondoliers and a tribe of alleged cannibals, as well as regular Joes off Chicago's mean streets, had all come together to see the wonders of the new age and celebrate the 200th anniversary of Columbus "discovering" America. Buffalo Bill, Susan B. Anthony, Teddy Roosevelt, Thomas Edison… Anybody who was anybody was there. With Isabella Tempest right in the middle of it, kicking up a huge scandal.

Jordan stared into space, imagining herself in the middle of the White City. It wasn't hard. It had happened practically on her doorstep, and the Midway Plaisance, the long, grassy area where the Ferris wheel and hot-air balloon and other popular attractions had sat, was still part of the University of Chicago campus.

Besides, the Chicago World's Fair had been the event of the century, so there were thousands of photographs and souvenirs of the place. Jordan had plowed her way through stacks of them since she'd started this dissertation. She'd even bought herself a coin on eBay, a commemorative half-dollar sold at the fair with Columbus's face on one side and one of his ships on the other, and she'd kept it on her desk for good luck ever since.

"I could use a little luck right now," she murmured, pushing papers aside to get to the cup where she kept it. Quickly, she found her lucky coin, held it tight and closed her eyes, picturing in her mind what it must've been like at Chicago's turn-of-the-century World's Fair.

The shining White City. Blue skies. A breeze off Lake Michigan. The world's first Ferris wheel twirling in the background. Art and treasures from around the world. And Isabella's outrageous arch.

Jordan opened her eyes. Ah, yes. The cool white marble arch, etched with figures of Greek gods and goddesses *in flagrante delicto*. Once displayed at the exposition, the piece had created a huge triumph and an even huger scandal. And then both of them—Isabella and her fabulous, scandalous arch—had simply vanished. Not one more word about their whereabouts, not in newspapers, magazines, books, journals, diaries... It was one thing for a woman to go missing. But how did a six-foot marble arch evaporate into thin air?

It was infuriating. And it had kept Jordan stuck for months. If only she could think of some new way to look at the facts.

"So Isabella creates the most sensual, most beautiful thing she's ever done," Jordan said out loud, spinning around in her chair to glance at the wall behind her desk, where she'd taped up pictures of all things Isabella

Tempest, including a poster-sized representation of the sculpture in question. "Her masterpiece."

Even in a poor re-creation like the sketch on her wall, the arch looked fantastic. And fantastically sexy, with all those nubile, naked marble bodies wrapped around each other, and all those women in the midst of ecstasy. Jordan couldn't help getting a little flushed every time she gazed at it.

She moved closer. Yes, the arch was a stunner. No question. Her finger traced a figure of Apollo on the upper curve of the sketch, where his mighty, muscular thighs pinned Daphne against a laurel tree. In the myth, Daphne had turned into a tree to escape the god's advances, but here, carved into Isabella Tempest's risqué arch, Daphne was clearly enjoying herself, tree or no tree. Head back, mouth open, nails raking Apollo's back, she looked as if she were in mid-climax, and a pretty steamy one at that.

"Isabella certainly knew how to heat things up," Jordan said with a shiver, her gaze sliding around the arch. "Daphne and Apollo up against the tree, Psyche blindfolded with Eros behind her, Artemis on top of Orion... Whew. Each one is hotter than the last."

Isabella had carved sixteen images like that, the extremes of pleasure and passion, up front and unashamed, into the pale, creamy stone. But all that flesh and all that ecstasy had apparently put Chicago society blood pressures in overdrive. And Isabella Tempest under arrest.

It was hard to pull herself away from the erotic power of the arch, but Jordan forced herself as she mentally went through the story one more time. Methodically. Dispassionately. Like a scholar.

"So Isabella gets a coveted spot in the Women's Building at the Columbian Exposition," she said out loud, looking for something, anything, she might've missed. "The World's Fair officially opens on May 1, but Isabella and her arch aren't there. Not finished, presumably. Sometime between then and June 16, she puts her arch in the Women's Building. And then, on the sixteenth, suddenly there's an uproar when society matron Mrs. Prentice Stanhope takes Susan B. Anthony on a tour of the building and one or the other catches sight of Isabella's 'indecent' creation. Shame, horror, outcry, all that good stuff. Isabella is arrested and then she and the arch vanish, never to be heard from again."

Jordan perched on the edge of her desk, gazing at the sketch, reflecting on what a shame it was that Isabella had only had time to make one masterpiece. Genius like that should never have been stifled.

"But where did it go?" she asked with an edge of frustration, tossing the Columbian half-dollar back into its cup with a loud, disappointed clink. "Where did Isabella go?"

She reached onto her desk, picked up and put down three large binders, crammed full of notes about Isabella's life, and riffled through a stack of folders containing information she already knew. She chewed on the end of a pen. She went back through her outline.

But there was nothing. No spark of inspiration. Just like every other time she'd tried this exercise.

She'd already tried to leave it with an ambiguous "we'll never know" ending and it just didn't work. It was like admitting that she was a failure when it came to research and analysis.

"Maybe I am a failure. Maybe that *is* the answer," she grumbled. She wanted to scream.

Finally, giving up, Jordan dumped the whole pile of folders back onto her desk and yanked open her desk drawer. She knew what she wanted, what she needed. It was getting to be a habit. She skirted away from words like *addiction* and *obsession*. It wasn't so bad, was it? To feel better because she could look at the two small pictures?

His pictures.

"Nick," she whispered, feeling a rush of relief just to look at him. "If you're going to keep driving me crazy like this, the least you can do is send me a psychic message from the Great Beyond to tell me where Isabella and the arch went. C'mon, Nick, help a girl out, will you?"

If only he could. She'd already spent far too much time examining every grain of the two existing photos of Nicholas Tempest, and she hadn't gotten any answers yet. But that didn't stop her from trying. She'd even made one of the pictures her screensaver, which meant every time she was stuck long enough for her laptop to go dark, she ended up gazing at Nick, daydreaming about him and drifting even farther away from working.

It was odd how attached to those photos she was. Nick Tempest, the man in the photos, who just happened to be Isabella's older brother, was only peripheral to her dissertation. But for some reason, Jordan kept finding herself coming back to him, somehow convinced that this man was the answer to every question she had, if only she stared at his picture long enough.

It was bizarre. It was unlike her. She'd never been one to sigh over rock stars or movie idols or sports heroes, not even when she was twelve. When her high school friends had swooned over Johnny Depp or Tom Cruise, she'd just rolled her eyes. No attraction there. Not even a flutter. How strange that Nick Tempest was her first fantasy crush, and he'd been dead for 110 years.

She'd stumbled over his photos on eBay when she went

searching for background on the Tempest family and their department store. Nick was one of the founders of Tempest & Trent, a stylish store that still sat, grand and imposing, in the exact same spot on State Street it'd occupied since 1894. In fact, Tempest & Trent had always been her favorite department store, and she and her grandmother had come to look at the Christmas windows every year when she was little. Funny she'd never wondered about its founder, not until she saw those pictures on eBay.

But once she saw them, she was determined to have them at any cost. Which meant she'd paid a small fortune and then agonized by the mailbox every day, waiting for the photos to arrive.

Even though she'd scanned them into her computer to use with her dissertation, she still kept the originals in her desk, safe inside small plastic sleeves. That made it easy to take them out and look at them if she needed to, which she'd found herself doing more and more often lately.

There was just something about Nick. Something that got under her skin, inside her brain, deep inside her fantasies.

"My dream lover," she whispered.

The first picture was ordinary enough, a sepia tone wedding portrait, with the words "Mr. & Mrs. Nicholas Tempest, May 1894," scrawled in spidery handwriting on the back. The other was a more candid shot, showing him standing next to an early version of an automobile. That one was marked simply "1895." He was unsmiling, even a little grim, as he stood next to his new wife in the first photo, and grinning with health and happiness in the second, but hot as blazes in both.

"It's not just the hotness factor," she argued to his picture, feeling a shade defensive to be this gaga over a guy she knew only from a couple of old photos. But the hotness factor was hard to deny. She whispered, "Okay, so you *are* totally hot."

Totally. Amazingly. Overwhelmingly.

Maybe it was just that she'd spent so much time looking at sketches of that damn arch, with all its salacious imagery, and in her mind, Nick Tempest had become part of those steamy couplings. She didn't want to think about it or admit to herself just how deep this went. But it was deep.

Almost immediately after she'd found his pictures, she'd started to have dreams about him. Erotic dreams. *Extremely* erotic dreams. Like nothing she had ever known. They always involved the positions and stories from the arch, and they always involved Nick.

In the first one, Nick was playing Apollo and she was Daphne, and he was naked and hard and taking her up against a tree. She could remember how vivid the images were and how potent the clash between them. As he thrust into her, slamming her into the hard trunk again and again, as she wrapped her legs around him and took him deeper, she knew she hated him, she loved him, and mostly she wanted him so bad that it didn't matter. It was plain, straight-ahead, no-frills, banging-up-against-the-wall sex, and it blew her mind.

She'd awoken in the morning, sweaty and exhausted, wondering if she was going to find splinters in her bottom from the tree. That's how real it was. But there were no splinters, just rumpled sheets and a sleeping boyfriend. He'd been studying late and spent the night at her place, and she hoped she hadn't thrashed or moaned too loudly, giving away just what kind of dream she was having. But he was oblivious.

And the dreams went on.

A few nights later, with Daniel, the boyfriend, safely in his own apartment, Jordan had dreamed that she was Artemis to Nick's Orion. Since in that story she was the goddess and he was the mortal, this time *she* was in charge, riding him for hours, teasing him, denying him, and then taking what she wanted and demanding more. And when she woke up, she'd actually felt as thoroughly sated as if she *had* been romping all night with a warrior.

Uh-oh. Not good. Remembering the dreams, staring down at Nick's picture, Jordan felt heat and moisture rush to her core. She squeezed her thighs together, willing the tingling to stop.

Now it didn't even take the dreams, just the *memory* of the dreams, to push her to arousal. In the middle of the afternoon. In her office! And that just couldn't be.

"Damn you, Nick," she said out loud. "First you came around, haunting my dreams, boinking me silly, and then you *don't* come into my dreams. I'm turning into a crazy person!"

This part had to be sheer frustration. While the visions were coming every night, she looked forward to going to sleep, just to meet and stoke the fire with her dream lover, eager to find out whose myth they'd be acting out tonight.

Until a week or so ago, when the dreams stopped. No nightmares, no fantasies, no Nick. Clearly, it was the disappointment over losing her dreams that was making her even nuttier than she was before, even more obsessed.

Jordan gulped and sat up straighter in her chair, deliberately putting the photos aside. "It's not my fault. It's just…stress. Stress over not finishing the dissertation."

But she grabbed the photographs back before they'd even left her hands. She couldn't *not* look.

So handsome. So mesmerizing.

In the first picture, the wedding portrait, he stood tall and starkly handsome, in an immaculate long, dark coat with a stiff white shirt and white tie, with a small flower pinned to his lapel. Nick's posture—shoulders back, chin up, facing square into the camera—was comfortable, assured, maybe even arrogant. Next to him, his new wife looked remote and unremarkable.

Jordan chewed her lip. Who cared about the wife? She was doing her best to block out the fact that he'd even had a wife.

"That's bizarre," she chided herself. "Why should you care if a guy from 1893 was married? For all you know, they were the love story of the century. Or he was a jerk, or she was a saint, or…"

But she did care. Because, in her heart, she was having a love affair with him, and she didn't want him to be married.

For whatever reason, she felt completely connected to Nick. She'd known from the moment she'd spotted those pictures on eBay that he was important to her. The over-heated dreams only made that more obvious.

And that was why she continued to moon over his photos during the day, and then toss and turn at night, hoping she could reach the dreams where the two of them tangled together, naked and aroused, in the very positions depicted on the arch.

"The dreams have stopped. So let's not even think about them anymore," she said quickly. But she couldn't stop thinking about them, not when she looked into his face in the pictures. It was that face that haunted her fantasies.

His features were beautiful, with high cheekbones, dark brows, a slightly crooked nose that gave him character, and perfectly shaped lips, a little fuller on the bottom. She really liked the look of those wide, sensual lips, with the hint of a dimple on one side. She remembered tasting and nibbling those lips in her dreams. She remembered those lips trailing fire up her thigh...

"Okay, not thinking about that," she ordered herself, squirming a little in her hard wooden chair. "Not!"

But if she didn't look at his lips, then there were his eyes. They were so intense and compelling, pinning her, pulling her in, hypnotizing her. They weren't exactly safe, either.

The other photo was a little less sharp, but even more attractive, because he was smiling. Hatless, with his dark hair tousled by the wind, he looked carefree and adorable, as if his whole life were ahead of him and he couldn't wait to jump right in.

It made it that much more affecting to realize he'd died just a few months after it was taken. The more attached she became to Nick, the more tragic that seemed.

"I feel like I know you inside and out, Nick," she said softly, fingering the hard angle of his jaw in the small photo. "And you know me. Like it's always been that way. But why?"

She'd felt guilty taking time away from her main research into Isabella and the arch, but she'd done it, anyway, to glean more details about Nick. Not that she'd managed to find much. She knew when he was born and married and when he died. She'd read about his travels to Europe with Isabella from reports in the society columns at that time, and it sounded as if the brother and sister were fairly close. But when he got married to Lydia Trent, and when he died just a year after that in, of all things, America's first car race, his beloved sister wasn't there. Not in the list of wedding guests, and not in the list of mourners at his funeral. She wasn't even mentioned in his obituary.

"Do I keep staring at you because it seems weird your sister didn't come to your wedding or your funeral?" Jordan questioned aloud. "Or because it's so hard to think about you dying just a year after your wedding?"

Or because he was handsome and tragic and amazingly hot?

"Or because I am one crazy, mixed-up chick," she whispered. "Because fantasizing about a guy who's been dead since 1895 is not exactly sane."

"Jordan?"

Recognizing the voice, she looked up, hastily shoving the photos back inside her drawer as Daniel edged into her office. Daniel. Her boyfriend. Sort of her fiancé. Really just her boyfriend, though. And she needed to get a grip and stop thinking about Nick and the tree and his thighs and her thighs and his lips and his…

Yeah, time to get a grip.

2

How to Be a Scandalous Woman, Rule 2:
Gossip is great. It's when they're not talking about
you that you have to worry.

1893

NICHOLAS BONAVENTURE TEMPEST was bored. Bored down to the soles of his fine leather boots.

Alone in the third-floor music room of his family mansion, leaning back with his feet propped on a wooden table, Nick aimed and then tossed a souvenir Columbian Exposition half-dollar into an empty china cup he'd set on a piano stool about five feet away. Clink. In again. Just like the past eleven times he'd played this game. After an even dozen, he supposed he ought to move on.

Not for the first time, he reached for the brandy decanter at his elbow. He'd already had quite enough to be thoroughly sloshed, but in the mood he was currently in, there just wasn't enough liquor in the world. Tedious dinner parties, tedious women, tedious conversation… Even his father's best Napoleon brandy wasn't enough to make that nonsense palatable.

"Ah, well. I'm done with it for one more night, at any rate." He saluted himself with his glass. "Until tomorrow."

"Nick, darling, it's already tomorrow," his sister, Isabella, noted sweetly as she swept into the room.

Nick sat up straighter. One look told him something was up. Trouble was pretty much the norm with Isabella, but the sparkle of mischief in her pretty blue eyes was even more ominous than usual. He hoped she hadn't fallen in love again. He didn't need to get into any more fights defending Isabella's honor. Not that there was any honor left as far as he could tell, or that she cared. Still, a good fistfight might provide a diversion.

"Are you just getting home?" he asked. "A bit late, isn't it?"

"Not for me. I don't believe in living my life by the clock. Besides, you're hardly one to talk," she pointed out. "You're the one who has to make an appearance at the store bright and early."

"Don't remind me."

Isabella was clearly too wrapped up in her own good mood to pay attention to his gloom. She discarded her cloak and gloves, dumping them on a nearby music stand. "It's not my fault you've become such a respectable citizen. I warned you time and again that Father would turn you into a drudge if you let him."

"I'm hardly a drudge. I run the place."

"You're a drudge. And you're much too good for that."

She began humming some cheery tune, dancing around in her loose artist's smock, the kind she always wore over her gowns when she was working on a sculpture. That explained why she was coming in so late. When she was in the middle of a project, she didn't notice anything else. It did not, however, explain her good spirits. Ever since she'd come home from Europe, Bella had been moody and unhappy about her future as a sculptress.

Spinning around to look at him, she set her pretty face in a pout. "Play something on the piano for me, will you, Nick? You're so much better at it than I."

"And wake up the entire household? I don't think so."

"Not just a drudge but a shriveled-up old prune," she mocked him. "I want the old Nick back. My dashing brother, always running off after some fast woman or fast horse. *He* would've played me a tune in the wee hours if I asked him."

"One of us had to grow up," he commented dryly. "It certainly wasn't going to be you."

She shrugged. "I hope I never grow up. It's quite disgusting."

Nick managed a smile. Lightly he said, "If everyone in this family were an *artiste* like you, you'd have no pretty dresses, there would be holes in our shoes, our stomachs would be empty, and we'd all be living in a shack in the middle of the woods."

"You stole that from Father. I've heard him say that a hundred times."

"Yes, well, he's right. Don't waste your time worrying about me. I've decided that if it's my destiny to mind the store, at least I'll do a good job of it." Nick purposely changed the subject, both because he was bored with that one and because he was still trying to figure out what mischief Isabella was up to. "What are you working on, Bella? Haven't seen much of you lately. Must be something big."

"Not that big," she murmured.

She unbuttoned her smock and tossed it on top of her cloak, revealing a frilly green dress with a nipped waist and the huge, pouffy sleeves that were all the rage. Isabella might consider herself a rebel and an artist, but she still liked to wear the latest fashions.

"Did you hear that, Nick? The grandfather clock in the hall just rang five. That means it's not late. Why, it's positively early. Almost time for you to do your duty and report to the store to play Lord High Pooh-bah." She raised an eyebrow as she picked up his still-burning cigar resting in a cut-glass ashtray. "Mother will have your hide for smoking up here."

"Mother never comes up here," he said coldly, rescuing the fine Cuban before she snuffed it. "Besides, cigars are a mere misdemeanor in the record book of my crimes."

"Ah. Ducked out of the Trents' dinner party early, did you?" She made a sympathetic face. "Father won't like that. He's determined to deliver you to Lydia Trent all wrapped up like a Christmas package."

The idea sent Nick straight to the brandy decanter again. "Yes, well, he has visions of a department-store dynasty. Tempest & Trent, purveyors of fine luxury goods, a step ahead of anything Marshall Field can come up with." Nick scowled, knocking back his drink. "All he needs is for me to marry Lydia."

"So that's what's got you up here at all hours, swimming in brandy and cigars? The specter of a future hog-tied to Lydia Trent?"

"I suppose. It was a dreadful party. Dreadful people. I stayed approximately five minutes past dinner before I pleaded a headache and got out of there."

"And then what?"

Putting aside his drink for the moment, Nick swung his legs off the music table and took a long puff on his cigar. "And then what, what?"

"Well, you can't have escaped from the Trents and come right here. You'd have been drinking for, oh, the past seven hours. Even you don't hold your liquor that well."

"I checked in at the club, played a few hands of poker,

won an outrageous amount of money, tried again to convince Freddy Montgomery to sell me his new horse, tried again to convince Freddy Montgomery to buy my old carriage… It's so dull, I'm boring even myself." Nick tried not to sigh. "Someone's got to find something more interesting to do in this town or I'm going to lose my mind."

"Face it, Nicky," his sister said, fingering the strings of a violin no one ever played. "You're just not cut out for the workaday world. You need to take me to Paris again. We're overdue for an adventure."

He eyed her warily. "When are you going to tell me what your new project is?"

Her lips curved into a very smug little smile. Now he *knew* he was in for trouble. "I don't know what you mean."

"I mean whatever it is you're working on that has you so excited. So excited you lost track of time and came wandering in at 5:00 a.m. with your hair all disheveled and smudged like a chimney sweep."

"Nonsense. And it's not new. If you must know, I've been working on it forever," she said saucily, her smile widening. "That's why I'm excited. I'm finally finished, Nick. I've finished my masterpiece."

It was his turn to raise an eyebrow. "I take it you're not talking about another statue of my hand."

"It's an excellent hand, but I've moved on to bigger projects."

"Such as?"

Isabella giggled, covering her mouth with one hand. He didn't like the sound of that. Finally, she whispered, "I don't think I should say."

"Why not?"

Her glance skittered away from him. "Maybe I want it to be a surprise."

Nick narrowed his eyes. "How big a surprise?"

"About six feet."

The same height as a man. Oh, no. Not again. When she was studying in Italy, Isabella had done several nude torsos of one of her beaus. When she brought the pieces back to Chicago, they'd set every tongue in the city wagging. Now he suspected she'd moved on to the entire body of a naked man, complete with genitalia. Maybe Nick could convince her to add a fig leaf…

"Who's your subject?" he asked. He wasn't sure which would be worse—an anonymous naked stranger or someone recognizable by Chicago society. If she'd sculpted the son of a prominent family without his trousers, the entire Tempest family might have to pick up and move far, far away.

"Apollo, Zeus, Eros…" Her words trailed off dreamily. "They're all there. And they're spectacular."

He allowed himself a sigh of relief. Greek gods didn't sound so bad. Representing them in stone was quite popular, as a matter of fact. Except… Except he knew his sister. "What have you done with these Greek gods? Are they clothed?"

She shrugged, looking pleased with herself. "I told you, they're spectacular. Stunning. I've added something new this time. I've added *passion*. Far and away my best work ever."

Given the fact that she had sidestepped his question about clothes, he could only conclude that all these Greek deities were, in fact, naked. That wasn't unusual, either, as far as classical or modern sculpture went. He'd seen enough of it on his travels with his sister to know that much, and also to know that she was fascinated by the human form.

"Is this a commissioned piece?" he inquired, trying to pin her down. "Is someone going to pay for this and hopefully whisk it away to Outer Mongolia?"

"Of course not. My art is intended to be seen. I want people to experience it, to feel and change because of it. This sculpture is definitely going to change people." Isabella swished her skirts as she began to pace back and forth. "I'm counting on this piece to make my name."

"That's exactly what I'm afraid of."

She shot back, "Don't mock me, Nick. You wait and see! By morning, when it's on display, people from around the world—artists and collectors and scholars—will be smitten. I wouldn't be surprised if potential patrons waving huge sums of money were breaking down my door tomorrow, begging me to create pieces just for them."

"Where?" he asked suspiciously. Isabella had no gallery, no studio, where buyers could see this supposed masterpiece. "Where is it on display?"

After stewing for a moment, she confessed, "It's at the Women's Building. At the fair."

"But I thought…" Nick stubbed out his cigar. "I thought they didn't want you there."

"Well, they didn't." She shrugged again. "But Mother got me in."

Isabella and their mother had argued about this very subject for months. The last Nick had heard, Mother wasn't budging and was not going to use her influence as a member of the prestigious Board of Lady Managers to find a spot for Bella's work, specifically because she didn't approve of her daughter's preoccupation with nude male torsos or female faces with a lascivious look in her their eyes. So far, thank goodness, Isabella had not combined the strapping males with the provocative females, because that would…

"Good God, Bella, you didn't."

All innocence, she inquired, "Didn't what?"

"What exactly is the theme of this work, this masterpiece with all the Greek gods and goddesses? Have you named it?" he asked impatiently, standing up and advancing on her.

"It doesn't have a name yet, actually. Maybe you can help me with that, Nick." Eagerly, she perched on a stool near him. "At first I thought I would call it *Erotikos*, but then I thought perhaps *Sexdecim* would be the right name. It has an intriguing ring to it, don't you think? It's Latin, though, and I'd prefer Greek, since my figures are Greek."

"*Sexdecim* just means sixteen," he told her. "How can the same statue fit either *Erotikos* or *Sixteen?* Good Lord." He'd just had a horrifying thought. "You're not sculpting erotic sixteen-year-olds into a statue, are you?"

"Heavens, no." Isabella twirled the other way on her stool, avoiding his eyes. "It's not exactly a statue, anyway. It's an arch. I've intended it as a stand-alone work, something like a mantel for one's fireplace, but much more beautiful than that. It's marble. I love working in marble. It's so unforgiving, and yet so stunning if you get it right. Father had a fit, of course, since it was also wretchedly expensive. But I think it was worth every penny."

"Sixteen?" he prompted.

"Oh, about the sixteen. Yes, well, there are sixteen couples on my arch. Sixteen pairs of gods and goddesses. So…"

"Couples, you say?"

That whole *Erotikos* thing was becoming clearer. And more unpleasant, all at the same time. Sixteen couples on an arch, all carved to look lusty and sensual. Bella wouldn't have done that. Not after their mother had put her own reputation on the line with the ever-so-lofty Lady Managers to push her daughter's work into the Women's Building. Isabella might be foolish, but she would never abuse their mother's trust and good name, would she?

Of course she would. With a sense of dread, hoping against hope that the sixteen couples were merely *looking* erotic and not *acting* erotic, Nick asked, "What are your gods and goddesses doing, precisely?"

"It's a depiction of the mythology for each of the couples," she explained. "So, for example, Apollo and Daphne are depicted wound 'round a tree, while Perseus and Andromeda are chained together. I was rather proud of that. Using the chains, I mean, since she's chained to a rock in the myth." She sighed deeply. "The chains give so much more urgency and tension to that particular coupling."

"Coupling?" he echoed. That sounded so much worse than mere *couple*. "You have all of these Greek gods in the midst of *couplings?* You've actually thrown them together and portrayed them while they're…" How did one say this to one's sister? "While they're *in the act?*"

"Well, yes, actually." His sister—his infuriating, irresponsible, reckless sister—ducked around him to pick up his brandy snifter. She held it out to him like a peace offering. "Do you remember, Nick, when we were in Italy, and you went off to Germany to look at somebody's engine or something?"

He grabbed the brandy and knocked back the rest of it, all in one gulp. That demonstrated a reckless disregard for good brandy, but he didn't care. "The motor-wagons, yes. I spent a few days in Stuttgart."

"Right. That was when Franco asked if I'd like to see his private collection."

Nick tightened his jaw. He'd never much cared for Franco, the count his sister had carried on a brief flirtation with while they visited Rome. He'd tried to keep a careful eye on her, but it appeared he had failed miserably, if she was off looking at the private collections of oily Italian counts the moment his back was turned. "That sounds ominous."

"Not at all," she assured him. "Franco had acquired a most intriguing volume, with sketches and poetry to illustrate something called the Sixteen Positions. Apparently it was quite scandalous in the sixteenth century, and the author and artist were excommunicated and burned at the stake or drawn and quartered or something equally dreadful."

It sounded pornographic. Sixteen positions? *He* didn't even know sixteen positions, and he was a man of the world! Nick's hands clenched into fists. If Franco had been in front of him at that moment, he swore he would've knocked the count's teeth in.

"Sixteen sexual positions, you see?" Isabella said helpfully, as if he hadn't already figured that out on his own. "My inspiration was to combine those positions with characters from Greek mythology to say something about how earthly passion and supernatural power combine."

As she gazed into space, enraptured by her idea, Nick didn't know how to respond.

"It's very strong, Nick," she said dreamily. "Very beautiful. Simply bursting with lust and ecstasy and all of the things I wanted to—"

"Lust and ecstasy… You've gone too far this time," he muttered. Clearly, they never should've let Isabella study in Italy. Or get anywhere near the depraved Franco Pirelli, Conte di Bassano. "Much too far."

"But, Nick, you haven't seen—"

"I will soon enough," he growled. As he glanced around to find his jacket, he hastily redid his collar and began to tie his cravat. "Where is it? Where are you working these days?"

"It's not at my studio." She folded her arms, laying the immense puffs of her sleeves over the dainty bows on her bodice, looking defiant and stubborn, as well as about twelve years old. But twelve-year-olds didn't create artwork bursting with lust and ecstasy and the lewd sexual encounters of Greek gods.

"Where then?"

Isabella lifted her pointy little chin, so much like their mother's. "By now, it should already be in place at the Women's Building. The delivery men had already arrived and carted it up before I left. So you see it's too late for you to stop it."

This time, he didn't bother to keep his voice down. "How exactly do you think Bertha Palmer and the Lady Managers are going to respond to something like that? If your statue is one-tenth as lurid as I'm imagining it, there will be a scandal that even you can't live down."

"Nick, really," she said indignantly. "There are nude statues all over the fair. Have you seen the naked mermaids frolicking in the fountain in the Grand Basin? Perhaps you noticed one or two of the gigantic, half-draped women called Lady Victory or Spirit of Discovery or Westward Ho or whatever it is they've named them. As long as they're not real people, but some sort of symbol, nobody minds if their breasts are spilling out all over the Fine Arts Building."

"It's not the same, Bella," he insisted. "And I don't have time to discuss it with you. I have to find this monster you've created and get it out of there before anyone sees it. The Women's Building, right?"

"The fair isn't open yet," she called after him as he dashed out the door. "Not for several hours. When you see how beautiful it is, you won't be able to destroy it. It's a fool's errand, Nick!"

He ignored her. Bored no more, energized by his mission to find and do away with whatever it was his sister had created, Nick Tempest set off for the grounds of the world-famous Columbian Exposition.

3

How to Be a Scandalous Woman, Rule 3:
There are times you have to draw a line in the
sand. Any crab that crosses? Dead.

"HI THERE," Jordan managed, doing her best not to sound flustered or guilty in front of Daniel. "What are you doing here? I thought you'd already left for San Francisco."

"San Diego."

"Right. San Diego. I meant San Diego." How lame was it not to know where your boyfriend was taking off to for a week? Okay, so she was too busy cheating on him in her dreams to notice where he was going. Not exactly a good excuse. "Sorry. But I thought you'd already left."

He stood there on the other side of her desk, holding a briefcase in one hand, shifting from one foot to the other. "I canceled my trip."

"The whole thing?"

That was surprising. Daniel never canceled anything, especially not a trip like this, where he was combining a conference with a job interview. Unlike her, with her never-ending dissertation, Daniel had already finished up his PhD in economics, and now he was scoping out the best job prospects at the best universities in his usual precise and methodical way.

Looking him over, Jordan asked, "Are you okay? You're not sick or anything, are you?"

"No, no. I'm fine. I just had a change of plans."

"That's…not like you."

"I don't need to go." He gave her a small smile. "I just heard from Princeton. I'm in."

"In? You mean they offered you a position? At Princeton?" He nodded, his smile still firmly in place.

"Daniel, that's amazing. Wow. When did this happen?"

"I got the call this morning."

She blinked. "And this is the first you're telling me?"

He lifted his narrow shoulders in a half-shrug. "I needed to get my thoughts in order, come up with a plan." Propping the briefcase on the edge of her desk, he flipped it open and rustled around inside. "This will mean a lot of changes for both of us."

"So…that means you said yes?" she asked slowly.

"Of course I said yes. They were my first choice."

"Well, of course, but…" But it involved her, too. In ways she didn't even want to think about. She put that aside for the time being. "Maybe we should, you know, celebrate." She wasn't sure what she was supposed to do. Leap over her desk and hug him? Pick up the phone and get some champagne delivered? Daniel didn't seem all that excited, though. More…determined. Which was odd.

"I'd rather get things squared away first." He pulled a sheaf of papers out of his briefcase, reaching over the laptop to hand her the top sheet. "This is the schedule I came up with. I thought we could go over it together."

Princeton, changes, schedules, all pondered, decided upon, and neatly typed up and printed out, without even consulting her. Jordan felt her hackles begin to rise as she glanced down at the paper.

"You'll see," he went on, "that item one is me moving out there, item two is finding a place for us to live, and item three is the wedding. Something small, just the two of us and maybe my parents, is probably best. We could do it after we get to New Jersey, since that's so close to where my parents are. You wouldn't need yours there, would you?"

She glanced up from his list. "What? I'm sorry. What are we talking about?"

"Your parents. Our wedding. I didn't think you'd want them there. I mean, no offense, but they're sort of problematic." Daniel grimaced. "They haven't laid eyes on each other in twenty years, have they? And your father's new family with Stacey… What's the total? Four kids under five?"

He was waiting for an answer, but she was still way behind in this conversation, back where he'd said, *Item three is the wedding*…. "I'm sorry, but I'm lost."

"Your dad," he prompted. "Stacey. Four kids under five."

Jordan lifted a hand to her head, mumbling a response on automatic pilot. "Not Stacey. Michelle. Stacey was his second wife. Then Tracy. Michelle is the new one."

"Right. The thing is, both your parents are, well, kind of nutty," he told her. "Your mother would probably want to write us some erotic Ode to Fertility or something, and your dad would bring his new wife who's younger than you are, not to mention their passel of toddlers, and my parents would go through the roof. They have very specific ideas about what my wedding should entail."

She was well aware that Daniel didn't like her parents. They didn't like him, either. Or each other, for that matter. They hadn't been married very long—actually, no one was sure if they'd bothered to get married at all—and they were crazy, unconventional and high maintenance in all the ways she wasn't and Daniel *certainly* wasn't. But still… Moving to New Jersey and dealing with his parents and—

A wedding? Was he insane?

"I don't mind postponing a honeymoon till later, do you?" Daniel rolled on. "I put that down as item twelve, if you want to look ahead on the schedule."

She frowned. "Daniel, I need you to stop. This is… impossible! I can't do it."

He didn't look pleased, but he did pause at least. Finally, he asked, "Which parts?"

"All of it!"

"Why?"

"Because…" She leaned forward to push her stomach into her drawer, just to make sure it clicked shut with Nick's pictures inside. "Because I'm not ready. I'm teaching a class this semester. And I'm not finished with my thesis. You know all of that. I'm not at a place where I can leave Chicago, let alone think about weddings."

He sent a pointed glance at the jumble of notebooks and folders on her desk. "Maybe it's past time you cut your losses and moved on."

"Cut my losses?"

"Maybe you should find another dissertation topic," he said coolly.

"Dump my dissertation? Are you kidding?" First he blindsided her with this marriage stuff, and then he went totally off the deep end. "I've worked my butt off to get this far. And what I have is really good material. I'm not going to abandon it."

He shook his head. "You still don't have an ending, do you?"

No, she didn't have an ending, which he very well knew. But that didn't mean she was going to give up.

After a long pause, Daniel added, "I've been as patient as I can. But we had a plan, an agreement. I'm on schedule. You're not."

Jordan already knew the rest of it. *If you don't finish your dissertation, we can't move on to the next step of the life we've so carefully planned…. Remember, full professor by forty…*

It was the mantra he lived by, not just for himself, but for the two of them. Daniel wanted them to be the perfect faculty couple, brilliant in their own fields, moving toward the top of the academic ladder faster than anybody else. She'd thought that was what she wanted, too.

At some point, however, the whole idea had become suffocating. She thought of the scandalous women she'd studied and taught about. They would've laughed at a "full professor by forty" decree.

"Maybe I'm sick to death of living my life by a schedule," she began, thinking things through as she spoke. It was a radical idea for her, not to have a plan set down, but this whole freedom and spontaneity thing was starting to sound really good.

Daniel just regarded her balefully.

"Maybe it's time to rip up the schedules and throw away the rulebook," Jordan said with more conviction than she felt. "Maybe it's time for me to do what *I* want to do."

"When have you ever done anything else?" Daniel scoffed. "I don't know what's going on with you, Jordan. Really, I don't. I didn't want to say anything, but, well, you've been acting strange for months. I've been trying to plan ahead for this new phase of my life, all the while wondering why my fiancée is dragging her heels."

"I'm not dragging my heels. I'm just…" What? What could she possibly say to explain why she didn't want to marry him now? And maybe not later. Because there was clearly something wrong with their relationship if the sex was way hotter with her dream lover than with her real one? "I have to point out that I'm not technically your fiancée. We agreed that we wouldn't talk about marriage again until I was done."

"But you may never be done."

"I will finish, Daniel. You know I will." She stopped, not sure what to say. "I love this project. Is it so wrong to hold out for the perfect ending?"

"I don't think this has anything to do with the ending," Daniel retorted. He turned away, muttering, "That's a symptom, not a cause."

"What's that supposed to mean?"

"It means that yes, you're a perfectionist. So am I. But…" He spun back to face her, pinning her with his gaze. "You know as well as I do that there are a million ways to finish the damn thing whether or not you know where the twit disappeared to. Hypothesize that she fell off a cliff or ran away to Mexico or her family got tired of her acting out and stuck her in a loony bin or sent her to a nunnery. Go with one, argue it and be done with it. See? Problem solved."

"I can't even believe you're saying this!" She stood up, pacing back and forth in the small area behind her desk. Who did he think he was, ordering her around? And calling Isabella a twit? The two of them prided themselves on never arguing, but this seemed like a perfect time to start. "Actually, I do believe it. You never did respect anything except your own field. As if economics is next to godliness. Ha! Heaven forbid anybody else care about their own work."

He looked shocked. He wasn't used to being insulted. But she couldn't seem to stop herself.

"Numbers aren't everything, you know," she said angrily. "I happen to think that Isabella and her arch say something very important about women and sexuality. I argue in my thesis that she was the first mainstream female artist to give women orgasms. Did you know that? Huh?"

His sneer was very unattractive. "And you really think that's an appropriate topic for a *real* scholar?"

"Absolutely. Just because you're not interested in whether Victorian women were completely repressed sexually and even denied the right to their own orgasms—"

"Oh, please!" he interrupted. "We both know the reason you're not finished has nothing to do with Isabella or her pornographic arch or the repressed orgasms of Victorian women."

"What's that supposed to mean?"

"It means…" His eyes narrowed. "It means that you'll never find the right ending. Because you don't want to."

"Why? Why would I not want to?"

"Because that would mean being done with *him*."

The word *him* hung there in the air between them for a long moment. Jordan started, stopped, and started again. Finally, she hedged with, "Him who?"

"You know who! The brother. You're obsessed with the brother."

She backed away from her desk, shaking her head. Did he know? About her dreams? No, he couldn't. Keeping her dignity, she declared, "My only interest in him is because he's important to the project and hopefully to *finishing* the project."

"Why?" he snapped. "Do you think he had something to do with her disappearance? What'd he do, kill her?"

"Are you kidding? Of course he didn't kill her. Nick would never have murdered his sister!" But she broke off when she saw Daniel's triumphant expression.

"You are completely obsessed," he declared. He came around her desk, grabbed her laptop and spun it toward both of them. "See? You can't deny it. He's your freaking screensaver!"

There it was, Nick's face, photoshopped from the picture with the car. Smiling, full of life, absolutely gorgeous... She gazed down at him. *Nick...*

"Jordan!"

She jerked back to real life. "Okay, yes, of course that's him, but—"

"Don't bother," he said flatly. "You've been distracted for months. Drooling over his damn picture for months. I wouldn't be surprised if you were spending all your days writing 'Mrs. Nicholas Tempest' and 'I Love Nick T' over and over in your spiral notebooks."

Her mouth dropped open. "I don't have any spiral notebooks."

"I'm not stupid, Jordan. Or blind."

She sat down in her chair with a thump, edging her laptop back to face her, then rolling the trackball so the screensaver would disappear. Too little, too late.

"I thought we were on the same page," Daniel argued. "I thought we were so much alike. Both mature, responsible adults, crossing our t's, dotting our i's, getting the job done, making each other proud. But ever since you started this whole scandalous women kick..." He shook his head in disgust. "I just don't understand why you ever got into it in the first place. You could've studied Lincoln's boyhood or

George Washington's teeth like everybody else. You just don't fit this scandalous women thing. You are the least scandalous person I've ever met."

She didn't know how to respond to that. Somehow, it didn't seem like a compliment. Stubbornly, she avoided the whole subject, insisting, "I'm not giving up now. I just can't. I need to know what happened to Isabella before I write the end."

"And if you never find out? What then?" Reaching once more into the briefcase, Daniel pulled out a glossy trifold brochure, slapping it down on her desk, next to her hand. "This was stuck to your door. It looks right up your alley. Maybe you can even take your class to it. Looks like a real magnet for ridiculous, sex-crazed women." And then he smacked his case closed and made a move for the door.

"You're leaving?" She couldn't believe he was pushing some silly ad for a campus film fest or rock concert into the middle of their first argument and then just walking out.

"I have things to do. Plans to make." Daniel sent her one last quick look. "Push has come to shove, Jordan. *I'm* moving to New Jersey. You're going to have to decide what you want."

"I know what I want. And it's not moving to New Jersey!"

But he was already out the door and stomping down the hall. Damn him, anyway. Was it so wrong to want to finish up her beloved project before deciding what to do with the rest of her life?

"I am not dragging my heels!" she announced to the empty room. "I'm just linear, that's all. I want to finish *this* before thinking about *that*."

Liar, liar, pants on fire, mocked a little voice inside. She ignored it.

"I am furious with you, Daniel," she shouted, even though he was long gone. "You're trying to make me sound like some irresponsible, juvenile, swooning nutcase, and I totally reject that. And I reject *you!*"

Jordan Albright, irresponsible or juvenile? Not likely. She'd been valedictorian of her high school class. Her undergraduate degree came summa cum laude and Phi Beta Kappa. Everybody knew she was someone who could be counted on, who came through, who sweated the details and produced great work on time every time. Well, she saw through Daniel's transparent attempt to bulldoze her into planning a wedding and leaving Chicago. So unfair. It was all because he was jealous of the attention she paid to Isabella and the arch. And Nick.

Okay, so probably the fact that he was jealous of Nick wasn't so unreasonable, considering the steam factor of those dreams and the level of her obsession. But still…

Fuming, she glanced down at the brochure he'd left behind, noting the words "Sex Through the Ages" and "Now in Chicago!" swirling over an illustration of two marble lovers tangled in an intimate embrace. Hmm…

Not the normal college promo piece, that was for sure. *Sex Through the Ages?* What did that mean? Some kind of art exhibit, apparently.

Maybe she should go. At least it would get her out of the office and she wouldn't have to think about Daniel and his outrageous insults anymore. Besides, the picture on the cover was reminiscent of some of Isabella's work.

Jordan always followed up on any exhibit, any museum show that had anything remotely like Isabella's work. You never knew when you might stumble over a small statue or a sketch. In fact, she had a piece of sculpture, a man's hand, sitting in her living room at home. She felt sure the object was Isabella's handiwork, even if she hadn't exactly proved it yet. There was just something about the power and the passion in those elegant fingers that cried "Isabella Tempest" to her.

Although "Sex Through the Ages" sounded like a theme Isabella's sculptures would fit, a lot of late Victorian artists had worked with nudes, and the chances that this show had anything of Isabella's weren't good. "Highly unlikely," she reminded herself as she peered at the pamphlet.

"'Many periods and cultures,'" Jordan read aloud off the front. "'Lingerie, lacing and leather. Fertility icons and totems. Erotic paintings, drawings, pottery and sculpture.'"

She scanned the rest of the flyer, looking for any details about the specific sculpture in the exhibit, about ninety percent sure there wouldn't be anything of interest to her. Maybe more details on Victorian nudes, but she already had plenty of sources on that, so...

"Wait a minute," she whispered. "It can't be."

But it was.

There, on the inside panel of the tri-fold brochure, was a small picture of an arch.

An arch just like Isabella's.

4

How to Be a Scandalous Woman, Rule 4:
Leap before you look.

THE PICTURE WAS TINY, and there wasn't a lot of detail, but it was definitely an arch. Could it be Isabella's?

"Too small to tell for sure," she decided, peering at the picture. Her eyes swept over the poster-size reproduction on her wall, and then back at the tiny illustration in the brochure. They looked the same, but...

Stunned, Jordan took a deep breath. It couldn't be Isabella's arch! Not in some crazy advertisement stuck to her door. That was too easy, too weird, too coincidental. Her arch? The one that might provide the missing piece of the puzzle she needed so desperately? Showing up out of the blue?

Jordan had done all the research, looked high and low for references to the arch in every collection, every museum, every estate, leaving no stone unturned. How could it turn up like this?

It would almost be insulting if it were her arch.

"Okay, this is no time to stand on pride," she chided herself. "If there's even a tiny possibility it's the right one, I have to go. I have to find out. If this is it, there could be a paper trail to tell me where it's been all the time. Maybe all the way back to Isabella. Oh, my God." She gulped. "That would be *huge*."

Even without a paper trail, the arch would be a crucial, dramatic addition to her dissertation. Exactly what she needed to finish and prove to herself and to Daniel that she was a serious scholar.

"Art Institute, opening Friday," she read aloud.

Damn. It was only Tuesday. Maybe if she grabbed a cab and got to the Art Institute right now, she could talk her way into the gallery where they were setting up the exhibit.

Deciding quickly, Jordan pulled open her yellow messenger bag and stuffed the slim brochure in there, alongside her wallet, cell phone, PDA, keys, an umbrella, a package of gum, a small notebook, several pens, aspirin, a lip balm and all the other things she usually carried. She liked to be prepared.

But then she looked down at her outfit. It'd been blazing hot and humid all week, and she'd planned to be in the office with no appointments for most of the day, so she hadn't exactly dressed professionally. In fact, she'd thrown on clothes that made her feel more free and saucy, in the hope of sparking enough creativity to get around her dissertation impasse. Which meant she was wearing a too-short jeans skirt, a slinky camisole with a bold red-and-black print on it, and her favorite high-heeled sandals, the ones that made her taller and more confident. For a woman who believed in emphasizing brain over body, it was actually kind of a shady outfit. One not likely to convince museum officials that she was a trustworthy academic type.

She briefly considered going home and changing into something more businesslike—at least throw a jacket over the cami and change into a longer skirt—but she was too impatient. This might be *the* arch. *Her* arch. It might be a breakthrough. Finally!

Jordan had never believed in karma or fate or anything crazy like that. Never. But maybe this was the time to start.

"It can't just be a coincidence that something so close to my arch showed up in that brochure. It was meant for me," she said with determination. "It's the message I've been waiting for."

Hefting her bag over her shoulder, she took two steps toward the door. But at the last minute, she turned back and scooped up her lucky Columbian Exhibition half-dollar out of the cup, sticking it in her pocket. And then she leaned over far enough to edge open the drawer, grab the two photographs of Nick Tempest in their plastic sleeves, and carefully slide them into the bag next to the "Sex Through the Ages" brochure. It didn't make any sense to take Nick with her, but she didn't care. She wanted him along for the ride.

Jordan stewed all the way to the Art Institute on the "L", wishing the train would move faster, pulling out Nick's pictures to make sure she hadn't lost them, rubbing her coin for luck, and then checking the "Sex" flyer one more time to be sure she'd really seen what she thought she'd seen.

"It sure looks like my arch," she whispered.

But what would she do if it was? Actually locating Isabella's arch would change everything. How far back into the dissertation would she have to go if it was the right arch and it had a paper trail? What if it wasn't as magnificent as she thought from the sketches and not a masterpiece at all? What if Isabella was just a mediocre artist with a smutty arch that didn't mean anything to anybody?

What if it *did* provide the answer and she could now write the ending and that was it? Over? Done? No more Nick haunting her dreams?

Jordan closed her eyes and tried to stop herself from coming up with more questions and driving herself even crazier. "If it changes everything, maybe it'll be in a good way," she said out loud, getting a strange look from the person across from her on the train.

Finally, she hit her stop and practically ran over to Michigan Avenue, hustling down the sidewalks and then huffing and puffing up the stone steps of the Art Institute. Luckily she was a member of the Institute, so she didn't have to wait to pay. Still, she stopped at the information desk.

"'Sex Through the Ages,'" she said impatiently to the woman behind the desk. "Which way?"

"Well, it will be in the Beckwith Gallery, southeast side of the second floor," the clerk responded, "but that exhibit isn't open yet."

"Yes, I know. Thank you!" Jordan called back, already dashing for the stairs.

If she'd been anxious before, she was practically humming with impatience by the time she ran up one flight of stairs, down two long halls and into an elevator, until she was finally standing in front of the tall, imposing doors to the Beckwith Gallery. Unfortunately, the doors were closed, with a chain fastened between the handles, and a sign placed in front of them that said No Admittance During Installation Of New Exhibit.

She stopped for a minute, testing the chain, noting that it wasn't tied or secured, just dangling there. She bent closer to the crack between the doors, squinting. There wasn't much to see. It was dark and quiet on the other side.

Quickly, she made up her mind. Jordan wasn't exactly the breaking-and-entering type, but she could at least try to get in there. After sending a quick glance around, seeing no one, hearing no one, she drew back carefully on the chain.

It jangled loudly, surprising her, making her drop the end, which caused even more of a racket when it banged against the brass handle. She jumped away, all ready to act innocent if a guard came running.

But no one came. Thank goodness. After waiting for one long minute and then two, Jordan gathered her courage and sidled up to the door again. This time she pulled the chain all the way through to one side, with a fast yank, ignoring the noise. And then she grabbed the handle, tugging, expecting the doors to be bolted, wondering how she was going to jimmy the lock.

But… Her eyes widened and her hand trembled around the knob. She couldn't believe it. There, under her fingers, the handle was turning. *It wasn't locked.*

The massive wooden door creaked as she dragged it open enough to sneak through, and the sudden sound almost gave her another panic attack. She figured at this point she should be immune. She would have plenty of time later to reflect on just when she'd decided to break and enter and become a criminal. It wasn't like her at all. The usual her, anyway. So she was acting like somebody else, somebody wilder and more reckless. Too bad. For now, she was going to get into that gallery and find the arch come hell or high water.

Once the doors closed behind her, the air felt hot and stuffy. Or maybe it was fear making her overheat. It was also shadowy and dim, but she didn't dare search for light switches. She crept along, as quiet and careful as she could manage. The only thing she heard was her own heartbeat, pounding in her ears.

Jordan sneaked farther into the gallery, peering into corners, her eyes adjusting to the dim surroundings as she tried to figure out if there was any rhyme or reason to what was where. There were no guards, no museum staff puttering around, just paintings and pottery here and there, some unopened crates and boxes, and quite a few placards already in place on brass stands, detailing the exhibits to come. She saw parts of "The History of the Condom" in one room, and a display of phallic-shaped household items recovered from the ancient city of Pompeii in another.

"Who knew Pompeii's patron god didn't wear pants?" she asked out loud. Every piece of art devoted to him was all about his huge, erect penis, right out there in the open. It seemed the citizens of his town celebrated his amazingly large asset with all sorts of things shaped in its image. There were spoons, cups, vases, jewelry and more penis-shaped wind chimes strung up than seemed reasonable. They tinkled when she walked by, as if they were happy to see her.

Jordan backed away from the Pompeii exhibit, only to find herself up close and personal with a series of gorgeous Japanese woodcuts depicting women having sex with sea monsters.

"I guess I'm in the right place," she murmured uneasily. This was definitely all about sex. Everywhere she looked. Sex, sex, sex. It was making her a little dizzy.

Under other circumstances, it might've been a fascinating exhibit and she might've been able to switch gears into Jordan Albright, Academic, so she could look at it objectively, without all the funny feelings. Hot, lightheaded, starting to perspire…

"They really need some air conditioning in here," she muttered. Sure, blame it on the lack of AC.

She raised a hand to swipe at the moisture on her forehead, reminding herself fiercely that she was on a mission, a *professional* mission, and she needed to block out all the salacious etchings and naughty bits of pottery if she was going to find the elusive arch before anybody noticed she was there.

As she turned into a larger room, she noticed tall statuary shrouded in white drapes. It created an eerie mood, with giant, looming figures casting deep shadows into the rest of the space. She reached out to test the edge of a drop cloth.

And a hand touched her elbow.

Jordan jumped about a foot, shrieking something indecipherable, as she spun around to face the intruder. She raised two fists in the air, prepared to act menacing.

But all she saw was a small, older man in a uniform, with wisps of silver-gray hair escaping from under a smart military cap. He sort of looked like Captain Kangaroo in that uniform. He was even smiling kindly. Nobody scary. She set her hand over her pounding heart.

"So sorry to frighten you," he declared. "I'm the curator of this exhibit. May I help you find something in particular?"

What? It took her about two beats to get the sense of that. He wanted to help her? She was expecting him to kick her out or have her arrested for breaking and entering and skulking suspiciously around a museum full of priceless objets d'art.

She inhaled, trying to get her breathing back to normal. If only the air weren't so hot and heavy in this place. Her silk camisole was sticking to her skin, and she felt as if she were suffocating. "I'm so sorry. I know I'm not supposed to be here, but I—"

"No, please, don't worry." His smile widened, and there was a definite twinkle in his bright blue eyes. "'Sex Through the Ages' is a very unusual collection, and not everyone's cup of tea. So it does my heart good to run into someone so eager to see it that she couldn't wait for the official opening."

"That's true, I suppose," Jordan managed. "You're sure you don't mind?"

"I'm here to help," he said in a conspiratorial tone.

"Okay, well, there's one piece in particular I need to find." She scrambled to pull her bag around to the front, quickly tugging out the flyer for the "Sex" exhibit and opening it to show him the tiny picture of the arch.

"Oh, that's a spectacular piece," he said with hushed awe. "One-of-a-kind."

"Do you know who the sculptor is?" she asked quickly, but he didn't answer.

Without another word, he turned and marched from that room, motioning for her to follow. She did. She didn't have much of a choice.

Down the hall, around a corner, passing several dark rooms, he led her into a narrow hall lined with statues. If possible, it was even more stifling and confining in this small space, even harder to breathe. The curator was wearing a long-sleeved jacket over a shirt and tie and he had set a brisk pace to get to this corridor, yet he looked immaculate, without a hint of perspiration. It was freaky.

"Here it is," he said quietly, flipping a switch.

Jordan blinked. *Holy hell in a handbasket.*

With one lone light bulb shining directly above it, the marble sculpture gleamed like a beacon in front of her. Isabella's arch?

Isabella's arch.

Six feet tall, Greek gods and goddesses entwined in eternal embraces, oozing sex and sin from every marble pore... She took a deep breath, exhaled and then just stared. She dropped her messenger bag next to her feet with a thump, edging closer, wiping her sweaty palms against the fabric of her denim skirt.

She'd never really believed she would ever see it. But this had to be it. Even without authenticating the marble or the signature or anything else, Jordan knew in her heart that this was Isabella's arch.

"Wow. Just… Wow," was all she could get out.

In person, it was so much more than she expected. So much more everything. It was powerful and beautiful and overwhelmingly sensual. All Jordan could do was gape. Even in the midst of "Sex Through the Ages," with flesh and passion depicted at every turn, she could feel the erotic power of the arch reach out and wrap around her, pulling her closer.

Leaning in, mesmerized by the sensuous figures carved into the cool, creamy stone, she couldn't seem to breathe or move. Her skin was glazed with sweat and there was a haze in front of her eyes.

She couldn't get her fill of gazing at it. Just taking it in.

The people on the arch pulsed with life and vitality, wound together with their blatant sexuality. It felt like an invasion of privacy even to look at them.

Jordan blinked again, seeing stars dancing in the air between her and the statue. But she couldn't glance away.

Her fingers ached to feel its surface. If she touched the piece, she was afraid she might combust right there. One touch and poof, she'd be a pile of dust under winged Eros's foot, down there at the base of the arch, where he was making love to blindfolded Psyche as she twisted with an orgasm so real that Jordan was surprised not to hear Psyche's cries of pleasure echoing right there in the Beckwith Gallery.

Her gaze trailed over Psyche and Eros, the back of Pygmalion's head between Galatea's marble thighs, Aphrodite and Ares, tangled in a net but more entangled with each other, Narcissus with Echo's eager mouth hovering near his erection…

Fighting against an arousal of her own, so sharp it threatened to topple her right over, Jordan glanced away. Was it just the effect of a stuffy room, too many oversized penises back in the Pompeii room, a day already marked by memories of Nick in her dreams, or was the erotic lure of Isabella's arch driving her mad all by itself?

The curator's voice puffed soft near her ear. "Would you like to touch it?"

She was dying to. But she still wasn't sure.

"Touch it," he whispered.

The statue was mesmerizing. Impulsively reaching out, she filled her hand with the marble curve of Apollo's sinuous buttock, three-dimensional now instead of merely sketched, flexing as he pressed himself into Daphne.

Her fingers closed over his flesh. Jordan gasped. How was it possible that marble could feel warm and alive against her skin?

She pulled back, shocked, burning, at the exact moment the curator said intently, "Don't forget, Jordan, you must come back the same way you go."

"What? I don't underst—" But there was no time to finish her words before he inexplicably shoved her. Hard.

One minute she was gazing spellbound at Apollo, and the next she was tumbling under the arch. She tripped, skidded, reached out to catch herself and…

And fell headfirst into open space.

5

How to Be a Scandalous Woman, Rule 5:
If you want him, grab him. You can worry about
the consequences later.

1893

NICK WAS HAVING a devil of a time finding his sister's out-rageous artwork.

"She wouldn't have lied to me about where it was, would she?" he muttered. "Damn Women's Building, any-way."

Like most everyone else in Chicago, he'd visited the fair several times, but he hadn't set foot inside the Women's Building. No wonder. The place was full of the silliest items imaginable.

To try to find Isabella's arch, he'd had to traverse a model kitchen and kindergarten, exhibits ranging from the latest in egg-beaters to frying pans, and an entire gallery crammed with dainty, hand-painted china cups and saucers. That was a lot more china than any man should have to encounter in a lifetime.

After the cups and saucers, he'd somehow wandered into an auditorium where a cadre of angry women, half of them wearing trousers instead of skirts, were carrying on a lecture about the evils of corsetry, complete with diagrams and a half-clad model who looked every bit as fearsome as the ladies in bloomers. He could see why she wouldn't be anxious to strap a corset on over that mountain of flesh. He'd barely escaped with his life, as the ladies of the Anti-Corset Brigade made it clear men were not welcome.

"What man would want to be welcome for that sort of thing?" he grumbled. "Teacups and lace doilies. Lectures on corsets. Talk about your bull in a china shop."

Finally, he took a path away from the general public, searching the second floor, away from the main atrium. Women were milling around downstairs, but absolutely no one was up here. After passing "Kentucky Home," which appeared to be a recreation of an entire rural household from some not-too-distant past, and "Women in Savagery," whatever that was, he saw a gallery that looked more promising. This one said it was "The American Sculptress," which sounded as if it fit Isabella. Better than "Kentucky Home" or "Women in Savagery," at any rate.

Although the room was crowded with display cases and small statuary, there wasn't a soul around. Thank goodness. If he was lucky, no one had seen the arch yet.

As Nick entered, he knew at once that he'd come to the right place. The marble arch she'd described was standing in the center of the room, all by itself, shining in the soft morning light. He set his jaw. So this was Isabella's handiwork.

It was lovely, in an obscene sort of way. As he came nearer, Nick wasn't sure whether to avert his eyes or appreciate the enthusiasm with which his sister had depicted the men and women pleasuring each other. There was a certain undeniable power to the blasted thing.

Nick shook his head. He simply couldn't look at it. It was too carnal, too raw, knowing that his own sister had created something like that.

One thing was certain—that arch was guaranteed to shock the petticoats off every society woman in town.

"I suspect the ladies of the Anti-Corset Brigade down in the auditorium wouldn't be too fond of it, either," Nick said dryly. Even if the women on it were certainly free of corsets.

Free of corsets, free of dresses, free of drawers… And free of good sense, it appeared. If anyone saw it, Isabella would be a pariah, and the Tempest family would no doubt be shunned along with her.

Which raised the question of what he was going to do with it. The piece was too big to carry away, and even he wasn't enough of a monster to take a sledgehammer to something his sister considered her masterpiece. This just wasn't the right venue for it. If she could take it somewhere less conspicuous—far less conspicuous, as well as far, far away—he supposed it might be of use to someone. After all, wealthy men the world over had collections of erotica.

"Perhaps if it were in a private collection in Siberia," Nick said with a certain edge. Anywhere but here.

He glanced quickly around the room, looking for some tool or device that might suggest a temporary solution to the problem. If he could move a marble stand or two in front of it, place some statuary there, maybe even shove a display case that way, he might be able to camouflage it. Awfully heavy work by himself, however. But if he went to get a crew of workmen, he risked them seeing and gossiping about the thing. Of course, Isabella had hired a crew to get it this far, so it seemed that genie was already out of the bottle.

Hmm… He noticed a pile of heavy canvas tossed in the front corner of the room, near the entrance, as if painters or movers had carelessly left a drop cloth behind. That might just do the trick.

But as Nick bent to unfold the fabric to see if there was enough to cover Isabella's sculpture, he heard a curious noise behind him, back by the arch. There was a distinct thump, and then, just as he spun around, a louder thud.

"What in blazes?"

Where there had been no one before, now a young woman lay under Isabella's arch. A very oddly dressed young woman. Pretty, too. He felt the strangest *zing* of awareness and recognition, as if he knew her, as if he knew her well. But he was sure he didn't. Not someone who looked like that. Her arms and legs were bare, her hair was loose, she had no hat or gloves or proper coat… In fact, she appeared to be wearing less than the lightskirts down by the river. Much less.

Plus there was the fact that she had appeared out of nowhere. First he was alone in the room, then he turned away from the arch for a few seconds, and suddenly, poof, a mysterious woman landed in the room as if the gods themselves had dropped her from the sky. Truly bizarre.

"Where did she come from?" he asked out loud, looking around. It just didn't make sense.

She would've had to walk past him to get into the gallery unless she'd been hiding behind a potted palm or something when he arrived. And if she had, why run out into the middle of the room and throw herself under the arch the moment his back was turned?

Given that she was still lying there, motionless, he took a step her direction. "Miss? Are you all right?" But she didn't answer, just reclined there with her eyes shut.

"Damnation," Nick swore.

He crossed immediately to her side, kneeling next to her. Quickly, he lifted her head an inch or two off the floor, feeling around for any sort of injury. She had a lump, all right, just at the crown of her head.

As he stripped off his coat and pillowed it under her head, he wondered what he should do next. "Damnation," he said again. Well, he'd wished for a diversion, hadn't he? It looked like he'd gotten what he wished for, in the form of one beautiful, strange young woman.

Glancing down at her, he concluded, "Definitely beautiful. Definitely strange."

People from all nations had gathered in Chicago for the World's Fair, including Egyptian dancing girls with their undulating bellies and barefoot Polynesian ladies wrapped in a few yards of bright cloth, but even so, he'd never seen anyone dressed remotely like *this*. In fact, she looked as though she'd cobbled together her small costume by grabbing a scrap of this and that from the flotsam of a shipwreck.

Speaking of cobbled... He gave her feet a gander. What in blazes had she done to her shoes? There were no more than a thin strap bound around her toes and another around her heel, balanced on very high heels, with more foot left bare than covered. And her toenails appeared to have been painted or dyed. Painted toes? He suddenly had visions of exotic women lying about in some tropical paradise, sewing together fragments of denim and silk for garments and carefully painting each other's toenails with the tiniest of brushes.

It was an intriguing image, if one he felt hadn't the slightest chance of being true. So where did she come from? And how had she come to be here?

He knew it was a risky maneuver, but he leaned in closer and began to feel around her waist and bodice. "Steady," he told himself. "It's not prurient. Has to be done."

Yes, indeed. No choice but to paw an unconscious woman.

"I'm not pawing," he argued with himself. "Just checking for hidden belts or pockets where she might be carrying something that could help identify her."

Right. That's why it was imperative, for example, to search around the plunging neckline of her silk camisole, revealing some sort of curious, even briefer undergarment, a sinful shade of red, peeking out around the edges of the first one. Or edge a finger or two up under the lace hem of her camisole, where her stomach was soft and warm, or trace a line all the way up her beautiful bare leg and under the brief slash of well-worn denim barely covering her hips.

So little clothing. So very dangerous to let his fingers roam around that skin. She was luscious, that was for sure, slender and yet curvy, with all the right assets in the right places. Her strange attire seemed to offer all of those assets up for his perusal, not covering anything completely, just teasing enough to stoke his appetite.

"Ah, well," he murmured, his hand flat over her left breast. "I can now safely say that she's still breathing, can't I?" He withdrew his hand, regretfully. No matter how fetching she was, it wasn't right to sample the wares when she was out cold.

In the end, his clumsy search produced nothing in the way of identification and nothing to explain her bizarre appearance. All he found was one small pocket right out in the open, over her hipbone, sewn into the minuscule denim garment. She let out a soft moan as he poked into the tight pocket, making him almost drop the lone coin he pulled out and held up to the light.

Hmm… Nothing earth-shattering, just a souvenir Columbian Exposition half-dollar, much like the one he'd been tossing around back home. Fifty cents would get her one camel ride down Cairo Street on the Midway Plaisance, or two trips on the World's Fair steamship. Not much. And she didn't appear to have anything else.

Strange. The coin he'd extracted from her pocket had a small scratch across Columbus's eye. So did the one he'd been playing with in the wee hours of morning. After throwing one coin into a cup for hours, he'd gotten pretty familiar with it.

He examined this one more closely. There were thousands of the coins circulating around the fair and the city, but it looked *exactly* like the one he'd had earlier, scratch and all. Strange. Had she stolen his half-dollar in the past few hours? If so, how? And why?

Tucking the coin into his vest pocket, trying to stay dispassionate, he gazed down at her. "Who are you?" he asked out loud.

She blinked, opening her eyes. "Nick?" she mumbled.

He didn't move. *She knew his name.*

After propping herself up on one elbow, she opened her eyes wide and shook her head, as if trying to dislodge the cobwebs. Then she looked at him again, and smiled.

"Nick," she said, but this time it came out stronger and more sure, and she gazed at him with this dreamy, adoring gaze that shook him down to his boots.

Who was she? Why was she licking her lips at him as if she were the cat and he were a bowl of cream?

Quickly, before he had time to react, she slipped onto his lap, framed his face with her hands, and kissed him like there was no tomorrow.

Right from the start her mouth was wide open, wet and demanding, as if she was very familiar with how to fan his fire. She nibbled him, tasted him, owned him, sending the message that she wanted him down to his soul. *Now*.

At first he was so shocked he didn't do anything. But it didn't take long to start giving as good as he got.

He might be a gentleman, but he was no saint. If she was hungry for it, so was he. After all, he was already half aroused from sliding his hands over her sweet curves.

It had been a damn long time since he'd had a woman this delectable, this bold in his lap. He liked his lovers hot and fast, and that was exactly what she offered.

She moaned with pleasure, settling more closely into his lap, never breaking that stunning kiss. She wiggled her bottom just a tiny bit, plastering her silk-clad breasts against his chest and wrapping her arms around him. As she moved, the band of denim she wore in place of a skirt bunched around her hips, putting the slippery silk of her minute undergarment directly on top of his crotch. What *was* she wearing under there?

The friction was driving him crazy. He was a man, after all, and his entire body went rigid, pounding with desire. Even if he'd wanted to hold back, for the sake of good sense or propriety, it was too late now. So he hauled her even closer, shoving one hand into her soft hair at the nape of her neck, the other bracing her back as he slashed deeper in her mouth, taking everything he wanted from her.

It was the best kiss he'd ever had in his life.

He tightened his arm around her keeping her riding hard up against him as he edged her backward, closer to the floor. But just at the moment he was ready to lay her down, full-out under the marble arch, she went stock still.

Pulling her mouth away, gasping for breath, she shoved a hand against his chest. "Wait!"

He clenched his jaw and held himself tightly. Her eyes were wide and disbelieving and her lips soft and swollen as she scrambled out from underneath him.

"I thought…I thought it was another dream! I thought if it was you, then it must be a dream. But this is no dream!" she mumbled, gaping at him for a long moment. "What the hell is going on here?"

6

How to Be a Scandalous Woman, Rule 6:
It's always better to fly by the seat of your pants.
Especially if you're not wearing any.

JORDAN TRIED TO GET her bearings. Her head was pounding, and her vision was a little blurry. Had she hit her head? Where was she?

"Excuse me," the man she'd just been kissing interrupted in a very chilly tone. "I'd like to make it clear that you kissed me, not vice versa. I have done nothing improper whatsoever."

Her gaze skittered back and forth between him and the arch, and she saw the dark jacket that had been propped under her head. She picked it up off the floor, clutching the soft wool to her chest as she surveyed the room, desperate to get her bearings.

The last thing she remembered was following that funny man in the uniform, the one who resembled Captain Kangaroo, down a narrow corridor. It was blazingly hot and not very well lit. But now she seemed to be in soft morning light in a huge, all-white gallery stuffed full of statuary. There were windows all around, high, wide windows, and what looked like sunbeams streaming into the room. It also seemed to have dropped about twenty degrees. She shivered. She should be in a stuffy, humid hallway, not a bright, breezy gallery. Had there been a trapdoor in the floor at the Art Institute? A trapdoor that landed her *and* the arch a floor below, in a much different place?

She looked back at the man across from her. She'd imagined it was Nick. Her Nick, from the pictures. But it couldn't be. Could it?

"Oh, no," she whispered, not believing it herself.

How could he be Nick Tempest? Her ears were ringing and there seemed to be alarms clanging in her brain. She still couldn't quite focus. But she didn't need to. She knew that face as well as she knew her own.

It was beautiful, with high cheekbones, dark brows and a slightly crooked nose that gave him character. He had perfectly shaped, sensual lips, a little fuller on the bottom, with the hint of a dimple on one side. And his eyes…

They were blue. Crystal-blue. Like the clearest lake on a sunny day. In the black-and-white photo she'd kept in her desk, she hadn't realized they were blue. Even in her vivid, Technicolor dreams, she didn't remember his eyes being blue. They were so much more intense and compelling now, with a reckless fire she could never have imagined.

This was just so different. Three-dimensional. *Alive.*

Her mouth dropped open. "You totally *are* Nick."

"Yes, I'm aware of that." Moving a little stiffly, he removed his dark wool jacket from her hands and shrugged back into it, buttoning it closed in the front.

She had a pretty good idea why he'd buttoned his jacket, and why he was leaving his hands hanging there, jiggling the button. Because there was a noticeable tent in his pants. She felt her face flush. Yeah, she remembered feeling his rock-hard erection underneath her, too, when she was straddling his lap. Straddling his lap? *Oh, Lord, Jordan, what have you gotten yourself into?*

His gaze was steely when he announced, "What I want to know is who *you* are."

"Jordan. Jordan Albright," she replied automatically.

His expression was dark and forbidding. "I don't believe I know any Albrights. And Jordan seems an odd given name for a woman. I think I would remember that if I'd met you before."

"It's from *The Great Gatsby*. My parents were, you know, fans of the book. Both of them. Only thing they had in common," she babbled. But she couldn't talk about that. Not at the moment.

It was so weird how she had so little self-control. She still found herself wanting to grab hold of him, rip off his clothes, rip off her clothes, too, and do wild, crazy things right there under the arch. She felt as if she were stoked halfway to an orgasm just by virtue of being so close to the damned thing.

Or maybe it was the aftereffect of that runaway kiss, where she was squashing herself up against him and trying her damnedest to rub her moist panties into the hard ridge of his erection...

Oh, Lord. What was happening to her? Pressing one fist to her forehead, tugging her skirt down with the other hand, she had to fight hard to keep a lid on whatever was happening to her brain and her body.

"I've never heard of your Gatsby book," he announced, looking very suspicious and not at all like the sex-pistol fantasy man she knew.

That Nick had hopped to the main event without any preamble, any conversation, any *anything* except, well, straight-up sex. Sideways and upside-down sex, too, but that was beside the point and she was not going to think about that anymore. The important thing was that this man acted like slamming, jamming sex was not necessarily the most important thing in the world, and it flew in the face of her assumptions.

He seemed to be waiting for her to say something, and when she didn't, he inquired, "Who wrote your Gatsby book?"

Impatient, she couldn't stop herself from blurting, "F. Scott Fitzgerald. But of course you haven't heard of it. You lived in the 1890s and it wasn't written until the 1920s!"

"You're named after a book that hasn't been written yet?"

"No. It was already written when *I* was born, just not when you…" She held up a hand. "I can't explain. You're just going to have to trust me."

He didn't look as if that was very likely. In fact, the fish eye he was giving her had *let's get you to the nearest loony bin* written all over it.

Carefully, he asked, "Do you have people in town? Relations, perhaps, or someone you were visiting? Anyone you know here in Chicago?"

"I don't know," she told him truthfully, not at all sure what they were talking about. Her Chicago or his? Where was she, anyway? "I mean, I know you. Sort of."

"Ah." He frowned. "How exactly do you know me?"

What was she supposed to say? *Well, you see, I've been drooling over your picture for the past six months, and as a matter of fact, I was so obsessed that I had a hundred hot dreams about you. We had this Apollo and Daphne thing up against a tree, and ooh, baby…*

No. Not gonna happen.

Instead, she tried to keep her tone polite and even. It

wasn't easy. "I'm sorry, but I'm a little confused right now. I do know you, but, well, not the way you think, and *that,* what we just did…"

"The kiss?" he supplied, with a gleam she didn't like in his eye.

That was more than a kiss. A lot more. "It felt very… How do I put this?" She searched for the right word. Overpowering? Scary? Like being body-slammed by a tidal wave? "Real. It felt real. Up till then, I kind of thought I was having a dream, but *that…*" She let out a shaky breath. "That didn't feel like any dream."

"Because it wasn't." The barest hint of a smile played over his lips. "I can assure you it was no dream. And to think I expected Isabella's arch to be the most bizarre thing I'd encounter today."

She choked back a rising sense of panic. "So it's not a dream. Scratch that theory. Why would it be? I went to the Art Institute to see the arch. I was perfectly awake, it was the middle of the day, and then that creepy curator guy said something about coming back the same way I went, and then he shoved me—"

"I haven't seen any curator," Nick put in.

"Well, he was there. I can promise you that. I leaned in closer and I touched Apollo's butt." She paused, trying not to blush. There was no sin in touching a marble butt, for heaven's sake. *Get over it, Jordan! You have a lot bigger problems right now.* "Okay, so I did, you know, touch Apollo. Right…" She pointed. "There. And then the curator shoved me. The next thing I knew, I was kissing you."

"I found you on the floor," he told her coolly. "I was here by myself, and then suddenly, the moment my back was turned, you were lying prone underneath the arch. I checked to see if you had injured yourself—"

"I remember that," she said suddenly. She had this vague, fuzzy memory of Nick leaning over her and his hand on her breast and it felt really yummy… Hot color rushed to her face. "Oh, my God. I was out cold and you were *groping* me?"

"Heavens, no. I merely looked for identification labels in your clothing or some kind of purse or handbag." He shoved his hands in his pockets. "You have none of those, by the way."

"Well, I did." Jordan started pacing around the room, looking for signs of her messenger bag. "I had a big canvas bag, bright yellow, that says PBS on the side in big black letters. Channel 11, WTTW, you know? It was a free gift for being a member. All of my stuff is in it. My wallet, my driver's license, my cell phone…" But none of it was here. "Without my bag, I don't even have a Band-Aid! Not even a wet wipe!"

"You have the oddest way of putting things," he said thoughtfully, hanging back but keeping an eye on her. "Is this a dialect I've never encountered? Where are you from?"

"It's perfectly good English!" she returned, still searching behind display cases. "You'll have to excuse me, but I don't really have time to deal with it right now if you don't know what a Band-Aid is!"

"Well," he continued, "I'm beginning to think you may have been set on by thugs of some sort. That might explain the missing bag as well as the head injury. Did you happen to arrive in Chicago by train? Thieves are known to lie in wait at the train station."

"No, no," she assured him, but he went on.

"But that would make sense, if they were the ones who hit you on the head and stole your purse and, uh…" He seemed pensive as his gaze skated up and down her. "And stole the majority of your clothing. But why would they have dropped you here?"

"No, no, I'm telling you. There were no thieves or thugs, just that one curator at the Art Institute. And nobody stole my clothes! This is what I was wearing!" She was trying hard not to freak out. But what was a person supposed to do when she had no idea where she was, she didn't have her wallet or her phone, and she woke up to find herself kissing a fabulous man who was a dead ringer for someone who'd been dead for more than a hundred years?

And right now, she wanted to have sex with him so bad it made her teeth ache?

Damn those erotic dreams, anyway. She felt as if she was in an experiment cooked up by some crazy mix of Pavlov and Dr. Ruth. *See Nick, have sex.* Only this time everything was different. He had clothes on, for one thing. And so did she. Plus he was actually talking. The Nick of her dreams never said a word because his mouth was too busy elsewhere. Like in the Pygmalion position, with his mouth on her thigh and his tongue flicking… She shivered again, and this time it wasn't because of the temperature in the room.

"This can't be," she muttered, pacing back and forth in front of the arch. "Stuff like this doesn't happen."

"Ah, I think I understand. This is some scheme of Isabella's, isn't it?" He was wearing a smug expression she didn't care for. "She knows that presenting a mystery like you would definitely get me off course. Let me guess—she threw you into my path to stop me from destroying the arch, didn't she?"

"Destroying it?" Horrified, she moved to set herself in front of it. She didn't how she knew it, but she was absolutely certain that the continued existence of the arch was incredibly important. A whole battery of images and ideas started to pelt her brain. *Isabella, scandal, arrest, disappearance, legacy, dissertation...* It was as if there was a big neon sign in her head flashing *Don't let anything happen to the arch!* "You wouldn't destroy it, would you?"

"I was merely planning to move it," he said grimly. "But I wasn't aware how large it was until I got here. I can hardly drag it away by myself, can I?"

"Phew." She sagged in relief against the cool marble, bracing herself against one side.

Across from her, Nick clenched his jaw. He seemed to be staring at her arm. "Miss Albright, would you mind?" He waved a hand. "You'll probably want to move away from the, uh..."

She followed the path of his gaze. What she saw was her own hand, resting about an inch from a perfectly carved, fully erect penis. Not only was that definitely an erection, but there was a female face carved in stone right next to it, eager to pounce.

Her fingers burning, Jordan yanked back her hand. "Oh. Narcissus and the blow job. Well."

"I'm not familiar with the term, but...yes. That." He shook his head fiercely, looking about as uncomfortable as Jordan felt. "Damn Isabella! What was she thinking? And how does she know enough about *that* to have carved it for posterity?"

"But you see," Jordan tried, "that's why Isabella is important. Not the, uh, blow job specifically, but the idea of women owning their own sexuality. That's so crucial."

He didn't say anything, but she saw the question in the sardonic lift of one dark brow. *Do you own your sexuality?*

Yes, yes, I do, she wanted to shout. *But I'm willing to share it with you!*

She turned to look at the arch more fully, stiffening her resolve and trying once again to act like a professional and not a sex addict who had imagined herself in all those positions with, you know, *him*, the guy who was standing right next to her. "Plus there's the fact that it's beautiful."

"Yes, well, that's debatable."

"No, it's not," she protested. "The arch is gorgeous. I can't believe, as her brother, you don't recognize that your sister is a genius."

He pressed his lips into a thin line. "If you really knew my sister, you would understand that she is a far more of a nuisance than a genius."

"But nobody else is doing stuff like this," Jordan argued. "And it will take until Georgia O'Keefe and Virginia Woolf, ages in the future, before women get their due in art as sexual beings."

He sighed. "So you're back on about the future again?"

In her enthusiasm for her dissertation topic, she'd forgotten she wasn't supposed to talk about that. *Way to kill the buzz, Jordan. Every time he starts looking like he wants to lick you, you make him think you're cuckoo for Cocoa Puffs.*

"Well…your future. But my present." She bit her lip. "I know it sounds strange, but it's true. I know about Isabella, and about you, because I've been studying her for several years. I'm writing my dissertation about her and her arch."

"Right," he said, nodding slowly. "Your dissertation is about Isabella and an arch that's only been finished this morning and never been seen before today."

She saw that he was edging away, as if he were already on his way to find the men in the white coats. She could hardly blame him. "I swear I'm not crazy," she said weakly.

There was a long pause as he stared at her, taking her measure. "I don't see a lunatic when I look in your eyes," he admitted reluctantly. "But if this isn't some misguided plan of Bella's or you're not mad as a hatter, then why are you saying these things?" He stopped, but started again. "The only explanation I can think of is this is a badger game."

She blinked. "I don't know what that is."

"A badger game," he repeated. "When a mysterious young lady, wearing no more than a few scraps of clothing, suddenly appears out of nowhere and throws herself at me, knows my name, asks me to trust her when she offers only the most far-fetched stories to explain herself..." He stopped, worked his jaw a bit, and then continued, "Well, it begins to look like a confidence scheme. I'm a wealthy man, Miss Albright. People try to part me from my money on a daily basis."

"Really? That's terrible."

"Should I expect your compatriot to come dashing in at the door at any moment, demanding money to hush him up before he goes to the newspapers?"

All she could think of to say was, "I—I don't have a compatriot."

His voice grew more mocking. "I can see the headline now. 'Tempest Heir Ensnared By Scarlet Woman In The White City.' With my sister's outrageous artwork as a backdrop."

"Don't you think if I was planning this badger thing, my henchman would already be here?" she pointed out. "Like, when you were groping me? Or when you were kissing me?"

"I wasn't groping you, and you kissed *me*," he said coldly. "But you do have a point. There's nothing scandalous to interrupt at the moment, is there? Although I suppose just catching me in the same room as someone dressed like you might do it."

Jordan sighed. "Trust me, I'm no scarlet woman. Really. I'm totally the opposite. I'm even boring."

Actually, she wished she were a scarlet woman. After all, Daniel thought she was the least scandalous woman he knew and it rankled. If she were even a tiny bit scandalous, she would've already made love to Nick Tempest under that damn aphrodisiac of an arch. The thing wielded the power of a boatload of Spanish fly. She was ready to jump out of her skin if she didn't jump his bones within the next five seconds.

But then she processed the rest of what Nick had said.

"Oh, my God. You called me a scarlet woman *in the White City*. Is that where we're supposed to be?" Jordan took a good look around her. White room, full of statuary, morning light flooding in the tall, high windows… At this point, she was so dazed and off-balance she didn't have any room left for surprise. "I'm at the Columbian Exposition?"

"Yes," he returned. "On the second floor of the Women's Building. As I suspect you well know."

"No, I didn't know. How would I? How in the world…" Slowly, she made her way over to the far side of the room. Taking a deep breath, Jordan got a good grasp on the window sill and took her first look at the outside world. "Holy moley. This is the White City."

"Yes, of course," he said behind her.

But her head was spinning and she barely heard him. She didn't know whether to laugh or cry. If this was all a fantasy, it was the most elaborate thing she'd ever seen.

"There's the lagoon," she whispered, staring down, where she could see one of the famous gondolas sliding through the water. There was a gondolier in a funny little outfit, and two passengers, ladies, wearing long black dresses and fancy hats, shading themselves with an umbrella. She lifted her gaze, rattling off what saw. "On the other side of the lagoon, there's the Brazilian building, Sweden's building with the flag on top, then the Café de la Marine with the ice-cream-cone towers, and the big white one on the end with all the gingerbread is the Fisheries building."

"Well, clearly you've been to the exposition," he remarked dryly. "You know every structure by sight."

"I—I…" She pressed one hand over her mouth, took it off to gulp for air, and put it back again. Even if someone had hired a troop of actors to put on old-fashioned clothes, how did they manage such an elaborate recreation of the Columbian Exposition, with all the buildings in the right places, carving lagoons back into Jackson Park and ripping up all the roads that had been there as recently as this morning? Not to mention finding sedan chairs and gondolas to scatter around.

Slowly, she mumbled, "If I were on the other side of the building, I would see the Ferris wheel and the Streets of Cairo and the whole Midway Plaisance, wouldn't I?"

"Yes, of course."

Whirling, she raised terrified eyes to his. "Nick, I'm at the Columbian Exposition in what appears to be 1893. Every detail is here."

"Yes, I know."

"But how? Why? I don't belong here!" She crossed back to him, taking him by the lapels, shaking him. "I'm from 2006! I'm not supposed to be hanging around in the White City. With you!"

His expression was hard to read. "I think you may have hit your head harder than we thought at first."

"You have to believe me. I'm from 2006. And either this is one big kahuna of a nightmare, or…" She stopped, unable to finish that thought. "Or I've lost my mind."

7

How to Be a Scandalous Woman, Rule 7:
"Seize the day"? Seize everything you can get your
hands on.

JORDAN PINCHED HERSELF, and then did it again, harder, but that didn't clarify anything.

"Try to be calm," Nick ordered her, sliding an arm around her shoulders, making her even less calm. His hand was right next to the outside curve of her breast, and she could feel her nipple tightening under the thin silk of her bra, hungry for his touch. That's how easy it was for him to turn her on. The Pavlovian effect again.

As if she had time for that right now!

He brushed his thumb against her bare shoulder, making her feel even more rattled. In a tone that was supposed to be soothing but felt anything but, he added, "It won't help matters if you're hysterical."

"I'm not hysterical," she snapped. "I think I'm doing pretty well under the circumstances."

It *so* wasn't fair that he kept touching her and messing with her head. Shaking off his arm, she turned back to the window. She couldn't stop staring. It was an enormous vista. The White City was freakin' huge! And beautiful. Incredible, too, in the "unbelievable" sense of the word. She tapped the solid wood of the window sill, plinked the glass pane, even rapped the plaster wall with her knuckles. All of it felt as solid and real as Nick beside her, but she couldn't quite wrap her brain around how any of it could be.

"What am I supposed to do next?" she asked. "I'm a planner by nature, you know, a linear thinker, but this is totally beyond my experience. I'm not a gamer, so no D&D or anything where you role-play. I've never even done Choose Your Own Adventure!"

"Could you please try to speak in phrases you think I might understand? I'm trying to help you," he reminded her.

Point taken. She held her hair off her face, trying to think it through. She really shouldn't be talking about twentieth-century pop culture with a guy from 1893.

She put it as plainly as she could. "I don't know where I'm supposed to go from here. I mean, on a normal trip, if I found myself stranded somewhere with all of my things stolen, I would go to the police."

"Not your best choice," he said immediately. "They will take you for something else entirely."

She didn't know what that meant—either a hooker or a mental patient, probably—but she wasn't going to argue it. "But I can't go anywhere. I don't have any money or identification or even bus fare."

Suddenly, she remembered the coin she'd stuck in her pocket just before she left her office. Fifty cents was better than nothing. But when she checked the pocket of her jeans skirt, she discovered that it, too, was gone. "Even my lucky coin is gone!"

"Coin?" he asked, lifting one eyebrow.

"Yes. I had a Columbian Exposition half-dollar. I stuck

it in my pocket before I left my office, right before I came here." She threw up her hands. "But it's disappeared along with everything else."

"I have to say, a half-dollar wouldn't get you very far, anyway. But no worries," he stated sensibly. "The important thing is to get you out of here as soon as possible. You'll come to my home."

He said it like it was a done deal. Nick's home? That sounded both wonderful and frightening.

Nick went on, "We've had visitors for the fair coming and going since May. There's no one with us at present, so it will be fine. It's settled."

"Yes, but—"

"It's no trouble. We'll present you as a chum of Isabella's, just arrived from Europe." He smiled, and she remembered how charming he could be. Very charming.

Since she'd arrived, he'd mostly seemed honorable and upstanding, the perfect gentleman. But every once in a while, she saw this predatory, ruthless look in his eye. And he *had* groped her while she was unconscious. Hmm...

He added, "If I know my sister, she will find this whole escapade enchanting."

"All right," she said softly. "I guess." But she still wondered why he would want to help her. At the moment, he undoubtedly thought she was a few bricks short of a load *and* a slut who threw herself at men she didn't know. Why would he invite *that* back to his house?

Nick stopped, holding up a hand and dropping his voice. "Did you hear footsteps out in the corridor?"

"No, I didn't hear anything."

But he was already poking his head outside the room to check. Quickly, he returned. "No one there, but there could be at any time."

Without further ado, he grabbed up a dust sheet that had been lying near the entrance, and tossed it over Isabella's arch. Then he moved a small marble pillar to secure one of the corners, and plunked a bust on top of the pillar.

"That's not going to work. It's obvious there's something hidden under there, which I'd think would just make people more curious and they'll lift the cover," Jordan pointed out. She shook her head, not sure how she felt about hiding it in the first place. It made her feel kind of bereft to not be able to look at it anymore. "I really think it's important for the arch to be seen. I know it's going to be controversial, but still—"

"No choice," he said hastily as he finished planting another piece of statuary in another corner. "I'll think of something more permanent later. For right now, it will have to suffice." He turned back to her, frowning. "And then, what about you?"

"What about me?" she asked with a certain feeling of apprehension.

"We need to get to my carriage. But you can hardly wander around the fair dressed like *that*."

"Oh." She glanced down at her outfit. "I suppose you're going to want to throw a dust sheet over me, too. I can wrap it like a toga and pretend I'm the Spirit of Columbia. It would even go with my sandals."

"A toga?" He shook his head. "That would cause almost as much of an uproar as what you're currently wearing. I don't believe I've ever seen a woman in a toga walking down the street."

"What then?"

Nick stared into space for a moment. "What with the teacups and doilies and needlework, there's surely some exhibit on ladies' clothing somewhere in this building." He shrugged. "I'll just see what I can find." After taking a step toward the door, he paused. "I don't suppose you would consider ducking under the tarp with the arch until I get back?"

"No!" Claustrophobia City. Besides, as long as she'd been thrown into this bizarre alternate reality, she wanted to explore it, damn it, not be stuck hiding in the dark under a tent of fabric.

"All right. But at least stay on the other side, out of sight, will you?" He considered for a moment, adding, "And if anyone should wander in here, don't speak to them, all right? You have a habit of speaking in gobbledygook, and I fear someone who isn't as kind-hearted as I will have you bound for an asylum the first time you start talking about gamers or Band Aid."

With that, Nick dashed out of the room, leaving Jordan all by herself with her chaotic thoughts. "Just wait till I tell him Band Aid and Band-Aids are not at all the same thing," she mused.

But why did he invite her back to his place? Did he have ulterior motives or did she just have sex on the brain?

"He clearly thinks I'm crackers," she said out loud. "So why is he helping me?"

There was something going on there, but what? Maybe he felt the same strange connection she did, and he, too, was powerless to fight it. Maybe he had a white knight complex. Maybe the kiss had blown his mind as much as hers and he wanted to do it again as badly as she did.

"I don't care," she decided. "Just as long as he comes back."

What if he didn't? She glanced around the room, wondering if she was going to disappear as unexpectedly as she'd arrived. But that was the weird thing—this room, and

Nick himself, seemed as normal as anywhere she'd ever been. How long would this fantasy last?

Just in case it was going to end soon, she refused to cower behind the arch. She wanted to see the outside world! It was amazing out there. Besides, no one except Nick had ventured into this dusty gallery the whole time they were there. Why would stray tourists show up now?

Feeling like a child with her nose pressed to the candy store window, Jordan returned to the wide windows, squinting into the misty morning light. There was almost too much to take in, even if she was on the wrong side of the building to see the midway. But in this direction, she could almost make out Lake Michigan in the distance. She leaned forward...

And then a hand touched her elbow.

Jordan jumped about a foot, spinning around, her heart pounding. She had a major case of déjà vu.

"You!" she shouted.

It was the funny little man in the conductor hat. Captain Kangaroo! Except his uniform was different, with lots more frogs and epaulets and all manner of gewgaws, and instead of a name tag, he had a shiny star pinned to his chest. Now his cap looked more like something that would've been worn in the Civil War: it had a strap around the chin, and there was a perky little feather waving on the top of it.

"Just thought I would check and make sure you're all right," he announced.

"What in the world is going on?" Jordan demanded. She felt like smacking the smug little man on one of his spiffy epaulets. "I was at the Art Institute. Everything was perfectly normal. And then you shoved me and here I am, with Nick, in what appears to be 1893! Who are you?"

"I'm a member of the Columbian Guard just this moment," he said slyly. "Can't you tell from my uniform?"

"What is this? I feel like I'm in the Holodeck on the Starship Enterprise!"

"It's quite real, I can promise you that."

"Nick said the same thing, but it didn't make me feel any better. I am not the sort of person who goes in for wrinkles in time or quantum leaping or…" Shoving a hand through her hair, Jordan stopped long enough to take a breath. "I can't even believe I'm saying this."

"Yes, well, rest assured, you are exactly where you need to be." He patted her on the arm. "You're here for a reason, and that will all become clear. But for now, just concentrate on enjoying the trip. You needed a vacation, didn't you?"

"This is hardly a vacation."

"It would be if you had a better attitude." He swung out one arm, dripping with gold braid. "Millions of people are coming to the World's Fair for the holiday of a lifetime. Maybe you should appreciate the opportunity to join them."

Oh, that was rich. *Him* lecturing her on her attitude. "So you threw me under an arch just to get me to go on vacation?"

But he didn't answer. Instead, he tipped his head to one side. "Now, where has your young man got off to? You'll want to stick by him. That's important. Stick to him like glue."

"But he thinks I'm insane," she responded. "And I'm not sure he's wrong."

"You're fine," the curator reassured her. "Just remember, you can only go back the same way you came."

"Jordan? Is there a problem here?" Nick's cool tones interrupted them, and they both whirled. He was carrying a black garment of some sort over his arm, an umbrella, and a small hat with what appeared to be a dead bird on it.

"This is him, Nick! The curator I told you about, who shoved me under the arch." Jordan rushed to his side. "I told you somebody pushed me."

"The young lady is mistaken," the older man said sweetly. "As you can see, I am not a curator, but an officer in the Columbian Guard. I was just about to take her to the Security Department." He was doing this twinkly, innocent, I-wouldn't-hurt-a-fly thing with his eyes. Jordan realized she would've fallen for it if she hadn't known better.

"I am not mistaken," she maintained. "He *was* the curator at the Art Institute."

But Nick seemed to be in accommodation mode, and he ignored her. "I'm sure we can clear this up," he said, oozing charm. He handed Jordan the cloak and that nasty little hat, gesturing to her to put them on, and then drew the guard aside. He reached into his pocket and pulled out a wad of cash. "The lady is my friend and I would like to avoid her having to go down to the Security Department."

"I found her unaccompanied and acting suspiciously. Can't be too careful," Captain Kangaroo stated in an apologetic tone. "We've had any number of squatters trying to set up camp in the buildings."

"You have the nerve to call me a squatter?" she choked. "When you're the reason I'm here?"

Nick waved her off, pressing several bills into the older man's hands. "I give you my word she is a lady of quality. As a matter of fact, she is staying as a guest at my home. I assure you, there's a perfectly reasonable explanation for her current unorthodox appearance. You see, she was attending the lecture in the auditorium, representing a, uh, model of the corsetless future of American women." He chuckled loudly as he made a show of looking her up and down. "Those ladies of the Anti-Corset Brigade certainly have some strange ideas about what women should wear, don't they?"

Shooting him a dark look, Jordan pulled the cloak around her shoulders. How did he do that? Every time he gazed at her, she felt naked.

"She's a bit far afield of the auditorium, isn't she?" the guard asked, clucking his tongue.

Nick smiled. "I guess she lost her way. She has a terrible sense of direction."

Jordan bit back a denial.

"I see." The curator nodded thoughtfully.

"So," Nick went on, embroidering the story, "I've just gone back to get her cloak for her, so that we can go back to my home. We were just leaving."

"Mmm-hmm." He looked dubious, but Nick passed him another bill or two, which he immediately slid into the pocket of his uniform. "As long as you're willing to vouch for her, Mr. Tempest, I'll take your word."

And then he had the audacity to *wink* at Jordan. She was so mad she was speechless. But he just ambled toward the doorway, holding out an arm as if they should go first.

Nick caught Jordan's elbow, trying to move her toward the exit. "Will you put on the hat?" he whispered. Raising his voice, he added, "Don't forget your umbrella, Miss Albright."

While he fastened the last hook at the collar of the coat, she tried to figure out whether the bird, which was fake rather than dead, went in the front or the back. Whichever way, the thing was nasty. She leaned in close to his ear. "I can't believe you gave that man money, Nick. He's the one who started all of this."

"Shh. Put on the hat. I told you not to talk to anybody. Now it's best if we can just get out of here without further incident."

She got the underlying message. *Don't cause a fuss and don't make waves.* "But he's the only one who can explain this," she said under her breath. "I think we should twist his arm until he talks."

Nick winced. "I'm not in the habit of twisting police officers' arms. It's not good for one's health. Besides, he knows my name and he's standing within five feet of Isabella's *thing*. What with you and the monstrosity in the vicinity, there's scandal at every turn."

She sent a glance over at smug, satisfied Captain Kangaroo, who appeared to be holding all the cards. What could she do?

"I've fixed it. Let it go," Nick commanded.

Right now, her choices were to bicker some more with the curator, probably to no avail, or go home with Nick, the man of her dreams. True, she couldn't know if he would be as wonderful here and now as he was in her fantasies, but she didn't know he wouldn't, either. Her heart sang, *Take a risk! Live in the moment!*

Carpe diem wasn't exactly her favorite motto, but she decided to embrace it. What did she have to lose?

Quickly, she twisted her hair into a knot, squashed the hideous hat on top of it, and tied it under her chin. With a long black coat that covered her from neck to ankles, that creepy little hat, and a black umbrella, she felt like Mary Poppins.

"Take good care of our damsel in distress, Mr. Tempest," the curator called out.

"I shall. Very good care," Nick responded warmly, nudging her along.

Why did those three little words sound so ominous?

"And, Miss Albright, remember what I said about going back the way you came." The curator tipped his cap and strolled off down the hall, whistling some merry tune she didn't recognize.

Jordan narrowed her eyes. She really, really didn't like that man.

Feeling ridiculous in her Mary Poppins getup, she kept her head down and tried not to look conspicuous as Nick led her down a staircase and out into the main hall. There were people around now, and she could hear animated conversations every which way. Yeesh. It was one thing to be a stranger in a strange land while she was alone with Nick, or even with the annoying curator, but quite another when that world was suddenly populated. With real people. Since they were all female, they were also wearing long dresses with wasp waists and long sleeves and gloves and hats...

Jordan couldn't help gawking. She'd always thought that people in old photos looked different from her, like a different species. But these people didn't. They looked just like the women she knew in 2006, like her friends and colleagues, except dressed in really weird clothes. Somehow, seeing them made 1893 that much more tangible.

Suddenly Nick grabbed her hand and began steering her a different way, down a corridor away from all the women, picking up speed rapidly.

"What are we doing?" Jordan asked breathlessly, trying to keep up. "I thought we were leaving. We were almost at the front door."

Swiftly, he told her, "Yes, I know. But we're going out the back way. We don't want the Anti-Corset Brigade, all those ladies milling around in the main hall, to realize that you are wearing a purloined cloak."

"You stole a cloak?"

"Where did you think I got it?" He gave her a mischievous smile. "I went to the cloakroom off the lecture hall, and grabbed the first coat I saw. It's Mrs. Anthony's. The famous suffragette. She's attending the lecture, I think, and her cloak was on the first peg. It looked to be the right length, so I borrowed it. Exigency makes thieves of us all." There was a reckless light in his eyes, as if he were daring her to object, but he whipped them both around a corner before she could.

"You stole Susan B. Anthony's coat?" Jordan slowed so that the bird on her hat would stop bouncing up and down on her forehead. She shoved it back into place and then held the sides of the cloak together more tightly. Talk about a brush with history. It wasn't every day you wrapped yourself in a legend's clothes.

"I prefer *borrowed* rather than *stole*." He shrugged. "Don't worry, I'll return it."

Jordan giggled. What was wrong with her? She was *so* not a giggler. "Me. In Susan B. Anthony's coat. That is just so cool."

"Good," he said, gallantly sweeping open a door to the sunshine outside. "Then I won't return it. I think you are a woman after my own heart, Jordan Albright."

And why did that make her feel so warm and fuzzy inside? *He likes me because I approve of theft. That's not a good thing.*

But as he hustled her between the flower beds and around the building, she found herself in an excellent mood. Maybe it was the flowers and the warm sunshine and all the beautiful sights around them. Maybe it was her handsome companion. Maybe it was that she had stopped tying herself in knots trying to figure out the whys and the wherefores of this crazy trip into *The Twilight Zone,* and just decided to be *here* now, wherever here was.

Jordan's step was lighter and her mood brighter than at any time in recent memory as he set a brisk pace down the Midway Plaisance. She wanted to see the exotic animals and vendors, smell the spicy foods at the bazaar, touch the Oriental rugs and treasures. She wanted it all. Instead of being the little girl with her nose pressed to the window, now she was the kid *in* the candy store.

"Can we get some Cracker Jacks?" she asked. "Or visit the Blarney Stone? Maybe sneak in and get a peek at Little Egypt, the belly dancer? All the pictures I've seen make her look short and dumpy and not that hot at all."

"I agree. I did not find her 'hootchy-kootchy' very entertaining."

"You saw her? You saw Little Egypt?"

His wicked grin was his answer. His voice was low and intimate when he confided, "I find your curves much more appealing than anything Little Egypt showed."

Jordan paused, feeling the impact of his gaze even though she was covered with heavy black fabric from stem to stern. She couldn't believe how sensual she felt. Mary Poppins never had it so good.

This time she couldn't blame it on the arch, either. Nope. It was just her and Nick, with no props and no outside influences.

"Um," she started, but it came out husky and funny, and she had to clear her throat. She'd been called a scarlet woman, she'd decided to seize the day and abandon linear thinking, and she was an accessory after the fact to cloak theft. This was a very unusual day.

Pulling away from his gaze, she glanced around for a distraction. How about the Ferris wheel? It was certainly big and obvious. She craned her head to look up at the dangling cars. Awkwardly, she offered, "I would love to take a ride on that baby."

"It's not open yet."

"No?"

"Soon," he said hurriedly. "But until then…I think we should get back to the house as soon as possible. You really need more proper clothing before we risk you being seen in public." Leaning in closer, he whispered in her ear, "Your toes are peeking out under your cloak. They're as unusual as the rest of you."

His breath puffed warm against her ear, tickling her. She really didn't care about her toes at this particular moment, not when she was getting overheated again just because he breathed on her. When she glanced down to check out her toes, the bird fell forward on her hat, plopping onto her forehead again, wrecking her mood. It was impossible to feel sexy with a bird banging your forehead. This time, she just reached up and yanked it off, swearing a blue streak.

Nick's eyebrows arched upward. Not used to women cursing like sailors, apparently.

"Let's forget about the hat and the Ferris wheel just now, all right?" he inquired. "Mr. Ferris's wheel is due to open later this week. We'll come back then. Will that do?"

But I'm not sure I'll still be here…

The curator's cryptic words about going back the same way she came popped into her head. What did it mean? Did she have a choice about when she arrived or departed this strange place? Would she at least get to assuage this terrible hunger and sleep with Nick before she got snatched back?

I'll worry about going back later. Right now I'm with Nick and I'm happy and that's all that matters.

As long as she didn't have to wear the stupid hat. She

held on to Nick's arm and smiled up at him. "Sure. Later would be wonderful."

But for today… Carpe diem, she told herself.

Seize the day, seize the moment, seize the man and seize everything you can get your hands on.

8

How to Be a Scandalous Woman, Rule 8:
They're called assets for a reason. If you've got
'em, flaunt 'em.

"STAY HERE," Nick ordered from the doorway of the guest bedroom. He'd managed to get Jordan up to the third floor of the house without incident and he was feeling pretty proud of himself.

It wasn't easy to stay inconspicuous when traveling with a woman like her. Especially given the fact that she wanted to know every single detail of every sight she saw. She was driving him crazy.

The simple fact of getting into his carriage seemed a big occasion to her. She watched him handle the horses with wide eyes, commented on the idiosyncrasies of the other vehicles and the roadways themselves, pointed excitedly to the brand-new, steam-powered train put in place just for the exposition as it rattled past on elevated tracks, and gaped in awe at her first glimpse of Prairie Avenue and its imposing mansions. Rosy color stained her cheeks and bright fire lit her eyes, making her look kissable and adorable. As well as, of course, quite mad.

He caught her sending wayward glances his way, too.

The well-bred ladies of his acquaintance did not have desire and longing written all over their faces like Jordan Albright. For whatever reason, that sexual connection between them throbbed below the surface constantly.

She chattered on, and he wondered if her conversation was intended to disguise what she was really thinking, what he was really thinking. Their encounter at the Women's Building had been barely enough to whet his appetite. He wanted more from Jordan, and he meant to get it.

I will make love to you, he thought as he pulled the carriage around to the back of the Tempest home and threw the reins to a coachman. *Or perhaps I will let you make love to me.*

Ever since she'd leaned on the arch near what she defined as a "blow job," he couldn't stop thinking about that act involving *her*. Every time her lips parted, he thought of the woman carved in stone, the one on her knees before Narcissus, her mouth poised to take him, and it made him hard all over again. He feared that Jordan and "blow job" were now inextricably linked in his brain. It wasn't healthy.

Nick stared at her under hooded lids while she went on about the individual features of the Tempest home, with its twin conical towers and abundance of gingerbread. How did she know so much about his house? She'd never seen a streetcar before, but she knew every architectural detail of his family home? She certainly was a puzzle. One he intended to solve one way or the other. If he had to seduce her secrets out of her, well, he would certainly enjoy that journey.

"Queen Anne," she said awkwardly, looking right into his eyes as he helped her descend from the carriage. He had her securely, but he didn't swing her down, just left her there with his hands at her waist and hers on his shoulders. She whispered, "I've always loved Queen Anne houses."

He was a betting man, one who always played the odds, and he would've laid a bundle on the fact that her thoughts had nothing to do with houses.

It was amusing to sneak her up the narrow, dark servants' stairs with no one in the house any wiser. She seemed to enjoy the subterfuge as well. Of course, bringing a woman into the Tempest home was nothing new for him, even if his parents weren't aware of that. They seemed to have ceded the top floor of the house to their children long ago, and Nick and Isabella had taken advantage over the years. This wasn't the first time he'd smuggled in a lady friend and then passed her off as a guest of his sister. Never anybody as distinctive as Jordan, however.

And now that he had her here, safe in his own home, what was he going to do with her? Funny that he didn't much care. He just knew he wanted her there, where he could keep an eye on her.

Isabella was the one person he risked running into upstairs as he ushered Jordan into his bedroom. But he wasn't concerned. Isabella would love a plot like this. He'd need her cooperation to get Jordan properly outfitted, anyway, plus he was counting on Bella to provide a cover story. He was interested in hearing whether she recognized the mysterious Miss Albright. His gaze settled on Jordan as she shed her hat and cloak and tested the feather mattress on the carved mahogany bed.

"I don't know how everybody isn't dying of heat all the time, wearing these heavy coats in the middle of summer," she commented as she discarded the cloak. "Whew. Heaven forbid an inch of skin shows, I guess."

A lot more than an inch was showing at the moment.

He didn't how much more he could handle. He'd better make finding proper attire his first priority. Maybe if she were wearing the right clothes, he would be less likely to be thinking with his cock all the time. He set his jaw. One could only hope.

Even putting aside the strange clothes, she was altogether too outspoken and audacious for polite company. If he told the truth, that was exactly why he liked her. But if she were ever to leave this bedroom she needed a bit of polish.

"The bathroom is next door if you need to freshen up," he told her, hesitating in the doorway with his hand on the glass knob. "I'm going to see if my sister is about. But until I come back, please stay in here, all right?"

Jordan was fooling with the lamp next to his bed. "I wondered whether you had electric lights. The Tempests keep up with the latest, huh?"

"When you live on Prairie Avenue, you must stay abreast of the neighbors," he said mockingly. "Besides, my sister is quite spoiled. Only the most up-to-date accoutrements will do."

"Good for her." She began gleefully examining the books on his bedside table, pulling open the drawers in the highboy, and generally poking into every corner in ways that no well-bred guest would. Jordan was unique, that was for certain.

"I don't mind if you look at the books on my table, but I'd really prefer you not go rooting around in my belongings," he said stiffly. *Good Lord.* He sounded like his father. Was there really anything she couldn't see in his dull, boring drawers?

"I'm sorry. You're right. That was rude of me." She sat down on the bed, but she brought with her a sculpture from his bureau. It was a marble hand. His hand. He should never have indulged Isabella by letting her sculpt it, but at the time, it had seemed harmless.

"What are you doing with my hand?"

"Your hand?" She glanced at him and then back at the chunk of marble cradled in her lap. She ran her fingers lovingly over the curve of the wrist, down to the ends of the fingers, making him decidedly uncomfortable before she raised dazed eyes to look at him again. "But this is *my* hand. I saw it sitting there on the top of your dresser and I recognized it immediately."

"I assure you, my sister sculpted that piece more than a year ago." He laid his own hand in her lap, right next to the marble version. "I think you will find they match."

Now she examined his real hand, feeling it up and down and around, in the same intimate manner she'd stroked the marble one. Perhaps offering his hand had not been the wisest idea.

"Totally the same," she said in awe. "But…" She broke off, pushing away from him, leaving the sculpture on the bed. "I don't understand any of this. This is your hand? But how did I get it?"

"You found it on my bureau," he reminded her.

"Not this one. The one in 2006!"

He had no reply to that. After a long pause, he simply suggested, "Why don't you pick up a book and read something while I go to check on Isabella?"

She closed her mouth, grabbed the nearest book and took a chair, propping her long, bare legs up on his desk. He couldn't take his eyes off those beautiful limbs splayed out for his inspection.

He retreated from the bedroom, hoping to clear his head and cool his blood. He checked the music room, but there was no Bella there. Not in the library or the ballroom, either.

"Isabella?" he called out, knocking on her bedroom door. But there was no answer. Nick slowly edged open the door, but saw only an empty bedroom with clothing articles scattered everywhere. Bella was not known for her neatness.

Quickly, he crossed to her closet, grabbing the first likely outfit he saw off the hooks. He was no expert on ladies' fashions, but the pale yellow, lace-edged walking suit looked acceptable to his eyes. Rummaging in the drawers of her dresser, he also found new white gloves and stockings, still pinned with the price tags from the family store.

He paused. What should he do about the more intimate details of the lady's toilette?

He'd undressed enough women to know she was going to need drawers, a camisole, petticoats, and a corset, no matter what the ladies back at the Women's Building thought, or Isabella's fashionable wardrobe would never fit the way it was intended. She was also going to need someone to lace her into that corset.

Nick smiled. Maybe this task had an upside after all.

Armed with everything he could think of, he returned to the bedroom. Jordan was sitting on his bed, barefoot, her legs stretched out in front of her and her nose in a book. Once again, she looked adorable, and his jaded heart began to beat a little faster. He frowned. Jordan in his bed was fine, but Jordan lodged in his heart was something else altogether.

"I have some things for you," he told her, trying to sound matter-of-fact and cheery. "Isabella's. I think you are approximately the same size."

"Thank goodness," she said with a sigh, slapping down the book and hopping off the bed. "I feel like a prisoner or something. When you're having an adventure, you want to get on with it, you know? Not sit around reading *Oliver Twist*."

"You're not a prisoner," he objected. "But you certainly can't see anyone until we've found proper clothes."

She took the bodice out of his hands, holding it up to her frame. "Good heavens, this is a lot of fabric. I could make six or seven tops out of the sleeves alone."

"That's what all the ladies are wearing," he assured her, setting the rest on the bed.

She slid her arms into the sleeves, trying to start hooking it on over her camisole. "The waist is so tiny."

"It's not meant to be worn that way. Here." He undid the one hook she'd fastened and then helped her pull it off, letting his hands rest on her shoulders longer than absolutely necessary.

His eyes lingered on her lips and he bent in closer. That spark—the one that said she wanted him and she was afraid of him, all at the same time—was glowing behind her amber eyes. She licked her bottom lip, sort of quivering with anticipation.

But he didn't kiss her. Nick smiled. It was rotten of him to tease her, but he liked keeping her off-balance. After all, that was the way her very presence kept him.

Softly, precisely, he said, "You'll need to remove what you're wearing. Every stitch."

"Why?" she asked uneasily. "Is this about giving me a makeover? Or getting me to strip for you?"

Nick backed away, adopting an innocent air. "It's the way the garments are made, I'm afraid." He picked through the pile of clothes on the bed, pulling out the camisole and the lace-edged drawers and holding them up. "You have to wear a camisole and drawers under a corset, and you'll need a corset for the dress to fit properly."

She started to object, but he refused to listen. "I'm not the person who sets these standards. It's what all the ladies wear. And in my experience, any lady who does not conform is treated as a social pariah. So I'm afraid there's no choice. You have to remove the clothes you're wearing now."

"I guess so," she said doubtfully. "But there's no reason you need to watch. Just hand me the stuff and I'll put it on."

"Stop being silly. I've already seen most of what you have to offer," he lied. "What difference do a few more scraps of fabric make? We're both adults." He laid down the challenge, holding the bloomers just out of reach. "Take off the denim item first."

"Doesn't the idea of me in even less clothing create even more risk of scandal?" she asked saucily.

"Not at all." He crossed his arms over his chest. "You're in my home. There is no risk of scandal here."

"Oh, all right." Awkward, blushing a most becoming shade of pink, she unfastened the metal snap at the waist of her skirt. Nick stood where he was, leaning casually against the bedpost, soaking in every detail.

Her eyes met his and she dropped the denim skirt to the floor. Now all that remained below her waist was a sliver of red silk. That was the silk he'd felt pressed against him when she was in his lap. His grip tightened on the bedpost as his body stiffened, responding to the memory and the picture of her in front of him, so prettily exposed. He was just glad he was wearing a suit coat, disguising the telltale bulge in his pants.

His gaze raked her long, slender legs and the inches of

skin just above the line of those ridiculously small knickers. He could see her hip bones, her navel, the soft curve of her belly as she stood before him, biting her lip, shifting slightly from foot to foot. Under the striped silk chemise she wore, her nipples hardened, peaking under the fabric. He let his eyes light there, then sweep the rest of her, well aware that his scrutiny was arousing her. He could see it written on her expressive face. She would never make a poker player.

Smugly aware of his own powers, he thought, *How far will you let this go, Jordan? How long before you beg me to take you, the way you wanted to under the arch?*

"What do I put on first?" she asked, glowering at him.

"Whatever you like," he said, his voice coming out gruff and raspy. He cleared his throat. "But you'll need to remove the rest of your garments first."

He could see her swallow. But she gave him a defiant stare, ripping the silk chemise off over her head in one quick motion, dropping it on the floor, revealing the most intriguing fragment of clothing yet. It was red and didn't cover much, but it hugged her soft, round breasts, binding them and displaying them to their best advantage, as if offering them up for a man's pleasure.

"Your undergarments are fascinating," he murmured. They covered so little. "Fascinating, but inappropriate."

"Now wait a minute—"

"The colors are too bright. They'll show through the fabric of the dress. And besides, a corset won't fit properly over that. Whatever that is." He pointed at the red binding over her breasts. "What do you call that, anyway?"

Jordan lifted her chin, sending him the message that she wasn't falling for his game. But it was a bad move, since it made her breasts rise, so firm and round, and his breath caught in his throat. "It's a bra. A Wonderbra, actually."

"It is a wonder," he said with more heat than he'd intended. His fingers were white as he clutched the bedpost, not trusting himself to let go. "But you'll still have to take it off. Unless you need my help to unhook it?"

"No, thank you. I've been taking my own bra off since I was twelve." Scooping up the fine linen camisole and bloomers, she waved a hand at him angrily. "But you need to turn around. Turn around."

He did as he was told, not bothering to tell her there was a mirror over the chest of drawers off to the side, and he could see her entire body shimmering in its reflection.

Working swiftly, she peeled off the Wonderbra and those tiny knickers, making her stunningly nude for just a second before she hastily pulled on the lacy camisole and stepped into the frilly drawers. It was a charming view, with her rose-colored nipples and the shadow of her thighs easily visible through the gauzy fabric. He felt his erection strain even harder against the fly of his trousers.

"Do the bloomers have a front and back?" she asked, trying to button them at her waist.

"What?" He had to get his mind out of his pants or lose it completely.

"The bloomers, the pantaloons, whatever you call them."

"I don't know. Just button them on best as you can. Petticoats, too."

"This is weird," she commented, adjusting a long petticoat over her knickers. "The crotch in the pants is open all the way from front to back. Are they ripped?"

"No, I'm afraid that's the way they come."

"Weird." She wiggled a little, testing them. "Kind of breezy down there."

"That's the way they are," he muttered. "Even ladies need to be able to…" First he discussed intimate sexual acts with her, and now bathroom etiquette. While she was squirming around taking the breeze on her nether regions! It was absurd. "They are open so that you may use the water closet if necessary."

"Well, yeah. I mean, easy access and all that, but… It just feels strange for the crotch to be open like that when you're used to something else."

"May I turn around now?"

"I guess," she said reluctantly. She was holding up the corset, examining its fasteners and laces. "Are the hooks in the back or the front?"

"Come over here," he motioned, moving aside, waiting for her join him at the foot of the bed. "I'll help you."

As she did, he took the corset from her, wrapping it around her middle, and bending to start hooking it up the front. His nose was practically buried in her round, firm breasts as he set to work. She just stood there, still as a statue, clearly uncomfortable as he fastened the corset. He yanked the last hook closed right under her breasts, jerking her forward.

Nick swallowed, his pulse pounding in his ears. He'd been trying to undermine her self-control, but it was his own he was fighting with. *Hoist with his own petard…* If he'd wanted her before, that desire had increased tenfold while he had his hands on her and his face practically buried in her cleavage.

His voice dropped into an even huskier register when he ordered, "All right, now turn around and grasp the bedpost."

"Is this really about the corset, Nick? Because I…"

"Be quiet." He drew the laces back, cinching her waist, and she inhaled sharply.

"I can hardly breathe," she complained, huffing and puffing a little.

"That's the only way Bella's dress will fit you," he told her. But her bottom was jiggling against him, weakening any shred of good intentions he had left. "Hold on to the bedpost as tight as you can."

"I'm going to pass out."

"You're doing just fine." Peering over her shoulder, he watched her breasts overflow the top of the corset, pushing against the thin muslin of her camisole. Her nipples were hard and distended and his hands ached to slide around to the front of the corset and fill his hands with her flesh.

She pushed her sweet little derriere back even more into the hard ridge of his desire, leaning forward to get more air into her lungs, and he knew he was moments away from taking her, right there, over the foot of the bed.

"Jordan…" he began, trying to hold himself back. "I don't know if I can…"

There was a loud knock on the door.

"Nick, are you there? It's Bella."

He went stock still.

"Come on, Nicky. I know you're there. I need to talk to you. Did you find my arch? You didn't do anything to it, did you?" She knocked again. "Nicholas Bonaventure Tempest, open this door!"

Jordan turned her head to look at him over her shoulder. "You can't let her in. I can't breathe! This thing is like an iron lung."

"Nicky!" his sister shouted. "I can hear you in there. I'll go get Mother if you don't open this door right now."

Nick pressed a soft kiss into the slope of Jordan's neck. "Nothing shocks Isabella," he told her. "Besides, you're wearing more than you were when I found you."

"Nick, undo my laces!" she protested hotly. "I'm not kidding—I can't breathe."

"Nicky?" Isabella shouted.

"There's no time," he whispered to Jordan. "Take smaller breaths."

"I'm already panting like a poodle!" she wheezed.

"Nicky!" Isabella began pounding on the door.

As he crossed to the door, Jordan grabbed up the jacket of the yellow suit, dragging it on over her arms, trying to make it meet in the middle so she could fasten it.

Nick paused at the door. His sister's timing had never been worse. "I'll be right there, Bella. Patience."

Behind him, Jordan was still attempting to do up her shirt front. He saw her attach the wrong hook to the wrong eye, but there was no time to fix it.

"Nicholas!"

He had no choice. He opened the door.

"Well, what took you so long?" Isabella demanded, barreling in. She blinked, getting a look at the other occupant in the room. "Oh." She smiled. "Well, well. My brother's found a new and very pretty diversion. How entertaining."

Jordan blushed about six shades of hot pink as Nick announced, in a tone much too formal for the surroundings, "Miss Jordan Albright, may I present my sister, Miss Isabella Maria Tempest."

"Pleased to meet you, Miss Albright," Isabella said cheerfully, circling around Jordan, looking her up and down. "Why, I do believe that's my dress you're wearing. Or half of it, at any rate. My petticoat, too? At least my brother has borrowed my newest items. I've never worn those. Nicky, is there a reason you're outfitting your lady friend from my closet?"

Jordan squirmed under Isabella's gaze, looking as if

she hoped another hole would open up and swallow her. "You're right, these are your clothes, but I can explain—"

"I gave them to her, Bella." He paused, trying to decide upon the best explanation. "I found her at the fair. She seems to have been set upon by thieves and all of her possessions stolen."

Bella bent to pick up one of Jordan's discarded sandals as well as her other two garments, examining the denim item and the brightly patterned chemise. "And all they left her were these bits and bobs?" She turned the shoe over, taking stock of its odd appearance. "My, those were thorough thieves."

"Yes," Nick agreed, "they were. Poor thing. They left her in nothing but some unsubstantial undergarments. As a gentleman, I felt it was my duty to bring her here and offer her shelter and clothing."

"Wasn't that sweet of you, Nicky?" Bella arched one golden eyebrow. "I take it you're not sputtering about my artwork anymore? Now that Miss Albright is monopolizing your attentions?"

"Lucky for you," he said darkly. "I saw it, Bella. I can't believe you abused Mother's good graces that way, displaying that piece of pornography at the Women's Building."

"It's not pornography!" Isabella and Jordan both chorused.

Bella glanced over, clearly surprised to find herself with an ally. "So you've seen it, too? How did you like it, Miss Albright?"

"It's amazing," Jordan told her, regaining some of her composure as the subject moved to her favorite topic of conversation. She was still breathing oddly, but she was definitely picking up speed and passion as she spoke about that blasted statue.

Nick rolled his eyes. With a defender as ardent as Jordan, Isabella was going to puff up with pride and become even more impossible.

"Your arch is a masterpiece," Jordan concluded. "Not only is it beautiful, but it represents a major turning point in the history of women in art."

"Really? How flattering." Bella linked her arm through Jordan's. "Go on."

"Don't encourage her," he tried, not even sure which one he was talking to.

"Well, you are the first female artist to give women orgasms," Jordan began with a good deal of enthusiasm.

Nick started to choke as his sister asked, "Am I really? I didn't realize."

"Yes, and it's very important, especially in the nineteenth century, when the idiots in charge were going around telling woman they weren't sexual beings." Jordan warmed to her topic, starting to sound more like herself. Apparently, she'd forgotten about the constrictions of the corset. "I mean, it's ludicrous! So for these sexually repressed Victorian ladies to see your work, where there are obviously women who enjoy sex and climax and everything right there, carved in marble, well, that's a revelation."

"Fascinating," Isabella responded.

"Horrifying," Nick growled, jamming his hands in his pockets.

"One thing… Why did you say *Victorian?* Do you mean British ladies are the ones most repressed, or the ones who'll benefit most from my work?"

"No, it's just that in my field, history," Jordan explained, "we use Victorian as a label for this entire period for both the U.S. and Britain, until Queen Victoria dies in 1901."

Nick waited for it to sink in that she had just said *1901*.

As in, eight years from now. But Isabella didn't make the same conclusion he had. Instead of looking to him to confirm that Jordan was well off her rocker, Isabella simply frowned, digesting the information.

"I see. Well, that's good. Because I think American women are even more backward when it comes to this sort of thing. It was only when I went to Europe—"

"Really? Europe was the important factor?" Jordan smiled. "That was my conclusion, when I wrote my dissertation, but I wasn't sure. Oh, Isabella, I am so happy to meet you! I have so many questions."

"Are you saying you are writing about me? How exciting!" She poked her brother. "Did you hear that, Nick? Someone is writing a book all about *me*."

"Did you also hear that she thinks Queen Victoria will die in 1901?"

Isabella brushed off his objection. "She's clearly a woman of great spirituality. Perhaps she can see into the future. Or perhaps she communicates with the dead. Ectoplasm, table-tapping, spirit closets... I've heard of such phenomena."

"Bella, those fortune-tellers with their ectoplasm and table-tapping are simply cheating people," he growled. "It's just a game to fleece the gullible, like you."

"'There are more things in heaven and earth than are dreamt of in your philosophy,'" Isabella quoted in a superior tone. "I think my new friend, Miss Albright, is charming, and if she says she can see the future, well, then I'll believe her. Am I to be famous, Miss Albright? Do tell!"

"Yes," Jordan said slowly. Her color was high, and she'd started gasping again. She had a hand pressed to her ribs. "Sort of. More like infamous."

"Oooh, even better!"

"Jordan, please don't do this," Nick pleaded, but she shook her head.

"I just figured it out, Isabella. I just realized why I'm here." Looking quite dizzy, Jordan raised a hand to her forehead. "It's all about you and the arch. I couldn't finish my dissertation because you disappeared, and no one knew where you or the arch went to. So I think…" She paused, trying to take a deep breath. "I think I'm supposed to save you."

9

How to Be a Scandalous Woman, Rule 9:
When you're an enigma wrapped in a riddle,
they'll have to try harder to solve your mystery.

JORDAN PLUCKED helplessly at the stays in the damn corset, afraid she was going to pass out from lack of oxygen. "Could someone please get me out of this thing? It's so tight, I think my ribs are collapsing."

But the two Tempests weren't paying her any attention. Since Isabella was about her size except for the unnaturally teeny, tiny waist, she figured the woman wasn't going to be all that sympathetic to her plight, anyway. She probably went through it on a daily basis.

Isabella was gloating to her brother. "She's come here to save me. This is thrilling, isn't it, Nicky? From what, do you think? White slavers, perhaps? A fate worse than death?"

"It's poppycock," he said flatly.

His sister swooped back to Jordan. "Do tell, Miss Albright! You don't mind if I call you Jordan, do you? I feel as if we're best friends now, since you are writing about me and mean to save me. I want to hear all the details!"

"Okay, listen!" Jordan announced. She started to unfasten the few hooks she'd done up the front the jacket. "Get me out of this iron lung first, and then we'll talk."

"Oh, heavens. Let me have a look." Isabella peeked under the jacket in the back. "Nick has laced you much too tight." She sent him an accusing glare. "You poor thing."

"I only tried to close it," he shot back. "I never claimed to be an expert on ladies' lingerie."

"Here, I've loosened it now."

Whew. She was actually getting oxygen to her brain again.

"About saving me?" Isabella prompted. "From what, exactly?"

"Well, disappearing," Jordan confessed. There was no way the bodice would close now, with the loose corset, so she had to leave it hanging open. Crotchless bloomers, breasts pouring over a corset and a blouse hanging open to reveal way too much… It was official—nineteenth-century fashion was built to make you feel like a sex slave.

"Disappearing? How?" Isabella asked eagerly.

Jordan tried to hold the pieces of her flouncy yellow jacket together in the front. "I don't know. No one knows. You see, on Friday, June 16, Mrs. Prentice Stanhope will take Susan B. Anthony on a tour of the Women's Building. They will discover your arch, and then it's curtains."

"Curtains?" Isabella echoed.

"You'll be arrested."

"No!" She was bubbling over with excitement at the news, clapping her hands together. "But that's wonderful! The publicity! The uproar! My name will be on everyone's lips!"

"If this were to happen, and I certainly hope it doesn't, our family name would be ruined," Nick said darkly. "Have you forgotten that that same name appears on our store? Do you think ladies will want to shop at a place linked to someone so notorious?"

"Oh, it won't do any harm to the family name," Jordan

said quickly. "I mean, your store will survive, still on State Street, still bringing in the soccer moms who want to buy out the Lancome counter."

Isabella glanced at Nick, looking for an explanation. "No, I don't understand, either," he said. "It's her dialect, apparently."

Jordan sighed. "Okay, let me say it a different way. The family will not be ruined and, yes, Isabella's name *will* be made. But, most important, after she's arrested, Isabella and the arch will vanish, never to be heard from again."

"How dramatic," Isabella said in a stage whisper.

"I looked for any clue, any scrap of information, but there's nothing," Jordan went on. "And that's not good. I mean, it's great to be famous, but wouldn't you rather be around to keep making art?"

"Oh, I'm not worried. Now that you've come, all will be well. I feel it in my bones."

"Bella, she does have a point. Perhaps you should move your arch back to the studio. Or throw it in Lake Michigan," he suggested. "I'm not saying I think Miss Albright can really see into the future, just that predicting an outcry over that particular piece is actually fairly obvious."

"Nicky, you're spoiling all my fun." She pulled Jordan aside. "Tell me more about my future, Miss Albright. Would it help if we had tea leaves or cards? Perhaps you'd like to look at my palm or feel the bumps on my head?"

"I'm not a fortune-teller," Jordan tried. "I just… Well, I don't know. You see, I'm a history graduate student. I teach a class on scandalous women at the University of Chicago. I was living a perfectly normal life, boring even, in 2006. I needed to finish my dissertation, but I couldn't, because I couldn't figure out what happened to you."

Isabella's pretty blue eyes were round as saucers. "My

word, that's ages in the future. Did you hear, Nicky? Not 1950 or even 1993. Clearly she's telling the truth. Why would anyone pick such a curious year as 2006?"

Jordan didn't exactly know what to say to that. "I didn't pick it. That's just when it was. I don't know why any of this is happening. Your arch showed up in an exhibit at the Art Institute. I went to see it, and boom. Here I am, with you."

Nick interjected, "Actually, you were with *me*. If you've been sent by mysterious forces to rescue Isabella from cruel fate," he said in a mockingly melodramatic tone, "then why didn't you end up in her studio, perhaps? Somewhere you were more likely to fall into *her* lap instead of mine."

She didn't blame him for being skeptical. It wasn't exactly a reasonable idea for a woman from 113 years in the future to suddenly pop up in your life. "I don't know. I didn't ask for any of this."

"Of course you didn't. It's just like that book by Mr. Mark Twain. You read it, too, Nick." Bella paused for a moment, chewing her lip. "What was the title? Oh, yes. *A Connecticut Yankee in King Arthur's Court*. Do you remember that book? The gentleman got knocked on the head, I believe, and landed right at Camelot with Merlin and Guinevere and the lot. It was very trying for him. They all thought he was a wizard and he got into all sorts of trouble."

"Yes, actually, I do remember. But I believe Mr. Twain was trying for humor, not realism."

"That hardly matters. Nicholas, this young lady has traveled through time expressly to save *my* life." Isabella looked very pleased with herself. "The least we can do is make her welcome."

Traveled through time… It was the first time the words

were out in the open. Jordan couldn't quite believe it herself. Her thoughts had been leading her to the same conclusion; she just hadn't been willing to say so. *Toto, I don't think we're in Kansas anymore.*

"There's no such thing as time traveling," Nick said with an edge of annoyance.

"Then how do you explain Miss Albright's peculiar shoes?" Bella asked. She picked up the one she'd been examining before. "I've never seen anything like this, have you?"

"No, but the Dutch wear little wooden boats for shoes, and I don't suppose they're from the year 2006."

"But her toes and her clothing…" Isabella turned the chemise inside out, showing the tag. "Banana Republic. What do you suppose that means? Feel the fabric. Look at the stitching. And the other one, the denim belt—"

"It's a skirt," Jordan said helpfully. "Calvin Klein. He's a designer. Banana Republic is a store."

"You see? A skirt. Does that look like any skirt you've ever seen?" Isabella demanded. "There's also the issue of her manner of speech. What did you say again, Jordan? I believe you said something about products being sold at Tempest & Son in the future. Something German that reminded me of dessert. *Sacher Torte?*"

"Actually, it was *soccer mom.* Soccer is a sport. Mom is just, you know, like mother." Jordan shook her head. "It isn't really important. The big thing was that Tempest & Trent makes it just fine, not at all damaged by the scandal over the arch at the Women's Building."

"Did you say Tempest & *Trent?*" Nick asked. "That's not the name of our store."

"Well, it will be." Jordan searched her hazy memory. It was strange how clear and sharp some things were, and how fuzzy others. "Tempest is you and Trent is…" She remembered. Of course. One of her two pictures of Nick was a wedding picture. With a sense of dread, she said, "Trent comes from your wife, Lydia. Tempest & Trent is the merger of two great department store dynasties."

"I am not married. To Lydia Trent or anyone else," he said curtly.

"Yes, but you will be. June, 1894. I've seen the picture."

Nick swore under his breath, pacing back and forth at the end of the bed. "This is absurd."

Her heart did a small leap to hear that. *Don't marry Lydia!*

On the other hand, her head was telling her that he was going to do that very thing. She couldn't change history, could she? Well, she was already trying to figure out how to stop Isabella from disappearing. Maybe she could keep Nick from marrying, too.

"That would be wrong," she whispered. "You have to go back—Captain Kangaroo said so—and you want to leave him, not married, without his department store dynasty? That's pretty mean, Jordan."

Even if the idea of Nick married to the stiff, unpleasant woman in the picture was just plain nasty.

"What are you muttering about now?" Nick asked. "More prophesies of doom?"

It was too confusing. It made her head hurt just to think about all the problems with this time travel theory. She'd seen it in movies and TV shows, where somebody always screwed something up, changing the entire course of history, and then monkeys ruled the earth or something equally dire when they got back.

"I think she's telling the truth. How would she have known about Lydia?" Isabella argued. "Who besides us had any idea what Father was planning? You can't explain that away."

"No," he said tersely. "I can't."

"It's perfectly clear that she is a time traveler." She squeezed Jordan with enthusiasm. "It's wonderfully exciting. Do you remember anything else? I'd love to take you to visit some of my friends and perhaps foretell their futures, too."

"Isabella, this is not a parlor trick."

"No, don't try to dissuade me," his sister interrupted. "I won't be put off my theory. She's journeyed through time and that's that. The only question is what's to be done about it now."

"I think when I hit my head, it affected my memory," Jordan said woozily. Things only got worse when her oxygen was cut off by the stupid corset. Now, her head was crowded with fragments of history that might be important—stock market crash, Wright brothers, world wars, the Internet—and there was no way to warn them about all the calamities and craziness ahead in the twentieth century. "I don't seem to be able to predict what I will or won't remember."

"First things first," Isabella announced, sounding an awful lot like her pushy brother. "We need to get you properly dressed so we can feed you something and take you out. You must go out and about if you're to have any fun at all while you're here. How do you feel about the opera, Jordan? Oh, and the Fieldings are having a dinner party on Wednesday evening."

"I don't think—"

But Isabella stormed on. "My clothes are too small for you, so we'll need to see what we can find and then get the dressmaker to whip something up as speedily as possible.

You'll need an evening gown and perhaps an afternoon dress, and, of course, boots and slippers." She frowned. "Perhaps Mother has something we can borrow. Her feet are a bit larger than mine. If not, I'm afraid you'll be marching around in Cook's workboots."

"She's not going to the opera or the Fieldings. You may not show off Miss Albright like a trained monkey," Nick ordered.

"She'll want to have some fun!"

"I don't really know how long I will be here," Jordan put in delicately. Evening gowns and the opera and fashionable dinner parties? She'd never done any of that in her own time. She could just imagine trying not to make ten or twelve major faux pas her first trip into someone's drawing room. "I think I can probably pass on the parties. The Gilded Age is more formal than I'm used to."

"Is that what they call us? The Gilded Age?" Isabella tipped her golden curls to one side. "I like that rather better than Victorian. I am personally not under the old bat's rule and I don't see why Americans should have to bear that label. It seems wrong to me. What do you think?"

"Bella, leave her alone!" Nick commanded. "Promise me you won't share this outrageous tale of time travel. Frankly, Jordan's story is incredible. If you tell anyone else about it, I fear the two of you will end up sharing a room at the insane asylum."

"Pish tosh," Isabella scoffed. "Victoria Woodhull and her sisters claim that spirits from the Great Beyond knock out stock tips on their tea table and no one has them committed."

"Bella," he said sternly, "don't speak about this with anyone else. Especially not our parents."

"Oh, I don't tell them anything. They are dreadfully

dull, our parents." With that, she linked her arm through Jordan's again, leaning in close to whisper conspiratorially, "Come with me, Jordan. First we'll find you something to wear, something right for dinner, plus I shall do up your hair and answer all of your questions. I find it fascinating that you are writing about me. Ask anything you like, and I will be sure to answer in full."

"Jordan, wait." His expression was firm and unyielding. "I speak from experience when I say that letting Isabella run roughshod over you is a terrible proposition. She is impulsive and spoiled, and no good can come of it." As Isabella reacted by smacking him on the shoulder, he reminded Jordan, "We agreed that you would follow my lead."

He sounded an awful lot like Daniel for a minute there. Were all men control freaks, or was it just the ones she ran into?

Okay, so Captain Kangaroo *had* told her she was supposed to stick to Nick like glue, but that just didn't make any sense. *Isabella* was the one who was going to disappear.

Besides, with Nick, she'd be cooped up in his bedroom, laced into a too small corset and crotchless bloomers, thinking about nothing but his eyes and his body and…sex, sex, sex. It was inevitable.

Sooner or later, the two of them were going to explode, and that couldn't be good. They'd spend all their time in bed. She'd never save Isabella that way!

Besides, she had this new mission, this new seizing the day thing going on. She'd never been as brave and bold as the scandalous women she taught about in her class, but there was no time like the present—or the past—to start.

If 1893 needed to be met head on, then that's what she

would do. To Nick, she said coolly, "I need to figure out why and how Isabella was going to disappear so I can stop it."

"I can keep an eye on my sister," he snapped. "She hardly needs you as her bodyguard."

Jordan shook her head, following Isabella to the door. If she stuck with Isabella, maybe she could right history. And if she steered clear of Nick, maybe he would end up marrying Lydia and creating the department store dynasty, the way things were supposed to be.

"I'm going with Isabella." She met his eyes. Damn those beautiful blue eyes that made her melt him every time she looked at him. She wanted him so badly she couldn't stand up straight, and that couldn't be. Not when she was spinning more off-balance every moment. Not when she was apparently stuck in the middle of 1893, up a creek without a paddle, not sure how much history she was allowed to change.

It was one thing to stop Isabella from vanishing, righting something that definitely went wrong the first time around. But quite another to give in to desire and sleep with Nick, screwing things up in ways she couldn't even imagine. What if she got even more attached and wanted to stay? What if she got pregnant?

Women from 2006 were not supposed to have sex while visiting other times. That much seemed crystal clear.

10

How to Be a Scandalous Woman, Rule 10:
Fake it till you make it.

AS SHE AND ISABELLA descended the grand front staircase later that evening, Jordan felt like Eliza Doolittle, the cockney street urchin trying to be a lady. She had butterflies that had nothing to do with the whalebone sticking her in the ribs.

Well, she now understood why Victorian women were so repressed, didn't she? It was impossible to be anything else when everything was laced and buttoned and bound within an inch of its life, and you had to breathe very carefully if you didn't want to risk splitting a seam. What she wouldn't have given for a pair of jeans and a T-shirt.

Maybe she shouldn't have given Isabella free rein to turn her into some turn-of-the-century Barbie doll. In the end, wearing a puffy pink dress (she hated pink) that was covered in bows and lace, a pair of slippers that pinched her toes, with her hair arranged in silly curls all over the top of her head, she thought she looked ridiculous.

When Nick came to meet them at the bottom of the stairs, lounging there with his hands in the pockets of his black pants, she wanted to kill him. His outfit, with a black jacket and white tie and vest, was much more formal than hers, but so much more comfortable! It wasn't fair.

Jordan tried to swallow, hoping she wasn't going to fall out of her dress, as Nick pulled her over to introduce her to his parents. If that wasn't a situation fraught with peril, she didn't know what was. She and Isabella had rehearsed a story to tell them—something about meeting her in London, yada yada yada—and Isabella had also given her a crash course in dinner etiquette, but she felt woefully unprepared, especially when faced with florid, overweight Mr. Tempest, his mustache twitching as he looked down his nose at his children, and elegant Mrs. Tempest, who seemed as if she'd never laughed in her life.

Her mind suddenly blanked on the issue of which fork was which, and she felt panic begin to creep in. Was it silly to be so anxious about forks? She really had much bigger problems than that right now. Like her sleeves. They were beyond leg-of-mutton and into leg-of-elephant territory. If elephants had pouffy legs. And if she didn't concentrate, she could easily knock all the good china right off the table with one swoosh of a sleeve.

This was a formal, stuffy world, and she'd practically been raised by wolves. When she was little, she'd always dreamed of fancy tea parties where everybody held up their pinky fingers and daintily ate cucumber sandwiches, instead of her mother's "feel free to express yourself and fingerpaint the living room with your birthday cake" affairs. All those manners in old movies and books had seemed so civilized, so pretty. Now, faced with a world where etiquette was everything, she really wished she could throw out all the rules and be herself.

Anybody for fingerpainting with birthday cake? That I know how to do.

Yeah, sure, she could eschew etiquette and be herself.

If she wanted to find her pink-bowed butt out on the mean streets of 1893 Chicago.

It was too late for independence. Nick was performing the ritual of introductions. Who knew there was a whole set of rules about whose name you said first and whether bowing or handshakes were acceptable?

"Mother, Father, may I present Miss Jordan Albright? Miss Albright is a friend of Isabella's, visiting us to see the World's Fair," Nick announced, inclining his head at each of them as he spoke their name. "Miss Albright, may I present my parents, Mr. and Mrs. Tempest."

"I know you will love Jordan as I do," Isabella interrupted. She blurted, "I met her in an art class in London and we became fast friends. I extended an invitation to visit us for the fair and I'm ever so glad she decided to come."

Her delivery was incredibly phony. If anybody in the room didn't suspect that was a made-up story, Jordan would be very surprised.

But no one said a word. There was that polite veneer after all. It probably wasn't done to out your visitors. Still, Jordan could tell not much escaped Henry Horatio Tempest's beady eyes.

"Pleasure to meet you, Miss Albright," he barked, tweaking one side of his impressive mustache between his fingers, casting glances between his two children and Jordan. He paused, waiting, as Nick and Isabella both watched her, frantically trying to send her signals.

Okay, now was the time to bow, right? Don't take his hand. Unmarried women do not offer hands to married men. Bow. Not too much, just a little, and then he'll tip his head at you, and that's it, you're introduced. Phew.

He seemed satisfied. She'd made it through the first test.

"Albright, eh?" Mr. Tempest asked, extending an arm

to walk her into the dining room. "Are you related to the Philadelphia Albrights? I believe I know an Albright in Philadelphia, don't I, Maude?"

"Yes, Henry," his wife said politely. "I believe that's Wilton Albright, the shipping magnate."

"No, no relation." Jordan smiled weakly.

"Then who are your people, my dear?" Maude Tempest asked, casting an uneasy glance up and down the dress she was wearing.

Was something wrong with the dress? Jordan didn't exactly know what to say about her *people,* either, but Isabella took that one before she had a chance. "Jordan is an orphan. All alone in the world. Poor child." And then she sighed extravagantly. "Such a sad and tragic story."

Jordan could see the smile playing around Nick's lips as Isabella made up some fairy tale about overturned carriages and blizzards in the Alps. *Oh, dear.*

As dinner started, Jordan just tried to keep her mouth shut and follow whatever the others did. She was determined not to mention one thing that showed her up as a traveler from Future World. No television or movie or pop culture references. Zip that lip.

She sent Nick a surreptitious glance or two, wondering what he was thinking. He was so quiet, so reserved. He'd turned into a different person.

Dinner became a blur as they were seated and the rest of the group exchanged endless chitchat. They talked on and on about Maude Tempest's social obligations and H. H. Tempest's business dealings, with lots of back and forth between Nick and his father about the store, as they were served course after course of food she didn't recognize. Heavy, creamed soup with something green floating in it, everything drenched in thick sauces, and no way to refuse to eat any of it without looking rude… It took her about half an hour to realize that the tiny container in front of her plate held salt. Well, no salt for her. She had no idea how you were supposed to move it from the little cup to your plate.

The wine was excellent, however. Jordan kept sipping from her glass, tasting this and that as plates arrived and disappeared, trying to eat it all in good humor. Good heavens, dinner was a production. She lost track of how many servants there were and how many dishes came and went. Did they do this every night? She thought longingly of her TV tray at home, of eating dinner and watching *Survivor* in her flannel pajama pants.

She was hacking at a piece of veal with white sauce and what was either coconut or shredded crab on the top, when she suddenly realized everyone was looking at her. Quickly, she checked her silverware, but no, she was using the same fork and knife as Nick, so that couldn't be it.

"Miss Albright?" Mr. Tempest prompted, and she realized he'd asked her something she didn't hear.

"I'm sorry?"

"I asked if you dabbled in sculpture like our Isabella."

"Oh, no, nothing like that. I don't have any artistic talent, I'm afraid."

"Then what sort of class did the two of you share?" Mrs. Tempest inquired.

"Art history," Jordan made up on the spot. "Yes, art history. In London. At the Victoria and Albert."

"What's that?"

"The Victoria and Albert?" Ooops. Must not be there yet. "It's a, uh, museum. Very new. Just opened."

"I see." Maude Tempest smiled gently. "We shall be

sure to look for it next time we visit London, won't we, Henry?"

He was too busy tucking into his veal to answer.

"Our class—the art history class at the Victoria and Albert—is how Jordan came to appreciate my talent," Isabella said gaily, embroidering on her lead. "She thinks I am important to history. Isn't that so, Jordan?"

Nick shook his head as Jordan agreed, "Yes, I do."

H.H. frowned. "I'm not sure that's wise, to swell Isabella's head that way. Bella, your mother says you've talked your way into a space at the Columbian Exposition. What's that all about?"

"I have made a marble arch, and it's my best piece yet," Isabella confessed happily. Nick made a polite cough, but his sister ignored him. "Everyone will be talking about my arch. You wait and see!"

Mr. Tempest made a "harrumph" noise, his face growing redder by the moment, as Mrs. Tempest looked uncomfortable. She asked, "Is that really wise, Bella? To have everyone talking?"

"Of course it is. How else am I to further my career?"

"Your little hobby is no career," her father trumpeted. "Ladies do not need careers. All you're doing is ruining your marriage prospects."

"I do not want any marriage prospects!" Bella shouted right back.

Jordan glanced from face to face, worried about the fighting, which seemed to fly in the face of everything Isabella had told her about good table manners. Nick looked a little green around the gills, so maybe he didn't like it, either. But the Tempest parents seemed blithely unconcerned, except for Mr. Tempest's rising color.

Isabella slapped her napkin down next to her plate. "I

am not a piece of merchandise for you to sell at Tempest & Son," she said angrily. "Use Nick as bait for a merger if you must, but I shall not be used! I shall never marry just to line your pockets, Father!"

And with that, she slammed away from the table and ran from the room. *Uh-oh.*

"You see now why I do not support my foolish daughter's romantic notion of a career." Mr. Tempest puffed himself up. His face really was an alarming shade of magenta. "All it does is make her more rebellious and ridiculous. It's disgraceful for a well-bred young woman to act this way."

"She is very talented, Mr. Tempest," Jordan said softly.

But he just made that same "harrumph" sound, ignoring Jordan completely. "Nick, I've asked you time and again to take her in hand. I fail to see why you haven't made more progress in subduing Isabella."

Jordan's eyes widened. Subduing Isabella? What did that mean, exactly? She had visions of Isabella wrapped in a blanket and dropped in Lake Michigan. Was that how she disappeared? Her father ordered Nick to *subdue* her?

Why didn't Nick say something? Why didn't he defend his sister's right to create her own art and live out her passion? She felt like kicking him under the table, but he was too far away.

"Nick?" his father demanded. "Please tell me why you continue to fail on this very simple exercise. How do you expect me to trust you with running my entire operation if you can't control one small slip of a girl?"

Nick drained his wine glass. "Father, you couldn't control her, and that's why you turned the task over to me. How do you expect me to do what you couldn't?"

"Something must be done," H.H. blustered. "I suppose

this new masterpiece of hers is even worse than before. Maude, you should never have used your influence to get her a space."

Stiffly, Mrs. Tempest said, "Isabella would not embarrass me."

"There you're wrong, Mother," Nick said quietly. "I'm afraid I have seen it, and it's…outrageous. Even for Isabella."

Now Mr. Tempest also rose from the table. His face was so purple, Jordan wasn't sure he wouldn't topple right over into the fruit cup. "I knew it! Well, Nick, you must stop her. Do you hear me? This can't go on!"

"I think you should calm down, Mr. Tempest," Jordan ventured. She couldn't just sit by and let this go on. Maybe this was her moment to change history and save Isabella, right here, right now.

"Jordan," Nick warned. "This is not the best time for this."

"No, I'm sorry, but I have to say this." She lifted her chin. "I've also seen her new piece, and I think it's beautiful. It's stunning. It would be a terrible injustice if it were removed from the fair or if someone with her talent were lost to the world. That's just wrong."

"Talent? Isabella? She wastes expensive marble on crude figures of naked men. How is that a talent?" her father raged.

"Would you say the same about Michelangelo?"

"Isabella is no Michelangelo. He was a man! It's one thing for a man to sculpt classical nudes, but for a young girl…" He shook his head so violently his mustache whipped from side to side. "It is improper. It is obscene."

"Just because she's a woman," Jordan countered, "does not take away her right to express her talent and her sensuality in whatever form she chooses."

Her words incited Henry Horatio Tempest so completely that he just stood there and sputtered.

Finally, he shouted, "Women do not have feelings such as...what you said. They do not! Everyone knows that! Especially not amongst the upper classes. It isn't done!"

"Nick, would you please escort Miss Albright to her room? I think Isabella would like to speak with her," his mother announced in withering tones.

"It would be a pleasure." Nick pushed back his chair, moving around the table to take Jordan's arm.

"Don't you think maybe you should tell your father how wrong he is?" Jordan whispered.

His glare gave her her answer. She set her napkin neatly next to her plate and rose with as much dignity as she could muster in a pink dress with sleeves the size of sofa cushions. Nick escorted her from the table, but she could hear Mr. Tempest's raised voice behind her.

"I want her out of my home!" he bellowed. "It's no wonder Isabella behaves the way she does when her friends are even more impertinent than she is!"

"Now, Henry," his wife replied. "Your color is terrible. You must calm down. Nick will take care of it. He always does."

"Lucky you," Jordan said under her breath.

"Jordan, there was no reason to pick a fight with my father," he told her. "He says his piece, and I handle Isabella. It's the way we've always done things."

"Okay, first of all, I didn't start it. He did. I know, he's my host and I'm supposed to be all quiet and polite. But did you hear what he said? Women don't have sensuality?" She rolled her eyes. "I mean, you don't agree with that!"

He said nothing.

"Well, I know you don't, even if you won't say so," she

argued. "Your father is a bully, your mother is miserable, and Isabella is going to disappear on Friday! That's kind of hard evidence that your methods aren't working."

"It might be wise for you to hold your tongue, lest I lose the battle to keep you here." Shaking his head, he looked grim. "Why I choose to fight this battle is beyond me."

"Nicholas?" It was his mother coming up behind them. "Dear, may I speak with you, please?"

"Excuse me," he said coldly. Then he left Jordan where she was standing at the foot of the grand staircase and joined his mother. "Mother, can you please speak to Father? It's important to me that Miss Albright stay."

"Yes, of course, darling. He'll calm down in due time. But…" She touched his arm. "But I am worried about you. I saw you with your heads together, and now you tell me that she is important to you?"

Jordan couldn't hear his reply.

"She is not right for you, Nicholas. She seems cheap and common and I think she is wearing my maid's dress. I know I've seen it before." She squinted at Jordan, who pretended to find the painting next to the stairs fascinating. "Please, Nicholas, be careful. Scandal involving Isabella or her friend could ruin your chances of marrying the Trent girl."

"Mother—"

"I know you will do what's right." And with that, and one last anxious glance at Jordan, she swept back into the dining room.

It was clear the Tempests had bigger plans for their son than hooking up with some cheeky waif off the street who wore dresses borrowed from the hired help. Lydia Trent was the chosen one. It was all incredibly depressing.

She narrowed her eyes, thinking things over. Given how

attached the Tempests were to propriety, she was seriously wondering if they were the ones who somehow made Isabella disappear. Her father's words sounded very dire and very permanent. Definitely something to keep an eye on.

Scampering up the steps, Jordan went to find one of the maids to help her out of the horrible pink dress. Her mind was whirling, as usual. All the while the girl unhooked and unfastened her, she stewed about it. She wanted badly to put her thoughts in order, make a list and sketch out a plan.

But how could she make plans when everything was out of her control?

Drowning in a borrowed nightgown that was way too big, but felt terrific after the tight dress she'd had to wear to dinner, Jordan stretched out on the feather bed in the guest room, turned onto her side, and stared at the wall her room shared with Nick's. Was he going to bed, too? Was he undressing right next door?

She groaned. This place was so weird. It was as if all the pins and buttons and laces made thinking about sex even more potent, as if covering everything up made you want to rip off the cover that much more.

It was a theory, anyway.

"Aw, Nick, what should I do? I'm sorry if I made it worse with your dad, but he was really being an ass," she whispered into her pillow. "I don't know. Should I agree with you and ol' H.H. and squash Isabella long enough to get the arch out of the public eye?"

That was certainly one choice. If they succeeded in covering it up, then Isabella wouldn't be arrested and presumably wouldn't disappear.

"But that goes against all my principles," Jordan told herself sternly. "I believe in freedom of expression. I believe in the message of the arch and Isabella's right to own her sexuality. No doubt on that one. There has to be another way."

Not that she had a clue what that other way was.

"And here I am, going to sleep, not sure whether I'll even wake up in the same century." She took a deep, shaky breath. So many things to be unsure of. If she woke up here tomorrow, she had to find what to wear and how to wear it, she had to figure out what to do with her hair, and find some shoes that fit better than Mrs. Tempest's maid's spare slippers.

Given all that, would it be so bad to wake up home in her own bed?

Yeah, it would.

"This is where I need to be," she told herself. She remembered the curator's words. *You're here for a reason, and that will become clear.* "I have to keep Isabella from disappearing. I know I can. I just need to put things in order and think it through."

But as she fell asleep, Jordan's thoughts were not on lists or plans. Instead, she was Galatea again, only a statue made of clay, and Nick was Pygmalion. He was nude. He was always nude in her dreams, and it was wonderful.

"Mmm… Blue eyes," she murmured. Of course he had blue eyes.

She melted into the dream, ecstatic to be back in a world she knew. It was the White City, but not exactly, but a gallery, definitely. Very white. Filmy drapes. Blue skies. Blue eyes.

She was a statue, his creation, and he molded her with his hands. His fingers carved her out of clay, warming her, drenching her with hunger, shaping her breasts and her waist and her thighs, his hands everywhere, until she was desperate to become real so that she could make love to him the way that he made love to her as he sculpted.

His desperation was palpable, too. He grew increasingly frustrated, and she saw it in his eyes and felt it in his fingers as he teased her nipples into tight, hard points, as he stroked her folds, as he caressed her thighs.

It was maddening to be only a statue and unable to respond.

And then he knelt before her, his hands on her thighs, and he pressed his mouth to her very core, breathing life into her from the inside out.

"Just like that, Nick," she said drowsily, turning over onto her back, wet and ready to be loved. In her dream, clay had turned to warm, trembling flesh as his tongue flicked against her nub, sliding into the center of her being.

Clunk. Her head hit the carved mahogany headboard. She looked up at an unfamiliar ceiling, ornate with painted cherubs, plaster moldings and trim.

Still in 1893, clearly.

Damn. Why did she have to wake up?

11

How to Be a Scandalous Woman, Rule 11:
Don't waste your time on knights in shining armor.
Look for the tarnished ones.

"EXPLAIN YOURSELF, Nicholas," his father demanded.

Having just entered the library, Nick wondered how far the nearest Scotch decanter was. He could definitely use a drink, whether it was before noon or not. He rubbed his forehead. "What am I explaining?"

"Smithers tells me you did not even make an appearance at Tempest & Son yesterday. The entire day!" He shook his head from side to side. "And here you are again, at home this morning. I would never have handed you the reins of the company if I'd known you intended to ignore your responsibilities this way. Why, I was there every morning at eight, rain or shine."

Nick did not point out that the company had also faltered considerably during the time his father was making his regular appearances. After too many unwise investments and foolish expansion during economic hard times, Tempest & Son had been shaken to the core. The senior Tempest had retired from day-to-day management and put Nick in charge only because he had no other choice.

"I've been at the head of the company for less than a year, and I've already put us on a stronger financial footing, as you well know." He regarded his father calmly. "It's been a terrible year in the economy, with bank panic after panic, and yet we have survived and even prospered. I believe I am entitled to set my own schedule."

"It doesn't look right if the man in charge isn't on the premises. We have 400 employees at the store. Who's to watch over them?"

"Smithers, perhaps?" Nick suggested with more than a touch of sarcasm.

"And then there's Isabella's damned art project," H.H. went on, changing the subject entirely. "The last one was shameful enough. This new abomination must be destroyed. Simply must. And then we'll have to send Isabella off to a convent or some such, somewhere she won't be allowed to pick up a chisel."

He hadn't actually told his father anything about the particulars of the immoral arch, but he wasn't surprised he was on the warpath. Forcibly retired, the old man didn't have enough to do, so he was always chewing on something. If only *he* would take the trip to Europe that Isabella wanted so badly.

"I think Bella can be reasoned with."

"We're far better off taking matters into our own hands. And that young woman you brought into my home," his father continued to fuss. "That Albright woman. Entirely unsuitable."

"Unsuitable for what?"

"For you." His jowls quivered with indignation. "You are spoken for."

"You mean Lydia Trent, I assume." Nick tossed himself

into a leather wing chair. It was a very comfortable chair. He hadn't slept well, and this chair would be an excellent place for a nap.

Facing the door to the main hall, he wondered idly if Jordan had come down yet. He hadn't seen her. He hadn't seen her last night, either, after that unsatisfactory dinner. She'd disappeared upstairs before he'd finished talking to his mother, and he hadn't had a chance to catch up to her. He'd almost thought that a woman who talked as openly about sex as she did might be waiting in his bed. But it hadn't happened. Pity.

Without any real enthusiasm, he tuned in to what his father was bellowing about.

"The timing is crucial. The opportunities are there. And that is why you need to get onboard with the Trent girl."

"I've already told you I have no intention of marrying her."

"The company needs their money."

"Let's hope not." Personally, he would've preferred selling off the company tomorrow rather than selling himself to the Trents. He knew his father didn't share that opinion. Henry Horatio Tempest had made his fortune by marrying well, so he didn't see any reason his son should balk at a similar arrangement.

"It's good business," his father persisted.

"It's *my* life," Nick said flatly.

He and his father had argued these same issues too many times to count. *I don't like the way you manage the store, manage your sister, manage your personal life.* H.H. wouldn't let it rest.

The old man sniffed, "It's also our family's well-being and reputation. Nothing to be taken lightly."

"And that's why I'm not taking it lightly." Hearing footsteps and rustling skirts in the hall, just outside the library door, Nick sat up straighter.

"Is that Isabella? Bring her in here and let's give her a talking-to about this uproar she's trying to create at the fair. Let's get that taken care of right now. Let's get a crew with some hammers down there to do away with the infernal thing."

"I believe it was…" *Jordan*. Instead, he said, "Cook. I need to speak with her."

And with that, he was up and out of the library.

"What do you need to speak to Cook about?" His father bristled, but Nick didn't answer. He was already out in the hall, closing the double doors to the library, advancing on Jordan.

She was wearing the yellow walking suit he'd tried to get her into last night, but the jacket was open, instead of fastened, and she had a lacy white blouse underneath. Instead of last night's elaborate curls, today she wore her hair simply braided and coiled around her head.

"I thought that was you," he said, cornering her against the newel post on the landing. He reached out to touch a stray tendril escaping from one braid. "You disappeared last night. Avoiding me?"

"No. Why should I do that?"

"I thought perhaps you were afraid of repeating our encounter in the bedroom." He leaned closer. "Were you frightened of me, Jordan?"

"Our encounter?" She tipped her head to one side, looking up at him as if he were an exhibit at the zoo. "Do you mean when you were supposedly helping me with the corset and you made me strip and then you came on to me? Hmm? Is that what you mean?"

His lips curved into a knowing smile. "Something like

that. Since you…" He adopted her words, wondering what it meant that he was actually starting to understand her without translations. "Since you came on to me first, I thought I would repay the favor."

"Consider it repaid. Done. Over. Not gonna happen again." She tried to move past him, but he blocked her path, catching her hand.

"That's a shame."

"Not so much." She sent him an unamused look, attempting to pull her hand away, but there were spots of color high on her cheeks. Haughty all of a sudden, she declared, "You didn't turn out to be who I thought you were."

"And who would that be?"

"Someone like Zeus, Apollo, Hercules," she listed in a snippy tone. "A real hero."

Her cheeks grew pinker, and he saw the heat in her gaze. She kept stealing glances down his body, below his waist. The vixen.

Unless he was mistaken, all of the characters she'd mentioned were represented on the arch. So she thought he belonged on the arch, did she? No wonder she was getting warmer. If he pictured her in the poses of the goddesses on that arch for even a few seconds, he'd work up a sweat himself. He rubbed his thumb in the center of her palm, holding tight to her hot little hand.

She swallowed, finishing up with, "Someone who understands that women should be in charge of their own destiny." And then she wrenched her hand free of his grasp.

"I don't believe you've read the same Greek myths I have," he said mockingly. "It seems to me that Zeus is always looking to trick or deceive his next conquest. Apollo spit in someone's mouth because she refused his advances—"

"Cassandra."

"Yes, I thought so. Gave her some curse, didn't he? And then there's Narcissus, self-involved and shallow, and infamous recipient of the…" He paused. Would she say it?

"Blow job," she whispered, her face aflame. She made the mistake of licking her lip, too, and Nick wanted to laugh out loud.

"So I take it that all of this disappointment in me stems from the fact that I chose not to defend Bella to my father. Is that what this is about, your deciding that I am apparently not worthy of the, uh, same treatment as Narcissus?"

He let it hang there, so they would both have the same mental image for a good, long moment.

"You should have spoken up," she snapped. Her eyes were blazing as she crossed her arms over her chest.

"I think it's wonderful that you feel so passionately about my sister's art."

"You do not."

"Actually, I do." He smiled. "I think most everything about you is wonderful."

"You do not."

He raised a hand, palm out, as if taking an oath. "It's the honest truth."

Jordan chewed her lip, peering at him. He could tell she was trying to judge his sincerity. "I'm not kidding about this, Nick. If you love your sister, you'll make sure she's safe."

He sighed. Jordan was entertaining and appealing, but the fortune-telling was getting tiresome. "I don't want a scandal erupting around my sister any more than you do. But if I remove the arch, that will eliminate the scandal and ensure that she is perfectly safe. Until the next time she decides to sculpt erotica. I don't see the problem. Remove arch, remove problem."

Jordan shook her head. "You can't destroy it. I heard your father just now, in the library. What did he say? Something about sending men with hammers to take care of it?"

"He's not the one who makes these decisions." Nick shrugged. "I would prefer to move it out of there now, before anyone sees it."

"But it *needs* to be seen," she insisted. "Its message about the sexual nature of women is vital."

"Please don't start that again."

"But if you move it or smash it…" She broke off. "I'll never get home, Nick. I think it's my only way back to 2006."

He exhaled a long breath. Her time travel mythology was expanding in scope. "Now you think the arch is a magic portal to another time? My sister is not only a genius but a powerful sorceress who can suspend time?"

"No, not like that. I don't know." Agitated, she swooped under his arm to step onto the polished wood floor below the landing. "The curator—the man you saw yesterday in the Columbian Guard uniform—he told me that I had to go back the same way I came. I came under the arch. So? You see? I have to go back under the arch. And if you take a sledgehammer to it, how will I get back?"

He paused. "You do realize how that sounds?"

"Of course I realize! It sounds like *The Wizard of Oz* or something. Just click your ruby slippers together three times and say 'There's no place like home!'" Wincing, she tugged at a hairpin fastened in one of her braids. "I thought when I woke up this morning, I would be back home. But no! Here I am, still waiting for the maid to come and squash me into these horrible clothes and scrape my hair into these awful braids and lace me into boots that pinch my toes."

"You look very pretty in the yellow dress," he said kindly.

"I don't look pretty! I look stupid," she shot back. "My entire body would fit into one sleeve, and yet the tops are too tight around the middle. The poor maid had to find this blouse to stick under the jacket so I wouldn't have to close it. So the blouse is half unbuttoned in the back and the jacket is unhooked all down the front to account for my girth. And I am not a fat person!"

"Not at all."

"I'm not!" She shook her head angrily. "It's just that the corsets are warping all of your women and smooshing their internal organs. No one should have a waist that small. It's inhuman. And I can't stay here! I don't belong here. I want my jeans and my hoodie and my flip-flops."

"Well," he offered, feeling like an idiot for even saying the words, "if it would make you feel better, I can get the carriage and drive you back to the fair. You can try leaping under the arch to your heart's content and see what happens."

"Oh, yeah, right." Jordan rolled her eyes. "That's not the way it works. I can't go back until I do what it is I'm supposed to do here. You complete your mission, and boom, you get to go. That's the way it always works in the TV shows."

"TV?"

"It's…complicated. Transmission of sound and pictures through cable and satellites and…" She bit her lip. "Seriously. It's complicated."

His hands braced on his hips, Nick took a deep breath and looked down at his feet. There was just no rational explanation for where she came up with these stories. She was a regular Mark Twain in a pretty package.

Funny that didn't curb his desire for her one iota. If anything, it made him want her more. Who knew what her imagination could come up with in the bedroom?

"Okay, listen," she tried again. "Susan B. Anthony and Mrs. Stanhope see the arch on Friday. What's today?"

"Tuesday."

"Right. So we have three days to come up with a plan. Three whole days. We don't have to do anything today." Jordan was picking up speed as she went along. "We could, I don't know, lock Mrs. Stanhope and Susan B. Anthony in a closet so they can't make their tour."

Dryly, he noted, "I doubt either Mrs. Anthony or Mrs. Stanhope would appreciate being locked in a closet on the strength of your crystal ball."

"It's not a crystal ball," she told him. "I used newspapers, journals, books, primary sources… I did excellent and thorough research, okay?"

"I'm sure you did, but…" He shook his head. "I'm a rational, reasonable businessman. If you could tell me one thing that happens, not three days from now, but today, something that we could verify. A horse that will win at Washington Park. A stock that will rise or fall. Can you do that?"

"Of course not. Why would I know about horses or stocks?" She rubbed her temple. "I can tell you there's a big stock market crash in 1929, though. And it might be a good idea to buy IBM in the 60s and Microsoft in the 90s."

"I would prefer something a bit closer to 1893," he said, deadpan. "Any sort of verifiable proof will do."

"I know, but I don't have anything! Ever since I hit my head when I got here, my memory has been fuzzy. Things seem to come back in bits and pieces," she told him, looking quite upset. "Like the whole Lydia Trent thing. That just sort of popped up. I know I had a lot more details about you and Isabella. There's something important about you... I wish I could remember! But I seem to have some mental block or something. The information just isn't complete."

"In my heart, Jordan, I do not believe in fortune-telling or time traveling. If our situations were reversed, would you?"

"No," she admitted. "But when Friday dawns and Isabella is arrested, will you believe me then?"

As he pondered her question, Thomas, the second footman, tapped him on the shoulder.

"Excuse me, sir." He held out a silver tray with a calling card dropped in the center. "Beg pardon, sir, but there's a man waiting for Miss Isabella. A Mr. Franco, I believe."

"Franco?" He picked up the card, reading, "Franco Pirelli, il Conte di Bassano." The one who'd introduced Isabella to the sixteen positions and inspired that blasted arch. "Tell him she's not at home."

"I'm sorry, sir, but I did tell him that. He asked to see you instead. I've left him in the front parlor."

"All right. I'll see him. But don't tell anyone else he's here. I don't want either of my parents conversing with him."

"Yes, sir." With a half-bow, the footman and his silver tray retreated.

"Who's this?" Jordan asked, obviously curious about anything that had to do with Bella. "Franco who?"

"Pirelli. He's a count. We met him in Rome and he invited us to stay at his palazzo." He ground his jaw. "Has quite the art collection."

"You don't seem to like him much."

"No," he said darkly, "I don't."

"Could he have something to do with Isabella's disappearance?"

"She hasn't disappeared," he reminded her.

"Yes, but she will."

Nick shoved a hand through his air. "Well, if she were to run off, I wouldn't put it past the count to be involved. He's a patron of the arts. Erotic arts. And he's very interested in Isabella. He owns a volume called *The Sixteen Positions*. Have you heard of it?"

Looking very curious, Jordan said, "No. Sixteen? As in sixteen couples on the arch?"

"Exactly. While we were in Rome, I took a side trip and left Bella alone for a day or two." Flicking the card against his palm, Nick said pensively, "Apparently, this Franco fellow showed her his medieval manuscript describing sixteen…" He paused. "The sixteen most *fulfilling* sexual positions."

He couldn't believe he was discussing this with Jordan. After the fellatio of Narcissus and the orgasms of Victorian women, he supposed anything was fair game between them. But wasn't that the problem, that sex and lust colored every word, every syllable between the two of them, all because of Isabella and her damned arch?

"Are you saying that Isabella used those same sixteen positions on the arch?" Jordan asked slowly.

"She told me the volume sparked her idea. She wanted to call it *Sexdecim*. Sixteen in Latin."

"Very interesting," she mused. "I never knew what her inspiration was or that she had a title. Fascinating."

"Not really."

"Can I meet this Franco person?" she asked eagerly.

"I'd like to kill this Franco person," he said savagely. "He's in the front parlor. I suppose you can accompany me. It might keep me from throttling him. But please don't say anything to encourage him."

With his luck, Jordan would be falling at Franco's polished boots within minutes, and she would champion him and his pornographic collections simply because they were Isabella's inspiration. Nick shuddered.

"Say nothing," he ordered.

With her following behind, he marched toward the parlor, intent on quickly dispatching Count Franco no matter what Jordan did or said.

He pulled open the doors. "Count, how nice to see you. I wasn't expecting a visitor all the way from Rome."

"Ah, yes. Your charming sister, when we meet in Roma, she invite me to come to Chicago to see the Fair of the World," he said in a thick Italian accent. Nick had wondered when they were in Italy how much of that accent was pasted on for effect.

With Jordan right there, Nick had to introduce her. "This is Miss Albright, a friend of Isabella's. She also wanted to meet you."

"Charming," he said again, taking her fingers in his gloved hand and pressing several kisses into them.

As he kept hold of her hand, she looked as if she didn't know what to do. "Nice to meet you," she managed, making an awkward curtsey.

"So, now, here I find myself," Count Franco continued, squeezing her fingers. "I must come to Chicago, I think, because I am very anxious to see what Isabella, she has created. She tell me it will be magnificent, a triumph, on the tips of all the tongues."

"Right." Nick gave him a thin smile, ramming his hands

in his pockets so he didn't have to shake the unctuous count's hand. There were definitely tongues associated with that arch, in positions that haunted him.

"And where is the lovely Isabella?"

"She's not at home," Nick started to say, but the panel doors slid open behind him, interrupting his words.

"Franco," Isabella cried, bouncing into the parlor.

He dropped Jordan's hand to do the same oily kissing routine with Isabella, with even more enthusiasm. "Bella," he enthused between kisses. "I tell your brother, I cannot wait to see your creation. I shall buy it and it shall be the centerpiece of my new gallery."

"Where is your gallery?" Nick asked, brightening as he harbored a small hope that it was on the moon or somewhere just as remote. Perhaps Franco might have his uses, after all.

"Milano," he said. "I put my most magnificent pieces in my new *palazzo del arte* in Milano so I can keep them private. For me to see and enjoy and no one else."

In Milan. Private. Perfect. "Well, that sounds wonderful, doesn't it, Isabella? Your first big sale. Shall we hammer out the details?"

"Nick!" Jordan exclaimed with dismay. "You can't do that."

"Heavens, no," Isabella agreed. "Franco hasn't even seen it yet."

"But he wants it desperately, Bella," Nick persisted. "You wouldn't want to disappoint our good friend Franco."

Jordan widened her eyes and waggled her eyebrows, as if she were trying to send him important messages. *Right.* She didn't want the arch going to Milan while she still harbored delusions of vaulting through time underneath it.

Well, he couldn't be bothered with that. If the opportunity arose to solve his problem neatly and easily, he meant to take it.

As Isabella drew the count aside to chat privately in Italian, Jordan moved closer, whispering, "I thought you were going to throw him out. Now you want to adopt him!"

"I don't want to adopt him," he muttered. "I want him to give Bella wads of cash and at the same time, spirit away the entire problem. He lives in Milan and he has a private gallery. What could be better?"

"Oh, I don't know. Maybe a chance for *women* to see it? For it to be in the Louvre or the Metropolitan Museum in New York?" She was positively seething, and he wondered if steam was going to start shooting from her ears. "For it to be as famous and celebrated as it deserves to be, not stuck in a palace in Milan with some skeevy count fantasizing—"

That was enough. Nick stuck his hand over her mouth before she could say the rest.

"I'm taking Franco to the fair," Isabella announced as she paraded past the two of them, oblivious to the argument. "He's dying to see the arch, and so he shall."

"Cover it back up when you're done," Nick called out, leaving his hand over Jordan's mouth for the time being.

He hoped Isabella went straight out and didn't introduce Franco to either parent. It was rude and a complete breach of etiquette to do so, but Nick was afraid that Franco would start describing his collection or that one particular volume, and the senior Mr. Tempest would have a coronary on the spot.

Isabella paid her brother no attention, waving a dismissive hand and sailing blithely on, arm in arm with the Conte di Bassano.

Nick removed his hand, turning Jordan around and pointing her toward the door. "We should be off as well. I need to check in at Tempest & Son to placate my father and his notion of management, and you can shop for what you need at the same time. Since you don't like your borrowed clothing, perhaps you would like to choose something new? We have a dressmaking department, and we're just experimenting with ready-made pieces. Perhaps they have something that can be altered quickly to fit you."

The idea of shopping was apparently so interesting that she forgot to be angry with him for forcibly shutting her up.

Looking pensive, Jordan asked, "What did those women from the Anti-Corset Brigade wear? Do you have any of that at your store?"

"Pantaloons and bloomers? I don't know. We might have a bicycling costume."

"I'll take anything that doesn't require a corset," she said forcefully. "Anything."

Nick smiled. "But you looked so delectable in your corset."

"I'm not even discussing it," she told him, linking her arm through his. "After we go to your store, you're going to take me back to the fair. We're going straight to the Women's Building, and we're going to make sure that Franco doesn't make off with either Isabella or the arch. Right?"

Nick preferred not to answer that.

12

How to Be a Scandalous Woman, Rule 12:
Go ahead, wear red. They don't call them "scarlet
women" for nothing.

OUT OF WHACK, out of step, out of balance. That's how Jordan felt at Tempest & Son.

She couldn't get over it. The store was in the place she expected—on the same corner, with Marshall Field's across the street—but that was the only similarity.

In 2006, it was her favorite place, upscale but still warm and inviting, with everything she could want, all in one location, and loads of good memories. As a child, Jordan had often visited her grandmother in Chicago for the holidays, and that had almost always included a trip to Tempest & Trent. She'd loved the heady smells in the perfume department, the displays of fine crystal and silver, the endless escalators that got narrower and narrower as you went to the top. Her grandmother had bought her Easter dresses in the children's department on the sixth floor every year when she was little, and she'd seen Santa there more times than she could remember. Once she'd moved to the city for good, she'd lingered in their Starbucks, lusted after a pair of high-heeled red boots in the shoe department, and sat for more than one makeover at their cosmetics counter.

But this wasn't the department store she knew.

It was smaller, for one thing. Instead of an entire city block, it was about a quarter of one. Instead of twelve stories, it was four. It was also cramped and dim inside, not because of ambient light—there were plenty of windows— but because it was crowded with so much merchandise.

Before, Nick had driven his own carriage home from the fair, an open, fast one with hardly anything to it. Now, he took her to the store in what he called a landau, an elegant, closed-in carriage with a coachman and the Tempest crest on the door. Appearances must be kept up, he said cynically. It wouldn't do for the boss to drive himself to the store.

And when they arrived, Jordan had to wait for a footman to take the reins and help her out, and then for another footman to accompany them in the front door. Was she supposed to say thank you? They looked startled when she did. So much fuss, just to make a quick trip downtown.

Everything in this world seemed to depend on knowing the exacting standards of etiquette and good breeding. It was ironic that a woman who'd always prided herself on playing by the rules had no idea what they were. Was she supposed to be wearing her hat and gloves inside? When was it okay to take them off? How did you button and unbutton your own gloves without using your teeth? Who did she bow to when introduced and whose hand was it okay to take? How many faux pas could a person make before they were sent out of town for good?

Nick tried to reassure her by telling her that this was Chicago and not as hidebound or snooty as the East. But it wasn't all that comforting. The rules still seemed to choke all the life out of her.

As soon as they were inside the door of Tempest & Son,

Nick seemed to stand taller and look more imposing. His posture was perfect and his manner reserved. No smiles, no mischievous winks or heated glances. She tried to smile herself, to get him to laugh a little, but he wasn't biting.

He swept down the aisle between millinery and ladies' gloves, guiding her to the elevator, and she felt the eyes of every single clerk on her. Each one they passed murmured, "Good morning, Mr. Tempest," but Nick just inclined his head in response. Jordan saw deference and respect on their faces, as well as a whole lot of curiosity directed at her. She was no mind reader, but she suspected they were wondering who the heck the weird chick was, the one whose clothes didn't fit, who had scuffed boots and a funny walk and an unfashionable hairdo.

It was like Calamity Jane had hitched a ride with the King of England.

She glanced over at Nick to see what his reaction was to all the stares and whispers, but he didn't even seem to notice. Once the elevator man took them to the fourth floor, Nick went right to his office.

"Some matters have been brought to my attention that I have to handle," he told Jordan apologetically. "But I'll have my assistant, Mr. Smithers, take you to the dressmaking salon, all right? You'll have an open account for anything you want in the store. And then please come back here when you're done."

Cool, distant not-Nick went right to work at his desk. Since when did he turn into Mr. Conscientious? *This* was the Nick who was so set on snuffing out scandal and keeping everybody in line. But what did that Nick want with *her?*

She was puzzling that over the whole time Smithers, a non-descript man with a weaseley look about him, accompanied her to the area called "Modiste." He dropped her off with specific instructions to the clerks there, who were just as curious as the ones downstairs about this woman brought in by the boss.

"Modiste" was very plush, with small velvet couches to sit on while clerks and seamstresses brought out garments displayed on dress forms to show off the fashion possibilities. Jordan just wanted to grab something, anything, plus she was self-conscious about the way her borrowed yellow outfit gaped in the back and didn't hook in the front, so she didn't want to try anything on. But before she knew it, they had her in an alteration room, stripped down and then re-upholstered from top to bottom, in a corset that fit, silk stockings and shoes and boots and little tortoiseshell combs for her hair. They just kept piling up the boxes of her purchases.

She wanted to say, *I'm not sure I'm staying long enough to make this worth your while,* but she supposed if they had carte blanche from the boss to outfit her, they were going to do it up right. So she kept her mouth shut and let them pick out the whole enchilada. It was kind of interesting, actually, how they had these almost-finished skirts and bodices, the same flouncy, overdone things Isabella wore, and then they would measure and pin and take away the garments to make alterations immediately. It wasn't the "ready-made" she was used to, where you picked what you wanted from the racks, but it had to be better than wearing hand-me-downs from the Tempest household.

After she'd been buzzed over for what seemed like hours, the last seamstress went off to make the final fittings. She was a timid, wan little thing, and she curtsied, murmured, "Sorry to have kept you so long, miss. It will be a few more minutes."

That left Jordan alone on the tufted ottoman in the last dressing room, trying to get her mind back on important things. Once again trapped in half an outfit, she couldn't leave the small cubicle. But she was itching to get back to Nick. She knew she ought to be worrying about her mission to save Isabella, but her mind kept wandering back to Nick. Nick, sex, corsets, sex with Nick while wearing a corset… She was getting a one-track mind.

Her thoughts were blessedly interrupted by the arrival of a new customer in the next room. At first the woman dithered on about which fabric best suited her coloring and the optimum number of bows for one's sleeves, la la la, Paris this and London that.

But then she took a different, more gossipy tone and divulged, "I hear Nicholas Tempest has brought a lady friend into the store today."

Jordan's ears perked up. She knew no good could come from listening to gossip about herself, but what could she do?

"So unfortunate," the seamstress helping her responded with a tsk-tsk at the end. "I have a friend down in millinery on One, and they sent her to bring hats up for this girl. She saw the bill. Mr. Tempest is paying for everything."

"A kept woman?" the customer inquired with a note of interest.

"Indeed." There was a rustle of fabrics as garments were moved around inside the small dressing room. Finally, the clerk continued, "Poor Mr. Tempest. He's so handsome and works so hard. All the prettiest girls here have set their caps for him. I'd have thought he'd choose an heiress, a Palmer or an Armour, even a Vanderbilt or an Astor. One would certainly think he would set his sights higher."

"Not after being seen with that one," the other woman sniffed. "They say she's come straight from the country."

"What country?"

"No, no. The country. With cows and horses. Colorado or Wyoming or somewhere rustic like that. The other girl who was waiting on me in stationery said she's as vulgar as vulgar can be, just bold as brass. She said she walks with huge, long strides, talks and laughs right out in the open, looks people in the eye, and doesn't know a thing about manners. Wherever did he find her?"

"There's talk she knows his sister."

"Ohh." The word spoke volumes about what the woman thought of Isabella. "Maude and H. H. Tempest are very proper. I'll never understand how they raised that child. But at least Isabella is pretty and diverting. She knows a hat from a glove."

"She comes to the store quite often," the clerk confided. "She enjoys a pretty frock or a new pair of stockings as much as the next girl. But…" She dropped her voice. "She boasted to one of the other girls about how many lovers she'd taken abroad."

"No!"

"Yes." She giggled. "It's quite scandalous."

"And now Nicholas is bringing even more scandal down on their heads with his uncouth country bumpkin."

"Shameful," the clerk concluded.

"Shameful," her customer agreed.

Hmm… So it was more shameful to look people in the eye than to admit you had a string of European lovers? Not that Jordan cared about either one of them, but she would've thought sex would trump a little self-confidence. She just didn't get this world at all.

She leaned back against the wall, resting her head, staring at the ceiling and wondering how long it would be before she could go back to her time, where she fit in, where she knew how to dress and act and where it was perfectly okay to laugh or smile or look someone in the eye.

Mean girls are mean girls, wherever you are, she reminded herself. How funny that she had never been their target when she was in school.

Sure, she'd been teased every now and again for being a teacher's pet or a Goodie Two Shoes because she got perfect grades and didn't play hooky or skip class. But that was the extent of it.

"Jump me back to 1893 and hook me up with the coolest guy in town, and the Mean Girls are on my tail like nobody's business," she said under her breath.

"Did you hear something?" the matron next door asked suddenly.

"No, ma'am."

"Ow. You've poked me with a pin," she complained. "Be more careful."

"Yes, ma'am."

I'll poke you with a pin. Jordan had a deep desire to rebel all of a sudden. Growing up with a decidedly counter-culture single mother, she'd done her rebelling in the opposite direction, becoming responsible and reliable, the good girl. But now, stuck in a world where women couldn't vote, have birth control or lovers, where they were keeping each other down by not fighting the system, Jordan found herself becoming just as radical as her mother.

Scandal? She could write the book.

Suddenly, she wanted to find the ladies of the Anti-Corset Brigade and join their ranks, burning corsets and freeing women from tyranny everywhere. Or at least make a stand.

Grabbing up the yellow, too-small bodice she'd arrived in, she buttoned it on over her new red skirt as best as she could, intent on blowing this pop stand. She might just give the Mean Girls next door a piece of her mind, even if she had to do it in an ill-fitting, mismatched outfit. But the timid woman who'd been helping her chose that moment to return with her new top, so she relented and put it on instead.

"Would you like a mirror, miss?" the seamstress asked, helping her fasten the hooks.

"No." She lifted her chin. It was amazing how shoes that actually fit and a little anger could combine to make her feel fierce and assertive. "It's how I feel inside that counts."

"Yes, miss." But she didn't seem convinced.

"No, I'm serious. It's who you are inside. What's your name?"

"Delia, miss."

"Delia, you need to stand up for yourself. Do what you want to do. Don't let society pigeonhole you because of your gender."

"Yes, miss," she said doubtfully.

Oh, well. She might not have convinced Delia, but there were a lot more people out in the world who could learn a lesson. Like the two women in the next cubicle who peeked out the door, shocked, as she marched past them in her new red dress.

Like Nick Tempest, who was interested in a woman who spoke her mind even though he wouldn't back up his own sister's right to express herself.

"We'll just see about that. I know you better than you think, Nick. The inner Nick is going to come out," she muttered.

It was kind of fun finding her way back to his office, actually looking around and thinking about what would be where in a hundred years. She decided that Nick's office would turn into the lingerie department. The ladies' writing room was definitely going to become Starbucks. She'd been there a hundred times.

Although he seemed distracted, Nick rose as he heard her approach. He found a smile for her. "You look beautiful. Red is your color."

She smiled back, meeting his eyes as boldly as she wanted. "Thank you, Nick. I had to really talk them into finding me a less punitive corset. I'm happy to say I succeeded."

"So you've finished your shopping? I'm afraid I'm not done." He frowned down at his desk. "I may have to send you back to the house in my carriage alone while I stay at my desk."

"No," she said flatly.

"No?"

"No. I'm not going to sit in my room for the entire afternoon when I may only have a few days here. Besides, you promised to take me to the fair. We need to find Isabella." She shook her head, almost dislodging one of her new combs. "I am holding you to your promise, Nick. It's time to play hooky. You and me."

Something flickered in his eyes. The old Nick was hiding in there, the one who leapt in and picked up bizarre women from under marble arches and used the excuse of corset lessons to seduce them, who wasn't put off by exotic vocabulary words or miniskirts or deep, dark kisses from strangers.

"You know you want to," she whispered. "You know you want to spend the afternoon with me."

It took him a moment, but she could see it on his face the minute he decided.

His lips curved into a very charming smile. "You're right. These papers will still be here tomorrow. But you may not." As he reached for his hat and gloves, he called out, "Smithers, I'm leaving for the rest of the day. Everything is in your capable hands."

"Yes, Mr. Tempest."

Nick took her elbow and led the way the way to the elevator.

"What would you say if I suggested we leave the landau and take the special steamship to the fair, like the other tourists?"

Jordan laughed out loud, not in the least concerned who heard her. "I would love it! A boat ride on Lake Michigan? Who would turn that down?"

She was so glad he'd suggested it. Removing her hat, she loosened her combs and let the lake breeze ruffle her hair. Even with the five or six layers of clothing she was wearing, she still felt more like herself than at any moment since she got here.

And when they came in through the gates to the fair, she didn't push to go straight to the Women's Building to check on Isabella. This was about playing hooky and thumbing her nose at responsibility. She would never have another chance to sit in a chair next to Nick while the funky Movable Sidewalk lurched them in from the pier. Or to stand there and gawk at the Great Basin with its fountains and sculptures and the grand buildings of the Court of Honor, the centerpiece of the exposition. It was awesome.

She passed on the camel ride and the place that offered opossum stew, but did check out the 22,000-pound cheese, the 16,000 varieties of orchids in the Horticulture Building, a quick view of an exploding volcano, a sword fight on "A Street in Cairo," and a really good cup of coffee at the Brazilian cafe. Wow. Had it only been two days since she'd had decent coffee?

Nick took her anywhere she wanted to go without a peep, and she found herself laughing more than she ever had in her entire life just at the look on his face when they saw the map of the United States made completely out of pickles.

It probably wasn't done in this time and place to howl and hoot until tears ran from your eyes, but she just didn't care. She was having fun.

"This is so much better than Disney World," she told him, quickly adding an explanation of what that was until his eyes started to glaze over. She noticed he didn't bother to argue about her revelations anymore, just mostly ignored them until she went on to a new topic.

"What next?" he asked.

"Isn't there anything you want to see?"

He didn't say anything, just kept gazing at her, as if that were his answer. "Sometimes, Nick, I don't know what to do with you," she whispered, taking his arm. "You're so sweet. After the dreams I had of you and me together, I thought you were the perfect fantasy man. But I was wrong. There's more to you than that."

More to you than sex.

Right there, in front of a Cracker Jack vendor, he brushed his finger against her cheek, and she almost lifted up to kiss him. She remembered herself in time, though, pulling away. She was already dumping enough gossip into his life. If he was seen kissing the scarlet woman in the middle of the fair, word would get back to the biddies at the store within minutes. And then where he would be after she left?

It wasn't that she didn't want to make out with him, or even make love with him, because she did. Desperately. But she knew they were going to have to be discreet. Damn Victorian sensibilities, anyway.

Not for the first time, it occurred to her that her normal, no-nonsense 2006 life was pretty darn controversial compared to where she now found herself.

Nick turned back to the path they'd been walking, leading them on to the huge Manufactures Building.

"Anything good in here?" she asked lightly, trying not to think about any of the things outside her control, like staying or leaving or anybody's future plans…

"Actually, there is something in here I'd like to see," he remarked. "There's a jewelry display from a New York outfit called Tiffany & Company. We've been thinking of adding fine jewelry to our store, with some of their products."

"Tiffany's? Really? I'm all for that." She tried to overlook the fact that Nick was bringing up business and concentrate on the fact that it was Tiffany's. *Come on.* Tiffany's was worth a look, even if he did have his head back at the store.

Nick paid a penny for a map, and in they went.

Inside the Manufactures and Liberal Arts Building, which was so incredibly huge she had to block out about seven-eighths of it just so her brain didn't explode, she asked, "How does anyone find anything in here?"

He held up the map, trying to read the tiny type. It took a while, but he eventually located the Tiffany & Co. pavilion. "Beautiful things," Nick commented, glancing around. "I wonder if they would be a good fit for Tempest & Son."

"Did you ever think of doing anything besides working at the store?" she asked suddenly. She wasn't sure it was wise to ask, but she did it, anyway.

"I never envisioned I would be there, if that's what you're asking." He shrugged, looking distant again, the way he had the moment he'd walked into the store. "I don't know that it's my destiny, or even the best use of my talents. But it's a family business, it needs to be managed, and someone has to do it. I don't see it being Isabella, do you?"

Jordan tried not to laugh. "Uh, no. But that doesn't mean it has to be you." She hesitated. "You seemed like a different person at the store, Nick. Older, sadder…"

"You sound like my sister. She called me a drudge the other day."

"I don't know that you're a drudge. It's just…" She took his hand, unable to hold back what she wanted to say. All those years of studying the time period ought to come to some good. Impassioned, she announced, "The world is about to crack wide open. Telephones, the phonograph, movie cameras, the car, the airplane… Technology is exploding every which way at once."

"I know that, Jordan. I may not recognize the names of those specific things, but look around you. What do you think this World's Fair is all about?" he asked impatiently. "Progress. Technology and progress."

"I think about who you are and what's coming, and then I think about you fooling with whether to add jewelry to your store, when you could be…" She stopped, aghast. A memory had popped into her brain.

Nick. America's first automobile race, from Hyde Park to Evanston. With Nick in it. And Nick dying in it. September, 1895.

Back in her desk, she'd had a picture of Nick standing next to a prototype of the racecar, smiling and happy. How could she have forgotten? It was her screensaver!

She remembered now that the people who spoke about him afterward talked about his energy and how he loved speed and progress and was committed to this new invention, the motor car, and wouldn't have wanted his death to hold that back or scare anyone.

Back when he'd been a myth, a dream lover, she'd thought the stories of his death were tragic. But they hadn't hit her where she lived, blasted her right in the heart, like now.

How could I not remember how he dies? She raised horrified eyes to his. *So soon.*

Right now, gazing suspiciously at her, he was so alive, so vital, so beautiful. It couldn't be a lousy two years till he died.

"Forget what I said," she mumbled. "Forget about speed. Let's look at Tiffany's."

A bit bemused, Nick said, "All right. I'd like to know why you suddenly looked so stricken, but if you don't want to say…"

Jordan kept her mouth shut and headed for the famous 120-carat Tiffany Yellow Diamond, the centerpiece of their display. She was still mentally stuck on the revelation that Nick was going to die in a car race, and she basically stared at the diamond without really seeing it.

But right next to it was a stunning ruby ring. The stone in the center was the size of a walnut. As it sat there in the case, hazy under the thick glass, she couldn't take her eyes off it. She read the label. "This ruby is known as the Burmese Red Devil." Why would she know anything about a ring like that?

Without warning, that memory crowded into her mind, too. This was something from the other clippings she'd had on Nick. In the stories about his engagement to Lydia Trent, it talked about the ring he gave her. It was from Tiffany's, and had been displayed in their pavilion at the Columbian Exposition. *The Burmese Red Devil*. Worth a small fortune.

"Nick." She cleared her throat. "This ring. This ruby right there. Have you seen it before?"

He gave it a casual glance. "No."

"You're going to be giving it to Lydia Trent in just about a year. It's her engagement present."

But he only laughed, fondly putting an arm around her and leaning in closer. "Is that why you became so serious all of a sudden? You've had another of your visions? Don't worry. Yes, my father has been touting the virtues of Miss Trent for many years, but as I've told you before, I'm not going to marry her. And even if I were, I wouldn't be gifting her with something as spectacular as the Burmese Red Devil."

Jordan chewed her lip, looking back and forth between him and the ring. "I know what I read."

"You haven't seen Lydia," he whispered into her ear. "Its brilliance would overpower her completely."

He was humoring her because he still didn't believe her. That seemed perfectly clear. In the interests of keeping the peace on such a lovely day, she lightened her tone, too. "You could buy it for *me*," she joked. "I'll take it back with me when I go. Do you know how much that thing would be worth in my day?"

"Yes, yes. That's you. The Amazing Woman of the Future. Why, you belong on the midway next to the snake charmers and the world's smallest elephant."

Her mouth dropped open in mock surprise. "You want to stick me in the freak show?"

"Never," he pledged. But then he began to steer her away from the suddenly depressing Tiffany exhibit. "It's been lovely to play with you this afternoon, but I think we have ignored Isabella too long. If I know my sister, she will have created more trouble in this one afternoon than most people do in a lifetime. Shall we make our way to the Women's Building to see what new havoc Bella has wrought?"

Oh, right. Isabella. Her mission. Like, duh. She'd completely forgotten she was supposed to be saving Isabella.

13

How to Be a Scandalous Woman, Rule 13:
Sex is a potent weapon, whether you're having it,
promising it, rebuffing it, or just remembering it.

"Tomorrow, Bella!" Franco shouted. "I will carry you and this beautiful piece of art off to Italia tomorrow!"

They could hear him all the way out in the hallway. Jordan elbowed Nick. "I knew it! I told you she was going to disappear. Did you hear that? Franco is taking her and the arch to Italy tomorrow. Now do you believe me?"

Calmly, Nick slid his arm around her. "You said Friday. If Franco ships them off tomorrow, they'll be long gone before your mythical visit from Susan B. Anthony and Mrs. Stanhope. Isabella can hardly be arrested or disgraced in Chicago if she and her arch are already on a boat to Italy. If that did happen, in fact, it would disprove your psychic vision."

"It's not a psychic vision." She stayed where she was, not quite ready to go into the gallery. "But maybe I changed things enough by being here to mess the dates up. That's possible. So it will be true, but not at the exact time."

"This is how charlatans always operate," Nick grumbled. "They change their stories until one comes true. There's a man who stands in front of City Hall every day at noon, carrying a sign that says the world is ending next week. He's been saying it for at least five years. Obviously, the world hasn't ended yet, but he continues to claim that his prediction is accurate and will be happening at some conveniently postponed deadline."

His characterization of her had changed from snake charmer to crazy Chicken Little. Jordan tried not to feel wounded.

"Would it be so hard to have a little faith in me? I want the best for your sister. Is that so impossible to believe?"

"Actually, I do believe that. I just don't believe you can predict the future. And I wouldn't worry. I know Bella. And she won't be running off to Italy with him." He reached out to wind a stray tendril of her hair around his finger. Teasingly, he said, "I still enjoy your company very much. Isn't that enough?"

"No." Under her breath, she added, "Not if the arch is my only way back to my own time, and Franco has it carted off to Milan."

"Nick and Jordan!" Isabella said happily, waving her arm to tell them to come in. She and Franco were standing very near the arch, which seemed to be glowing all on its own. The cover Nick had thrown over it was nowhere in sight, and Jordan could once again feel its erotic pull. It was like a swift kick to the solar plexus. When she glanced at Nick, he was staring at her with the same strange blaze of desire she felt. Was it so wrong to want to end this frustration with a bang? Right under the arch, no matter who else was in the room?

"Yes, it's wrong," she said under her breath, trying to remember to stand up straight and not just crumple.

"What are you two doing lurking in the hallway? Please, come in. Did you hear? Franco loves my piece. Isn't it marvelous?"

"I adore La Bella Isabella and her bella artwork. I take them back to Milano where Isabella can make more beautiful works for me alone. I will be her patron. I alone!"

Noting the way that Franco was hanging on to Isabella, eyeing her rather possessively, Jordan began to have even worse feelings about his intentions.

"Nick," she muttered, turning so only he could hear her, "you need to tell her to stay away from Franco. He's creepy."

Nick said softly, "If she wants to sell her sculpture to him, I won't stop her." Louder, greeting his sister, he declared, "What a fine idea to put the arch in Count Franco's collection. He has exquisite taste. The sooner he takes it away, the better."

Damn him, anyway. Franco can't take the arch.

That damn arch was so powerful. She was feeling the heavy, aching longing again. Around the arch, around Nick, she was dizzy and confused and thinking about sex, sex and more sex, while not having any. Maybe if she just got it over with…

Focus, Jordan. Work on the problem at hand. You can't keep acting as if you have a fever 24/7.

She threw out a trial balloon to see how likely the whole Franco and Italy thing was. "Isabella, you don't want to abandon us to go to Milan, do you?" She tried keeping it light.

"Oh, my stars," Isabella said with a laugh. "I can't go to Italy right now. Dear Franco is just being silly."

"Oh, Bella, you wound me," he said, pressing kisses into her hand. "Come, we talk more. You tell me price and I make you very happy."

She adopted a peevish expression. "I haven't decided yet whether I want to sell it. They've stuck it in this dreadful gallery away from everything and no one has even seen it yet. I should've tried to get it into the Fine Arts Building. My work does not belong wedged between teacups and embroidered aprons."

"Not sell? Isabella, I know you don't mean these hurtful words."

"Franco, darling, don't be tiresome." Forcefully wrenching her hand away, she studied the arch from several angles, casting an eye back at the light source, as if she were wondering how best to show it off.

Catching the odd expression in the count's eyes, Jordan couldn't help wondering if Isabella was going to end up hijacked to his palazzo whether she wanted to go or not. There was naked lust burning there for a long moment. Lust and something else, more like possession.

The Conte di Bassano had a snarl in his voice when he announced, "Bella, I must retire to my hotel now. We will return to this topic tomorrow. Perhaps you will make yourself more sensible then."

He did a sort of heel-clicky Continental salute that Jordan had only seen in Marx Brothers movies, and then he slunk out of there, casting dark looks behind him. Isabella paid him no mind. She was busy humming to herself and circling her masterpiece, flicking at imaginary pieces of dust, examining it this way and that, pleased and happy with her creation.

"I don't like the way he looks at her," Jordan told Nick. She crossed her arms over her chest. "Somebody needs to keep an eye on him to make sure he doesn't pull anything funny."

"What do you mean?"

"Like kidnapping your sister," she said with spirit. "Isabella isn't taking him seriously, and he acted like he was ready to eat her for breakfast."

Nick arched an eyebrow.

"I mean it," Jordan continued. "Franco strikes me as a guy who doesn't like to be crossed."

"I can't disagree," he said slowly.

"So maybe," she mused, "maybe on Friday, he tosses her and the arch on his ship and sails off. That would fit perfectly with the facts. Jeez. Why didn't I ever hear anything about Franco? All that research, and never a mention of a slimy Italian count with a thing for Isabella."

"In this city, it would only cost a few dollars to hire a tough to break his kneecaps or throw him in the river," Nick suggested. "I'd prefer to do that after he buys the thing and sends it off to parts unknown, but I wouldn't mind doing it before if it helps Isabella."

Jordan stared at him. "You're not serious."

"You're the one who claims he's going to kidnap my sister."

"Not for sure. It's just a theory," she protested. "You can't go around breaking kneecaps and throwing people into rivers based on a theory."

"He's definitely the one who got her started on this Sixteen Positions thing." Nick sent her a dark look. "My father would kill him for that alone."

Jordan's eyes widened. "Are you serious?" She was getting the idea that people were a bit more bloodthirsty here than she was used to. "Okay, I don't like him, but...I'm not going to let you hire somebody to hurt him when we don't even know he's going to do anything wrong. I mean, I understand if it ticks you off that he corrupted your sister, but sheesh. She's an adult. She can decide for herself if she wants to know about the Sixteen Positions."

"And if she's an adult, then why don't you share your theory about Franco with her and let her choose what to do?"

"Fine," she shot back. "Isabella?"

His sister glanced over, but didn't leave her post next to her sculpture. "Yes? What?"

"Bella," Nick interrupted, "Jordan is worried about Franco. She thinks he's up to no good."

Isabella didn't bother to comment, just rolled her eyes.

"No, really," Jordan tried. "He's got this total stalker vibe going."

"Franco is harmless," Isabella said matter-of-factly. "I can twist him around my finger. He really does love my work, that's all. But he knows he can never own *me*."

With a sigh, she swept past them, languidly making her way out of the gallery. Nick asked, "Bella, where are you off to?"

"Oh, I don't know," she said airily. "I, uh, want to… I mean…" She stopped, chewed on the tip of her gloved finger, and then started again. "I need to think, to clear my head. I am simply going to wander around the fair."

She said it in the same patently phony way she'd related the story about Jordan's parents supposedly dying in a carriage accident during an avalanche in the Swiss Alps.

"Where do you suppose she's really going?" Nick demanded. He seemed as out of sorts and touchy as Jordan felt. Damn the arch, anyway, for clouding all their brains and making them act like randy teenagers.

Jordan watched his sister speed up and suddenly act a whole lot more purposeful the minute she hit the hall. "I don't know, but I think we'd better follow her. Something is definitely up."

Grabbing her hand, Nick pulled her along behind Isabella out the door of the Women's Building and over a bridge to the small island built in the middle of the lagoon, with its charming Japanese temple and pretty gardens.

They didn't bother to be careful or furtive; Isabella was clearly not paying them the slightest bit of attention.

The sun was dipping below the horizon, and the island's tiny colored lights, hung from trees and bushes, were just starting to brighten. The atmosphere was not lost on Jordan. Yes, she knew they were supposed to be following Isabella, but it was hard to focus on that when the little fairy lights were twinkling and the shadows were deepening and everything had this lovely romantic glow.

Besides, her hand was securely in Nick's and his presence was overwhelming, as usual.

"This way," he said, edging her into a small pavilion.

"Did you see Isabella come in here?" She lifted her skirts to take the step up, peering into the dim interior.

"No."

"Then what…?" But Nick cut her off, spinning her around, pressing her into an alcove, holding her securely as he covered her mouth with his.

"You drive me insane," he said roughly. "Ever since I met you… It keeps getting worse. I can't stop wanting you."

She knew that feeling. His kiss was softer and sweeter, but every bit as devastating as the first time. "Nick," she whispered, making a feeble attempt to stop before they started. But she didn't want to stop.

She'd been thinking about kissing him all day. *Oh, hell.* That was all she thought about any time she was near him. Even when she wasn't near him.

Her last dream had been especially maddening. One thought of Pygmalion and Galatea, of his head between her thighs, and she was already wet and hungry for his touch.

Her huge puffed sleeves just didn't feel right when she

slipped her arms around him, though, and he seemed to notice, too. It was just too much fabric wadded up between them. Smiling devilishly, he began to undo her bodice, one tiny hook at a time, all by feel in the faint light. It took forever, and the anticipation was killing her. His fingers grazed her stomach, her waist, every rib, all the way up, and she felt the impact even through her corset, gasping each time another hook was freed.

Finally, just when she was ready to rip the damn thing off, he eased it off her shoulders, letting it swish to the floor.

As cool summer evening air hit her shoulders, she had a moment's regret, but those thoughts evaporated quickly enough. With Nick pulling her up hard against him, dropping kisses down the slope of her neck, nibbling her earlobe, pressing his mouth to her breast and wetting her skin through the thin muslin camisole, she just didn't have the time to worry about wardrobe issues.

"You are wearing entirely too many clothes," he rasped, massaging her bottom through the heavy silk of her skirt and petticoats, forcing her closer.

There were too many layers of fabric. It was frustrating and a major turn-on, all at the same time. She felt twitchy and anxious, ready to explode. She wanted to hike up her skirts all the way to the waist and bare herself to him, feel his hands and his mouth right there, where she needed him most.

Instead, his left hand cradled the back of her head, tipping her up so that he could take the kiss deeper and harder, while his right teased her nipple through the lace of her camisole, tweaking it into a hard peak. Her breasts seemed to swell above the rigid edge of the corset, and she lifted herself up into the cool linen of Nick's shirtfront and the soft wool of his waistcoat, trying to breathe against the steely bonds of her stays.

His collar was stiff, but she slid her hands inside it, wanting to touch his skin, feel his pulse, slide her fingers into his soft, dark hair.

It was manic, frantic, with breathless moans and whimpers as they each tried to shove aside the barriers and take what they wanted. He pulled the straps of her camisole down over her shoulders, baring her breasts completely, letting the last pink streaks of sunlight coming in the doorway play over her naked flesh. Nick leaned her back against the wall, his fingers diving under her skirt, shoving away yards of fabric, dancing over her ankle and her knee, teasing the sensitive skin on her inner thigh, heading up and up…

She lost any semblance of reason, pitching herself up into his hand. His thumb grazed her clit and it felt so incredibly good, she just about jumped out of her skin. He dipped a finger into her wet, slick core, then two, keeping up the delicate rhythm with his thumb, and she tried to hold on, but it was too powerful.

Jordan's moans started in earnest now. She panted as she surged into his hand. The climax came fast and fierce, slamming through her like nothing she had ever felt. She needed help, she craved release, and she hadn't known it could be this raw, this hot, this hard.

"Oh, no," she whispered, burying her face in the soft wool of his vest, hanging on for dear life while his fingers were still inside her and the aftereffects were still rippling through her body. "We weren't supposed to do this. Nick, I don't belong here. You're marrying somebody else."

"Shh," he murmured, tracing the line of her chin with tiny kisses. "It's all right. It was stupid to start this here, I admit, but I couldn't stop thinking about you, every minute. It's something we've both needed since the first moment we met."

"Before that," she confessed. She'd been with him so many times her dreams. "But this, here, it wasn't enough." She met his intense gaze. "For me or you, I think."

"Shh," he said again. "It spun out of control so quickly. I didn't intend... Not here."

"I still need the real thing," she said urgently. "You. I want you inside me."

He shuddered, and she knew he was still as turned on as she was. But he murmured, "Not yet. I have a plan."

"Really? Did you plan this little rendezvous, too?" She was wobbly, but she managed to pull back far enough to smooth her skirt over her hips. It surprised her to glance down and see her bare breasts jutting out over the corset, her nipples still distended and tender. When did that happen? Quickly, she pulled her camisole back into place, holding her breath, trying to get her pulse back to a more steady pace.

"I didn't plan this. But the sunset and the smell of the flowers and the summer breeze..." His teeth flashed white in his handsome face. "I couldn't resist."

"Me, either," she said in a shaky voice. "Obviously. I mean, I didn't... Resist."

"I think they designed this island for lovers," he whispered, leaning in closer, nipping her neck again. "All the little nooks and crannies are perfect for illicit trysts. If there were more light, I think you would see the other couples out there in the shadows, doing precisely what we were doing."

Oh, God. Maybe it was her imagination, but she thought she could hear shivery, orgasmic sounds coming from somewhere near. Maybe it was the only the water lapping against the banks of the island, or the muted cry of a seagull. But now she had visions of an orgy happening around them on that island.

At least she and Nick had the arch as an excuse, branding their brains with sexual imagery. Like the pose they'd just tried out, which she believed was number fourteen, with Hercules's fingers enflaming Hippolyta.

Trembling, Jordan said, "I can't believe we did that."

Nick's grin widened as he slid his mouth down to her collarbone, his hands fast around her waist. "I can. But it was just a taste of what we can do."

"No, we can't. Never again," she said quickly.

"Well, we can put that one aside for the moment," he said lazily. "I might suggest we move on to other choices. Like Narcissus and Echo, for example. Your favorite."

Falling under his spell all over again, she leaned into him, sliding her hand down his torso, gingerly, ever so lightly brushing the front of his trousers. "I think it's your favorite since you keep bringing it up." Oh, things were *up*, all right, right there under her hand.

"Not here," he breathed into her ear, batting her hand away. "Too many people walking by. I want you all to myself, with no interruptions."

Signs of not wanting to get caught with the "Scarlet Woman in the White City"? At least not with his pants down. She could hardly blame him.

"Damn," he said. He went very still, edging around her and peering into the darkness.

"What? Is it Isabella? Did you see something?"

"No, I heard something. *Someone*." He looked grim. "I think it was Lydia Trent."

"Not her again. Every time I manage to forget about the whole marriage and merger thing, here she is." But she had to admit, she was curious to see what Lydia looked like, even if this was the worst possible time. No, actually, the worst possible time would've been if she'd done what she wanted, if she'd had Nick with his pants around his ankles and her on her knees… She inhaled sharply. *That* would've been worse.

Jordan gathered her missing bodice off the floor and began to hook up the front. "Where is she?"

"She and her mother are over there." He pointed to a flowery path curving behind their small shelter. "I believe I heard a discussion of roses."

She gulped. "Do you think she saw us? Or heard your voice?"

"No. Damn." He slid back into the darkness, sheltering her body with his. "They've circled back. They're coming this way."

A tinkling female voice called out, "Miss Tempest? Is that you?"

"Miss Trent?" Isabella's unmistakable tones responded from somewhere near a group of trees off to the left.

"Oh, Lord. This is like something by Shakespeare where everybody ends up in the same forest. All we need is Puck," Jordan groaned.

"You stay here," he said ominously. "Isabella is with a man, and I mean to find out whom."

"That's not a good idea, Nick."

But it was too late. In full-on older brother mode, he went striding across the grass. "Bella," he said in clipped tones. "Miss Trent. Mrs. Trent. How interesting to run into you all on the wooded isle this evening. Lovely place, isn't it?"

There were murmurs she didn't catch, but Jordan was too anxious to see Nick's future bride to stay hidden in the shadows. She peeked out just far enough to get a glimpse.

Lydia and her mother were both wearing dark brown dresses and hats, so they blended right into the vegetation under the weeping willow where Isabella sat. It didn't really give Jordan much to go on since she couldn't make them out very well. Should she be feeling massive guilt, that she was stealing this woman's future fiancé? Or triumph, to have maybe stopped the engagement from ever happening?

Meanwhile, Jordan noticed there was another person there, standing behind Isabella. He was almost completely in shadow, but it was definitely a man. It certainly didn't look like Franco. Who was he?

Eventually, Lydia and her mother broke away from the group, marching off in the other direction, casting curious glances behind them. Mother and daughter's heads tipped close together as they occupied themselves with private conversation.

"The rose garden isn't far," Nick offered in a jovial tone. "You're on the right path."

"Thank you," Lydia called back. But she and her mother hightailed it out of there, looking scandalized.

Waiting for them to pass her hiding place, Jordan held her breath. Finally, she scooted out, anxious to find out what was going on with Isabella and what it all meant.

She arrived in mid-argument, with Isabella pacing back and forth in front of a rustic bench, throwing words at her brother. Nick was doing his best to look menacing as he blocked the path of the other person, a handsome young Asian man who stood silent, glancing back and forth between sister and brother.

"I love him!" Isabella cried. "He's done nothing wrong, Nick, and you have no right to interfere. We've fallen in love!"

"Who is he?" Nick demanded.

"He is my friend. My lover. A wonderful artist," she said

passionately. "All of that." Isabella threw herself in between the two men. "I won't allow you to hurt him."

The young man moved protectively behind Isabella, but he bowed a greeting in Nick's direction. "Tadahito Kayama," he said in a formal voice. His English was a bit stilted, but he managed. "It is a pleasure to meet you. I have come here with the Japanese delegation. We bring many artists. When Isabella visited our temple here, we find we have much in common."

"You can't have known each other long," Nick argued. "Not long enough to be kissing in plain view and pledging your love in front of witnesses."

Jordan kept her mouth shut, considering what they'd just been doing was a lot worse than kissing.

"We weren't in plain view," Isabella countered. "We were safely hidden under the willow. It's just that that damn Lydia has eagle eyes or something. So unfair. Why does she care what I do, anyway?"

"Probably because she's still envisioning me as a matrimonial prospect," Nick said tersely. "Although after catching her future sister-in-law canoodling under a tree with a Japanese man, she may change her mind."

"You don't want to marry her, anyway!" Isabella took Tadahito's arm. "But I do want to marry Tad. We are planning to run away together at the earliest opportunity, and nothing you can say can stop us."

Run away? There was that "ding, ding, ding" alarm again. Run away, like maybe, on Friday?

The list of possible reasons for Isabella's vanishing act just kept getting longer. Under her breath, Jordan muttered, "Man, I sure missed a lot in my research."

Nick's eyebrows shot up. "You can't marry someone the family has never met that you've known for a few weeks.

He's from another country, Bella! A faraway and exotic country to which you've never traveled. Are you planning to go to Japan with him?"

Lifting her chin, Isabella answered, "I don't know. But we will be together. Tad is a wonderful artist. He works with something called *shunga* that is the most beautiful thing I've ever seen."

Jordan knew what that was. It was a discipline of Japanese woodcuts, known for its intricacy, delicacy and hugely erotic content, like the woman having sex with the octopus that she'd seen back at the "Sex Through the Ages" exhibit. Wow. That stuff was fierce and hotter than a five-alarm fire.

"Tad is the only man I've ever met who understands me or my art," Isabella declared dramatically.

Jordan had to admit, it made a certain amount of sense. There weren't many Western artists going for all-out erotica like Isabella's sculpture, but Eastern… The traditions of spirituality and sexuality entwined in art were long and rich.

But Nick was not as accepting. "Our parents will certainly not approve of your friend Tad or his brand of artistry. You know that, Isabella."

"I don't care whether they approve or not."

Jordan silently applauded. *Good girl!*

Nick was shaking his head, looking very sour. "You continue to seek new ways to embarrass the family, and it appears you've succeeded beautifully. Your arch wasn't enough, so you had to throw a Japanese man into the pot, and then you paraded him in front of Lydia Trent and her mother!"

"Speaking of pots," Isabella noted, inclining her finger at Jordan where she stood on the outskirts of their little party.

"Perhaps you and the kettle should have a chat, Nicholas. Since you brought your new lady love home, gossip has been raging." She clicked her tongue. "Are you, too, seeking new ways to embarrass the family? It appears you've succeeded even more beautifully than I."

Furious, Nick started to speak, stopped, and then cursed under his breath. He looked like he wanted to kick something.

"Nick, I think you owe your sister an apology," Jordan interceded. "She's absolutely right that she and Tad haven't committed any greater sins than you and I have." Remembering how his hands had felt under her skirt and how lost in the moment she'd been, she couldn't stop hot color from rushing to her face. She hoped it was dark enough not to show. Defending herself as much as Isabella, she continued, "I just can't see anything wrong with two people swept up in the passion of the fair acting on their impulses. Plus, I don't think Isabella should have to knuckle under just because your parents say so. Or you, either, for that matter."

She couldn't help thinking of that enormous ruby ring and how, if his parents had their way, it would be flashing on Lydia Trent's ring finger next year. That was just *wrong*. Resolute, she met Nick's gaze. "Sometimes you have to do what's right for you, no matter what the consequences."

Nick muttered, "I don't think we're talking about Isabella anymore."

"Thank you, Jordan. Tad and I shall leave you to your own discussion," Isabella said grandly.

"I am very happy to have made your acquaintance," Tad said softly, ducking his head. He looked like he would've liked to sink into the mossy ground under the willow tree.

Neither Nick or Jordan said a word. She figured he was mad at her, but really, she couldn't have kept quiet.

So what if Chicago society tongues were wagging? She knew from her work that scandalous women got a lot done in the world. A lot more than the meek, mild ones nobody ever talked about.

"I'll take you home," Nick announced.

She didn't like the hard set to his features. "I thought you had plans," she said softly. "You mentioned something about further plans for the two of us tonight."

"Those plans will have to wait."

Uh-oh. She might have stood up for her beliefs, she might have seen the answer to the Isabella mystery, she might have even seen the last of the competition, but her sex life was going nowhere.

Why did that continue to seem like the most important of the four?

14

How to Be a Scandalous Woman, Rule 14:
Secrets beat truth nine times out of ten.

MORNING CAME MUCH TOO SOON. Once again, Jordan didn't sleep well, but at least this time, Nick didn't visit her in her dreams.

In an odd way, that made it even harder to sleep. All night, she kept tossing and turning in the narrow bed, staring at the wall that separated their rooms, wondering what he was doing on the other side, trying to predict whether he might come knocking. He didn't.

He was, however, in the breakfast room when she arrived.

"Good morning," he said coolly, sitting down at the table with a cup of coffee. He picked up his spoon and began stirring vigorously.

"Good morning." She began to fill her plate from the breakfast buffet set out.

"Some packages have arrived for you. Your parcels from the store."

"Oh. Excellent." Now at least she would have a change of dress. She unbent far enough to say, "Thank you for giving me a blank check at Tempest & Son. That was very generous of you."

"You're welcome." He continued to stir coffee that must be whipped into a frenzy by now.

She didn't like the chill in the room. Somebody had to be a grown-up here. "Okay, so, what do you think we should do about Isabella and Tad? Is he the one who'll take her away? Or is Franco more dangerous?"

"I don't think we should speak of it."

Another wall came clanging down between them. Stung, she asked, "You think it's none of my business?"

"I do."

"So you're just going to let her disappear on Friday? Because that *is* my business." Starting to get cranky, she waved her hand in the air. "Hello? I traveled through freakin' time to make sure she doesn't!"

"Jordan, please," he said grumpily. "I can't take any more of your time travel nonsense. Suffice it to say that I have the situation under control. I will not allow my sister to run away with her new, unsuitable beau any more than I will allow her to sail off with that disreputable count."

"But what if she really loves Tad?"

"He lives halfway around the world, his occupation is dubious at best, he's probably poor as a church mouse—"

"And that kind of thing matters to you? Wow," she exclaimed, "I guess I don't know you at all."

She chose to ignore the fact that those things had once meant something to her, too, back when she was choosing Daniel because he fit so neatly and seamlessly into the life she wanted for herself, "Full Professor Before Forty" and all. No, it hadn't been about his money. Just the fact that he was a safe, sensible choice. And here she was, arguing to Nick that safe and sensible was all wrong.

"Of course you don't know me. You have this fantasy

of who I am that I never had a hope of reaching," he said angrily.

Stubbornly, she persisted, "I wasn't talking about you and me. I was talking about your sister and what's best for her. Maybe Tad is what's best for her."

"Who is Tad?" a loud voice blared from the doorway.

Jordan took her plate to the table, zipping her lip now that the steamship known as H. H. Tempest had arrived.

"Who is Tad?" he demanded again, even louder this time. "What's Isabella done now?"

Reluctantly, Nick said, "Isabella has met an artist. He's with one of the delegations at the fair. Apparently they've been meeting for some time, and…" He shoved his cup away from him, sloshing coffee on the snowy linen tablecloth. "She fancies herself in love with him."

"Good God almighty!" Mr. Tempest stalked closer. "How could you let that happen, Nicholas? What were you thinking?"

Nick's answer was swallowed up by the noisy arrival of another guest. "Hello and good morning!" Franco announced, slapping his walking stick to his chest as he charged right into the breakfast room. "I have come to purchase La Bella Isabella's erotica." He rolled the *r* on erotica for about thirty seconds.

"Her *what?*" Henry Horatio Tempest looked more confused than angry. "What did that man say?"

"You must be the father of La Bella Isabella. Good morning to you, sir! You are a businessman. I am a businessman. This is why I come to you to speak man to man, to take care of the small details, yes? We don't need to involve the women, for they don't understand." And with that, the count fastened an evil smile on Jordan, as if willing her to leave.

She stayed where she was.

Mr. Tempest turned to his son. "What is this man talking about?"

Emotionless and stoic, Nick summarized, "The count wants to buy the piece that Bella has in the Women's Building. He wants to take it back to Milan."

"So you, sir, are a count?" H.H. looked a lot more interested.

"Indeed I am," Franco agreed. "Franco Pirelli, il Conte di Bassano. And, yes, your son is right. I mean to take this arch, this *errrotica*, back with me tomorrow. My men, they will be arriving at any moment, to pack it up. It shall be mine."

"What do you mean?" This new, even more imperious voice belonged to Isabella. "Franco, I thought I heard you. What do you mean by coming into my home and demanding my father sell you my arch? It isn't his to sell."

"Isabella, what's this about someone named Tad?" her father blustered. "Nicholas says you fancy yourself in love with him, but I will need to know who his people are and his prospects before any further discussion."

Franco's lids lowered, giving him the general look of a lizard. "What does this mean, Isabella? Who is Tad?"

"I blame you, Nicholas." Mr. Tempest advanced on his son, shaking a fist. "If you had only taken Isabella in hand when I told you to—"

"It's not his fault," Jordan piped up, hoping to avert blows. "Isabella is a grown woman with wants and desires of her own. She chose Tad all by herself."

"Yes, exactly," Isabella confirmed. "I'm in love with Tadahito and I shall be with him. Neither you, Father, nor you, Franco, will stand in my way."

"Tada… What?" Her father glanced from face to face.

"Where in blazes is the man from? What kind of name is that?"

"He's Japanese," Isabella declared. "He's an artist, and he is the only person in the entire world who understands me."

"Japanese?" The old man's ruddy face darkened with rage. Once again, he turned to Nick. "You've let your sister run amok for far too long. No one in our circle has ever seen a child married to someone from Japan. The Mainwarings were ridiculed for allowing their daughter to marry a Russian, and Japan is even more outrageous! I order you to make this unpleasantness go away. If need be, we can make arrangements for a convent or somewhere she can think over her disastrous conduct for a good long time."

As they stormed at each other, Jordan added another column to her mental toteboard of Ways Isabella Could Go Missing. Kidnapped by Franco and taken to Italy, eloping with Tadahito to Japan or other parts unknown, or perhaps sent to a convent by her father. There were too many choices to cover at this point.

And right in front of her, everybody was shouting at cross-purposes. She wasn't sure she'd ever been in a room with so much conflict.

"Father, I am not a child. If you disagree with me, speak to *me*," Isabella insisted.

"I will not lose you to some Japanese interloper!" Franco announced with a dramatic flourish.

"You must have me before you can lose me, and you don't. You never will."

"What is it that the count here wants to purchase?" Mr. Tempest interrupted. "Sir, if you really want to buy it, I say we do business."

"You can't sell my arch, Father. It isn't yours to sell."

"You know very well that if I choose to sell it, you won't stop me," her father shot back. "See here, Count, what's your price? Let's make a bargain, shall we?"

"You have gone too far, Father," Isabella declared. "I have the right to decide what happens to me as a woman and as an artist. If I do not want my arch in Franco's palazzo, then it shall not be there. If I *do* want to make a life with Tadahito in Japan, then I shall!"

That was an impressive speech. Jordan felt like applauding. Surely now Nick would put an end to this. All he needed to do was take his sister's side, turn Franco out into the street, and tell his father where to stuff the sexist attitudes. She looked at Nick expectantly.

But no. He and his mother, the last member of the family to arrive, stood over by the sideboard, impassively watching it all unfold.

"Well," Isabella concluded, "I have had more than I can take. I am leaving. I am going to find Tad and I may never be back!"

With one last toss of her golden curls, Isabella stomped off. Franco left soon after, now that the object of his pursuit was gone, and Mr. Tempest continued to rail in general about the injustice of having a worthless son and a faithless daughter.

"I will not let this go on," the old man raged. "I shall send a wire to my sister in Baltimore to see if she can locate a suitable convent."

Since nobody else was stepping up, Jordan felt she had to. "Isabella isn't a bag of laundry you can send to the cleaners," she told him. "She hasn't done anything wrong. She wants to chart her own destiny. She wants to follow her passion, whether it's with a man or with her art. What's so terrible about that?"

"Would you please tell your suffragette friend to be quiet?" his father bellowed at Nick. "Impertinent! Insufferable! All this talk of women and passion makes my blood boil. Women were not meant for passion of their own. Women are simply vessels to carry men's passion."

"*Vessels?* You've got to be kidding," she muttered. Mr. Tempest wasn't even looking at her anymore. Apparently vessels weren't worth fighting with, either.

She thought sure that would kick Nick into action to defend her. But still, Nick said nothing.

His father lost some of his steam without anyone to fight with, and eventually he strode from the room, muttering about convents and telegrams, with the silent Mrs. Tempest following close behind.

"Nick? Were you just going to sit there and let him say anything he wanted?" she asked.

"It's all so very easy for you," he said with an edge of sarcasm. "So very black and white. But I've grappled with this before. There's no reasoning with my father and there's no point in trying. Of course he's wrong. But he won't see that."

"Maybe if you told him—"

Nick's hollow laugh cut her off. "Don't you think I've tried that? Once I decided that my duty was to run the family business and run the family as well, I knew I had to simply work around his shortcomings. You wait until the storm has passed and then you do what you would've done all along. It's a very simple strategy."

"But it's making your sister miserable. And you're miserable, too. You let your father tie you up in knots and it's just wrong!" She shook her head, getting madder by the minute.

"It's not your concern," he said evenly.

"Not my concern?" The hell with that! Before she knew it, the words she didn't want to say were spilling out. "Nick, you're going to die in a damn car race two lousy years from now. America's first car race. Do you know what that is? Automobiles, motor car, horseless carriage. Ring any bells?"

There was an odd expression on his handsome face. "Yes, I do know it," he admitted. "I have invested in some such ventures. A lot of work is being done in that area."

"I know. Because you like speed, right? Fast cars, fast horses, fast women. It's all over your obit." This was so gruesome she couldn't believe she was saying it. More softly, she added, "I remembered yesterday and it's making me sick because you don't believe me and there's nothing I can do to stop you."

He sighed. "Oh, so it's just more prophesies. You need to start writing these down. You can outpace Nostradamus."

"I wish I didn't know, but I do," she told him, wanting to shake him. She'd seen his photo, where he looked free and happy next to that car. "I really think it's because you need some kind of escape from that stupid store. You certainly need to escape from your father and his mean, nasty, sexist, control-freak opinions. You know that I think women have a right to speak up, but, you know, you need to have your say, too." Plunging onward, she concluded, "Someday all those repressed feelings are just going to explode."

But he didn't respond, just spun on his heel and left the room.

"I think I must be doing something wrong," Jordan said out loud. "It just shouldn't be this hard." She felt utterly defeated.

"Miss Albright?" It was Nick's mother, clutching a handkerchief to her breast and looking distressed. Jordan wasn't sure she could handle another member of the Tempest family at the moment.

Well, it wasn't his mother's fault, was it? *If I were his mother, I wouldn't want him hooked up with me, either.* "I'm sorry, Mrs. Tempest," she said softly. "I seem to be causing such a stir in your household."

"No, no, not at all, Miss Albright. It's not you. This has never been what you might call a peaceful household." She hesitated. "I just wanted to tell you that I heard what you said the other day, about women being passionate and, dare I say it, sensual creatures at heart. I know my husband disagrees, but…" She straightened her spine. "Well, I know myself to have sensual urges. And therefore my husband must be wrong."

Well, it was a start. Now if only she could get through to her son.

With everybody mad at her except Mrs. Tempest, she didn't have anything to do but wander around the house. She found a book in the library, but didn't really want to read. Worried that someone might remember there was an extra person sponging off their charity and kick her out, she retreated to her room for the day. Lying on the bed, she stared at the cupids painted on the ceiling.

"I must be here to do something. People don't just wake up one day in a whole other century for no reason." But whatever her purpose, she'd screwed it up. As far as she knew, Isabella was headed straight for the same old disaster and mystery she'd had the first time the history books were written, Nick was probably still going to marry Lydia and die in a senseless car wreck long before his time, and she…

Well, she would muddle along somehow until she either

found a way back or got people here so angry with her that they threw her down a well. "Maybe I'm really supposed to be a suffragette," she mused. "Maybe if I throw my lot in with them, they'll get the vote before 1921."

Try as she might, she couldn't come up with any concrete reason she was here. *You're here for a reason, and that will all become clear.*

"Not so clear, Captain Kangaroo," she whispered. "Am I supposed to save Nick or Isabella? Whichever one, it's not working."

It was already dark by the time there was a knock on her door. Time for dinner, apparently. That ought to be fun. Maybe they would bring her a tray in her room like Jane Eyre.

But it was Nick.

As soon as she saw his face, she felt much less sure about her self-righteous position. Even more than she wanted to stand up for what she believed in, she didn't want to make him unhappy.

"I'm sorry," she offered. "I shouldn't have tried to interfere in your family business."

"And I apologize as well. You've meant a lot to me in a short time, and I should have better defended you against my father." He braced himself carelessly against the doorframe. "Old habits die hard. But perhaps you're right. Perhaps I do need to face him down and make my own way."

"Really?" He'd actually listened and processed what she told him? She noticed he didn't bring up the part about him dying in a car accident. She probably shouldn't have shared that information, anyway. Nobody wanted to know when they would meet their maker. But Nick... She wanted so desperately to save him.

"Really." He smiled, reaching out to brush a finger

around the curve of her cheek. "I was bored and I wished for a diversion and there you were. Life hasn't been the same since. I hope you know that I find you utterly maddening and utterly enchanting at the same time."

She covered his hand with hers, holding it to her face. "I'll keep the enchanting part."

"Jordan, last night…"

"Yes?" Was he referring to the magical little island and their intimate encounter? She tried not to blush. Those bizarre crotchless pants were making her crazier than she already was.

"I had planned something for the two of us. A surprise."

"I remember." He'd mentioned that before they all got sidetracked with the latest in Isabella's parade of suitors.

"You seem to think you won't be here very long." He threw up his hands. "I wish I knew better where you were from or where you might be going, but… Well, I wanted to make the most of the time we had together."

She gazed deep into his blue, blue eyes. The man had charm, that was for sure. "I'd like that, Nick."

"Do you mind going back to the fair?"

"No, of course not." She sent him a quizzical glance. "Are you taking me to see the hootchy-kootchy with Little Egypt?"

"No."

"What then?" Why was he being so mysterious. "I don't want to see that pickle map again," she joked. "Once was enough."

"Not the pickles."

"Oh, wait. Of course. The arch." She was a little disappointed, even though it was absolutely the best idea. "Are we going to camp out near the arch just to make sure nobody sees it and Franco doesn't steal it?"

"No!" He framed her face with his hands, holding her still. "Forget about that. I've posted guards. It will be fine."

She swallowed through a suddenly dry throat. His eyes were so intense. "Okay."

"For just one night, I'd like to forget about my sister and her trials and tribulations and my father and your future and all of that. I would like to enjoy…" He smiled and it took her breath away. "Us. You and me. I want to enjoy the time we have because we don't know how long it will last. Is that possible?"

They were actually thinking along the same lines. She nodded. "I would love to."

15

How to Be a Scandalous Woman, Rule 15:
Top or bottom? It's all a matter of perspective.

As HE LED JORDAN up onto the first platform around Mr. Ferris's Wheel, Nick was gratified to see surprise written all over her expressive face.

"But I thought you said the Ferris wheel wasn't open yet?"

"It isn't." He grinned, hoping she wouldn't be put off by the risk involved. To him, that was all part of the fun. "But most of the cars are attached now. I convinced Mr. Ferris to let me rent out his wheel for tonight. The engineer will take us to the top and let us dangle there for a good, long while."

She looked a little uneasy. "Does this thing work?"

"Yes, I think so. He's been spinning the cars around as he adds them to the wheel, testing it out with everyone from Mrs. Ferris to the hardy souls who jumped the fence and forced their way on. Nobody's fallen off yet."

"Well," she began, and he could tell she was trying to be cheerful, "let's hope the good luck lasts. How do we get in there?"

Nick waved at the engineer down in the pit. "Bring the car around," he called out.

It was noisy as the large carriage ground to a stop right in front of their loading platform. The cars were big enough for forty people, but he had arranged a better use of that space.

"When I saw it, I knew it was big." Jordan stared up at it, judging how high it reached. "But I'm used to Ferris wheels with little swings where two people go. Not nearly this big. Each of these compartments is like a whole trolley car."

"Just wait," he said slyly.

He'd had a test run, and found the ride itself disappointing, actually. It swayed a little, but nothing major, and it was mostly slow and placid as it climbed to the top. But once you were up there, then it became something extraordinary. The view was astonishing, with the entire fairgrounds displayed like a magical fairyland before you.

He'd planned to bring her up as the sun set, but then that damn island had worked its charm and distracted him. So tonight he went for starlight. When you only had one night in all the world, it had to be spectacular.

He took her hand to help her into the carriage.

"Nick, you did all this?" Her eyes were wide and warm as she took in the Arabian Nights setting he had arranged.

"Not with my own two hands, I admit. I hired some help."

All of the chairs had been removed, and there were bright silk pillows scattered on an Oriental carpet laid over the bare floor of the carriage. A small, carved table sat to one side of the pillows, and the food he'd asked for, nothing more complicated than bread, cheese and wine, was set up next to the table.

"It's beautiful." She walked in slowly, examining every detail. "You did this for me?"

"I wanted you to get your ride on the Ferris wheel."

"I can't believe you." Her smile looked a little tremulous. "And you thought you couldn't compare to my fantasy man. Nick, you are so much more. Seriously. The fantasy man was all about sex. You're so much more than just sex."

Nick inhaled sharply. How would she know? They hadn't explored all their options yet.

Jordan really was unusual, to just blurt that out without preamble. But he found himself envying that fantasy man who was all about sex. It would've been so much simpler that way.

As they climbed higher in the night sky, he discarded his jacket and tie and helped her unhook her bodice, all in the interests of comfort, of course, as they reclined on the carpet and leaned against the soft pillows. He sipped his glass of wine, watching her over the rim, wondering, not for the first time, who she really was and how she'd managed to inch her way under his skin within five minutes of showing up in his life.

There were so many unanswered questions when it came to Jordan. Her attachment to his sister's career, her unorthodox wardrobe and shoes, the coin that was identical to his, her insistence that she knew what would happen days before it did…

Sometimes Nick wished he were a less demanding man. Others would've accepted her story, made her high priestess of a new religion and followed her around adoring the ground she walked on for the rest of his life. But that just wasn't him. He needed her to make sense in a coherent, reasonable way.

Not this thunderstruck lust or bizarre feeling of connection, but something more real and far more rational.

Not even for you can I believe in fairies and wizards and time travelers.

"What are you thinking?" she asked sweetly, licking at a drop of wine around the rim of her own wine glass.

That I want your tongue on my flesh. He swallowed. "That we're almost at the top and we should be taking advantage of the view."

"Instead of taking advantage of each other?" she asked with a saucy smile.

But the vista was amazing, and that distracted her enough to help him breathe and control his urges a moment longer.

"You can see the bobbing lights on the boats in the harbor," he told her, leaning over her to point out the right spot. "And those streaks of light are electric launches in the lagoon."

"They look like diamonds. And all the buildings lit up…" She shook her head in disbelief. "I mean, I've been to Disney World and seen the Venetian Boats right here on Lake Michigan, but this is better than any of them. It's so big. I know I keep saying that, but the fair is just so incredible. It's such a shame it can't stay. But how lucky are we, to get to be here now? How lucky is that?"

He could tell she was nervous. Her words spilled out too fast, too carelessly. But he understood. His own nerves were jangling, as well. He hadn't been this impatient with a woman since he was sixteen. Maybe never. But when you only had one night…

He was desperate to take it slow, make it last, make it more memorable than anything either of them had ever felt. And yet he wasn't at all sure he would be able to wait another moment.

"We're very lucky."

He couldn't help it. He dropped a small kiss on the nape of her neck, sliding his tongue up to her ear, enjoying the way she shivered under his touch. As she closed her eyes, leaning back into him, he pulled the combs from her hair, letting it flow over her shoulders and his chest.

"You should wear your hair down," he told her. "Fashion be damned. I love your hair."

She smiled. "Fashion be damned is an excellent idea altogether."

Clothing be damned is an even better idea. But not yet. Not in a rush like their brief encounter on the Japanese Island. *Slow down,* he ordered himself. But his fingers were trembling as he withdrew them from her hair.

"Are you hungry?" he asked, letting his hands barely graze her bodice, not actually touching, just teasing, as he reached around her for the bread and cheese. If he was going to play this dangerous waiting game, then so was she. And only when they were both breathless, panting with anticipation, would he take them both to the place they craved.

He took a plump, juicy grape, a perfect round morsel, holding it an inch from her lips, pulling it a little farther away every time she tried to take it from him.

Her eyes were dancing with mischief when she finally leaned far enough to capture his hand in both of hers, biting the grape right out of his fingers. "Delicious," she murmured.

He tightened his embrace, situating her more closely in his lap, one arm fast at her waist. With his other hand, he slid the next grape back and forth against her lower lip, pushing aside her hair to whisper into her ear, "Tell me how much you want it and I may let you have it."

She said nothing, trying to nip at the grape as he held her back, tight against his chest.

"Tell me," he prompted.

"No."

"Naughty girl." As quick as that, he tossed the grape into his own mouth, taking down the wet little treat with a greedy, smacking noise. "Naughty girls don't get what they want."

"Don't they?" Looking over his shoulder, sending him a mocking gaze that was much too wise, she pulled his hand away from his mouth, bringing it to hers instead. And then she slid his index finger into her moist, warm, soft mouth, sucking his finger, swirling her tongue around it.

She took each finger on his right hand in turn, sliding her lips and her tongue up and down, biting the tip ever so gently, driving him mad. All he could think about was that damn statue, with the beautiful girl's eager, open mouth so close to Narcissus's marble manhood, ready to gobble up every inch of him.

As Jordan's clever tongue sluiced over his thumb, his desire climbed higher and harder, and he shifted uncomfortably, unable to take the pressure of her bottom, swathed and hidden under layers of heavy silk, as she wiggled even the slightest bit against his turgid, throbbing member.

"Are you thinking what I'm thinking?" she asked innocently, leaning back full against him. And then she whispered, "Narcissus."

He groaned. That was exactly what he was thinking. The very mention was enough to make his painfully swollen cock jerk against his trouser buttons, demanding release. Damn. Way too much clothing and way too much haste. If he wasn't careful, this would be all over before it began.

Keeping himself fiercely under control, determined to be the one who set the pace, he gripped her tighter around the waist, holding her captive. He was enjoying the view over her shoulder as her breasts rose and fell with each unsteady breath.

Her open bodice gaped, giving him a generous view of her exquisite curves. Her breasts strained against the barrier of her corset and chemise, and he couldn't resist maneuvering enough to slip her jacket off over her shoulders to offer an even clearer vista of all that creamy skin. With his left arm back around her waist, holding her close, he dropped small, brief kisses along her shoulder, inhaling the flowery fragrance of her hair, licking the sweet, salty taste of her skin.

When she let out a little whimper of pleasure, he moved back up to her chemise, squeezing hard as he filled his hands with her flesh. Undoing one, two and then three of the tiny hooks down her front, he didn't stop until her beautiful, rosy-tipped globes spilled out completely.

Moaning louder, she closed her eyes and tried to rub back against his cock with her bottom, only partially succeeding because of the breadth of her skirts. He felt the motion and the ripple of sensation, so slight, so devastating, and he rocked her against his lap, trying for more friction, as dangerous as that was. He had both hands on her breasts now, rolling her swollen tips between his fingers and the scratchy lace edge of her chemise, enjoying the way she gasped each time he increased the pressure, setting up a definite rhythm that promised much more to come.

Her own hands fluttered in the air. She tried to wedge them in between her body and his, as if going for his fly, but he kept his grip too tight so that there was no space between them, not able to bear the thought of her hands on him just yet. Thwarted, she shoved both hands down onto the front of her skirt, clearly attempting to palm herself through all that fabric. But she swore in frustration, grabbing fistfuls of her skirts, still moving with him, dancing to the beat he'd set even as she was bound by his arms, captured between his thighs, unable to reach the spot she so desperately wanted.

Nick smiled. Finally, he had her where he wanted her.

He lifted her enough to undo the button at the back of her skirt, and then he shoved it down, over her hips, where she kicked it off completely with a cry of relief. She was still wearing her petticoat, though, so he dispatched that, too, preferring her in just the bloomers. As she scrambled around to face him, on her hands and knees on the Oriental carpet, her hair was wild, her chemise undone, and her whiskey-colored eyes hungry. For him. She crawled closer.

Nick had never seen a woman look so aroused and so damn sexy. Her lips were soft and plump, parted slightly as she struggled to breathe.

He rose to his own knees, planning to grab her and peel off the rest of her garments, but she smiled and shook her head no, raising a hand to stop him.

"Uh-uh," she murmured, her voice unsteady. "That's not the way Narcissus goes. Besides, you've already had me. It's my turn."

He tried to form an argument, to convince her that what they'd done on the island, when he'd brought her to release with his fingers, was only the barest beginning, that there was so much more he wanted to explore. But there was no way to pull his thoughts together when Jordan was so close, unfastening his shirt's studs, stripping it off him and running her fingers over his muscled chest, down to his navel.

He couldn't believe how good her hands felt or how impossible it was to cut her off. Suddenly, she bent to press her lips to his flat stomach, and then, unexpectedly, she began to work on his fly, trapping him as she traversed one button at a time, excruciatingly slowly, rubbing her hand along his rigid column through the fine wool.

His hands gripping the back of her head, plunging into her silky tresses, he stayed there on his knees, trying not to sway, wishing he were made of marble. This was pure torture.

Finally, she peeled back the fabric of his trousers, sliding them and his linen drawers down his hips. When she dipped her head to take him into her hands, holding him an inch from her lips, he almost lost his mind.

Nick groaned, wishing there was some way to steel himself, desperately afraid he would explode right there.

Panting, his hips arching into her, he groaned loudly as she took his entire length into her mouth. Her mouth was wet and warm and she was insatiable, nipping him, tasting him, sliding him in and out. She twirled her slippery, wicked little tongue around his tip, skimming her hand up and down his stiff length at the same time. He was ready to burst. Oh, God. So close.

He gritted his teeth. No. Not yet.

Exerting extreme effort, he managed to pull himself back from the brink. Still breathing heavily, he took her face in his hands, tipping her chin up, to look at him.

"Enough," he whispered.

"Nick," she chastised him gently, meeting his gaze. "That wasn't nearly enough. Besides, turnabout is fair play."

"That wasn't turnabout." He moved swiftly, grabbing her around the hips, flipping her onto her back on the soft Oriental carpet before she even knew what had happened. She went down with a soft "oof." "This is turnabout."

He pinned her under the full weight of his body, securing her hands above her head with his, propping himself up where he could look down at her. She tried to wiggle free, but that only made things worse, with her breasts so bare, so prettily outlined by the torn chemise and unyielding corset. Down below, the thin cotton of her bloomers was no barrier against his surging phallus, still wet from her mouth.

As he lazily stroked himself back and forth gently, carelessly, against the front of her drawers, he nipped her lips, delving his tongue inside her mouth, just long enough to make it clear who was in charge and leave her breathless.

Feeling triumphant, Nick rose up, curving his lips into a crooked smile. Settling himself between her thighs, he teased her, nudging his cock just barely into the long, gaping breach in her sheer lawn panties, far enough to make her whimper again when his tip brushed her clit. He could already feel the heat and moisture emanating from her nether regions, and it took everything he had not to plunge right in.

Instead, he dipped to nibble her neck and lick her ear. He said softly, "It's oddly sexy, the idea of making love while you're still wearing those drawers."

"Then do it," she urged, wriggling underneath him. "Your way. My way. I don't care. But I don't know if I can stand waiting one more second. Do it, Nick."

His manhood was throbbing with need as he poised himself at her entrance. He grazed against her nub again, enjoying the way it made her whimper and squirm. She bucked up into him, raising herself to try to push him closer to the brink.

"Nick," she begged. She tangled her arms around his back, fastening her knees at his hips, desperate to pull him down. "Take me. Now. Please?"

He wanted to give her what she wanted. He needed to take what he wanted.

His self-control shattering, Nick entered her with one hard stroke. Ah. So worth the wait. He shuddered, pulling back, plunging again, deeper and harder, faster, as she cried out with pleasure, wrapping her legs around his hips, arching up to meet every thrust. Any skill or experience he'd had as a lover was lost—all he could do was slam into her wildly, rocketing them both to the top with reckless abandon.

A low moan escaped her, her fingernails dug into his buttocks, and he let go, sinking into her, exploding in a ferocious, blinding, magnificent climax. She cried out louder, tightening her grip with her arms and her legs, melting around him, reaching her own release at exactly the same moment.

But there was a loud, ominous clunk—the sound of iron striking iron somewhere above their heads—as he drove home the final stroke.

Nick held himself still, gathering her to his chest as the car suddenly pitched and jolted to one side. Damn it all to hell. Nothing like technological disaster to punctuate a truly earth-shattering climax.

There was another thump, not as loud as the first time, and then the carriage began to list to one side.

"Whoa." His arms tightened while they waited to see if anything else would happen. But it stayed steady for several minutes.

"Do you think we broke it?" she whispered. "If the Ferris wheel is a-rockin', don't come a-knockin'?"

He couldn't help it. A laugh escaped him as he carefully set her down among the pillows and reached behind her for his pants. "I don't think it had anything to do with us. Just some small bolt that didn't hold, perhaps. I think we'll be fine."

"Are you sure?"

"As sure as I can be. But the engineer is likely to bring us down now, so we'd best get dressed. I fear you have the better of me in that regard since you stripped me down to my skin." He kissed her quick, backing away before he got too attached. Damn interruption, anyway. He'd hoped they could try another round or two or three. "Unfortunate timing. But you and I will have more time to make it right." He smiled. He brought her hand to his lips. "We belong together. I have no doubt of that."

"Nick?" She sat up, snatching away her hand, looking startled and uneasy, as if she hadn't heard a word he'd said. "You said the Ferris wheel has already had trial runs, right?"

"Yes, why?"

"Because…" Chewing her lip, she gazed around at the interior of the compartment. "Because I just remembered something. Something awful."

Nick fastened his shirt studs, hoping this wasn't going to be another one of her visions of the future. It was wounding to his pride to make love to her like that, only to have her turn back to her fantasies before their passion had barely cooled.

She shook her head, speaking slowly. "There was a trial run, with dignitaries, the mayor of Chicago, people connected to the fair, that kind of thing."

What did he care about that? "Yes? And?"

"I don't know. I think maybe it hasn't happened yet. I think maybe I have to prevent it."

Looked like his luck had run out. Nick sighed heavily. He'd never had sex like that. He'd never felt this deep, abiding connection to any woman. And the one he'd finally found—the only one—turned out madder than a hatter.

She went on, "They filled up two cars. But one of the passengers in the mayor's car, the one that went up first, was afraid of heights and he didn't realize it until they started to climb. The higher they got, the more he freaked out. By the time they got to the top, he'd completely lost his marbles and he tried to jump out. The other people tried to restrain him, but he was too strong. He not only jumped, but he landed on the other car, unhinging a cable. So the car he jumped out of was okay, but the other one, the one he landed on, fell to the ground, killing all thirty passengers."

"The voice of doom speaks again," he said grimly. The romantic mood between them had completely vanished, thanks to her newest prophecy of disaster.

"I'm not making this up," she contended. She looked very upset about it, holding her hair back away from her face, staring into space. "It's just one of the stories I read when I was putting together background about the fair and why the Ferris wheel was out of commission for most of it." She reached for him. "Has that already happened?"

"Nothing remotely like that. Very few people have been up yet, as I told you. I believe the mayor is scheduled for a test run tomorrow."

"Tomorrow?"

"Jordan, please. It's not enough that we must watch Isabella like hawks and that I am never to go near a motor car." He exhaled deeply, disappointed beyond belief. "Now you want to stop anybody from taking the Ferris wheel ever again?"

"No. Just tomorrow. The day the mayor is there. I'm not making it up. Where do you think I come up with this stuff?" she demanded, angrily smoothing her skirts into place and hooking up her bodice. "You don't think it's important that unless we do something, thirty people will die?"

He held up one hand, forestalling further argument. First she'd preferred to lambaste him for not banging a drum for women's rights and censoring his father, and now she was interrupting an incomparable, incredible event with her loony psychic powers and unreasonable demands to save the world.

He'd hoped against hope for one night out of time, where they could make love under the stars, high above the shining panorama of the fair.

Chances like that came once in a lifetime.

But no. Not with Jordan. Things were never that easy.

16

How to Be a Scandalous Woman, Rule 16:
It's okay to be good every once in a while. Just
don't make a habit of it.

AS THURSDAY MORNING DAWNED, Jordan couldn't find
Nick.

She didn't really want to see him, not after last night,
but he was her only choice. She couldn't ask Isabella, because she wasn't there, either. The upstairs maid looked a
bit stunned when she told Jordan that Miss Isabella had
moved out. Out of this house and in with Tad, wherever he
lived, would've been Jordan's guess.

She didn't have time to decide if that was bad or good,
because she was still really worried about the Ferris wheel
and the accident she expected to occur today.

"Worry about Isabella tomorrow," she told herself.
"Ferris wheel today."

It was kind of like being Superman and prioritizing
your cases.

Honestly, she would've just camped out at the Ferris
wheel overnight if she could have, but the Columbian Guard
kicked everybody out after a certain hour. Besides, grumpy,
unpleasant Nick made her come home.

"I don't blame him for being cranky," she grumbled.

"We have sex and the entire Ferris wheel almost falls down. Somehow I'm getting the idea that our karma is not to be together."

But then, why all the dreams? Why did she land under the arch at the one moment Nick was next to it?

"What does it all mean?"

What it meant right now was that she had to go back to the midway, to get to the Ferris wheel and the mayor's car before the crisis. She'd been back and forth to the fair before, but unfortunately, she was too inexperienced with the transportation choices to know where to get the street-car or find the pier for the steamboat again. And besides, she didn't have any money.

So there she was, dressed in a new ensemble that had been made up by the department store seamstress to her specifications, which was much more comfortable and reasonable, given that she had nixed the huge puffed sleeves and the severely nipped waist. In fact, she felt ready to go save some bootie on the Ferris wheel. If only she knew how to get there.

"Damn you, Nick, where are you?" she said out loud in the hallway outside his bedroom.

"What?"

Jordan whirled. That sounded like Nick. A little weird, but Nick. Where did it come from? Somewhere on this floor.

Okay, so there was her room, Nick's, Isabella's, and another guest bedroom, and the doors were wide open to all four of those. That left another five doors. Two were bathrooms, but she had no idea about the other three.

"Nick?" she asked again, louder this time.

"What?" he repeated in a muted and strange voice.

It seemed to be coming from door number two. She pressed her ear to the wood panel. Clink. Clink.

"So he's pitching pennies. Why not?" Jordan pushed into the room, which she quickly figured out was a music room, what with the piano, the violin and cello, and several dusty music stands. "What are you doing?"

"Something I'm good at," he declared loudly.

He didn't exactly look at her, but he was kind of a mess. He appeared to be wearing last night's white dress shirt and black pants, although his collar and cuffs were undone and his shirt was untucked. Nick was normally a pretty snappy dresser, so this was unusual.

She found herself wanting to comb his hair, stroke his beard-shadowed cheek, kiss his soft lips, make it all better.

Except, no. No, no, no.

The whole time she was looking for him, she'd promised herself she would be casual and remote. Friendly, but nothing more.

After the way they always ended up half-naked and tangled around each other, she knew it wasn't going to be easy. But she just couldn't play those games with Nick anymore. It had long since made her careless and distracted.

So now that she'd found him, she had to keep herself under control. Even if he did look terrible. And hot. He wore stubble better than anybody she'd ever seen. *Rowrrr.*

No, no, no.

He didn't seem to notice her discomfort. He was busy with some game he was playing with a silver coin, a bit bigger than a quarter. Tipping his chair onto the back legs, he held up the coin, judging the distance and arc between his hand and a china cup several feet away.

"Nick, are you drunk?"

He tossed it. *Clink.* "Not nearly drunk enough."

"I guess you can't be that drunk, since you made the

shot," she noted. She walked over to look inside the cup, planning to retrieve the silver coin and toss it back to him for another try. "Huh. A Columbian half-dollar."

She peered at it. The one she'd bought on eBay looked exactly like this one, down to the scratch marking Columbus's eye. She was very familiar with it, what with holding it in her hand, rolling it across her desk and staring at it practically every day while she used it as a good luck totem for her dissertation.

"Nick," she cried, "this is my Columbian half-dollar. Did you steal it from me?"

Why would he do that? He was floating in money and he'd spent a boatload on her at the store. Why would he need her lousy fifty cents?

"It's not yours. It's mine."

"But it looks just like mine," she protested.

"Well, they're all fairly similar, aren't they?" He tipped his chair back again. "I've been throwing that coin at that cup for the past month. I've gotten so good that I make ninety percent of my shots. That is not your coin."

Well, maybe they all did look alike. Maybe scratches over Columbus's eye were really common. It still seemed strange, though.

"So what are you doing this morning, Jordan? What is it you're looking for?"

Same old, same old. *I'm looking for you.* She put the coin back in the cup. "I know you're upset with me, but I need a favor. I need you to take me back to the fair."

"Still on your crusade to save the mayor?"

There was no real way to answer that to his satisfaction, so she just said, "Yes," and left it at that.

Nick got up. He pulled his jacket off the back of a different chair. "I'll drive you."

"Not if you're drunk, you won't."

"I'm not even tipsy." He sent her a dark look. "Believe me, I wish I were."

After the first mile or so in silence, she kind of wished he were, too. He'd probably have been a lot more entertaining and a lot less moody.

When he pulled up outside the main gate, he jumped down, holding the reins in one hand as he helped her descend from the low-slung carriage. After depositing her safely on the sidewalk, he reached into his pocket with his free hand. "You'll need money to buy a ticket at the gate. How are you planning to convince them to let you onto the Ferris wheel with the mayor's party?"

"I don't know yet. I'll think of something when I get in there."

With a resigned air, Nick peeled off some more bills. "If you make a donation to the mayor's next campaign, I feel certain he'll let you join the party." As she started to leave, he glanced at her outfit for the first time. "I'm not sure they'll approve of you in that get-up, however."

"I had it designed by one of the seamstresses at your store. Do you think I'll start a new fashion trend?" she asked with a smile, holding the panels of her simple, flowing skirt away from her body. "This is lots more comfortable."

He walked around her, looking her up and down. "I do believe you've joined the Anti-Corset Brigade. Loose tunic. No hat, no gloves. Nary a ruffle or bow to be found." He raised both eyebrows in feigned surprise. "There's bound to be talk."

"Talk is good. It's when they stop talking about you that you have to worry." She grinned. It seemed she had fully embraced the scandalous-woman lifestyle, and it felt pretty good.

"I think I should probably accompany you," he decided. He shook his head. "You may have some difficulty getting cooperation dressed like that. It makes you seem radical."

"Radical? You really think so? Why are you helping me, anyway?" she asked, suddenly suspicious. "We both know you don't believe me."

"Yes, but someone has to look out for the innocents in the world."

"Huh," she said mockingly. "Here I thought I was a scandalous woman, making love on the Ferris wheel and going out in public without a hat or gloves. Innocent? Me?"

"Yes, Jordan, you." His voice was suddenly much less sarcastic. "You're the only woman I've ever met who manages to combine scandal and innocence so completely. You make me almost believe in that Future World of yours." He laughed, and the teasing tone came back. "Where else would you fit? You need a place so advanced and evolved that even virtuous women can also be sexual tigers."

Jordan tipped herself up to catch his jacket lapels. She kissed him, hard and fast. "I guess I got through to you more than I thought, Nick." But then she backed away. "See ya. I'm off to play hero."

"I said I would accompany you."

"Nope," she called out. "I appreciate the fact that you like my passion. But if you can't believe me and trust me all the way, then I want to do this myself."

Even scandalous women had to have standards.

Well, she'd talked a good game, but she still had butterflies when it came to bullying her way into the mayor's party near the Ferris wheel. She didn't know the mayor from Adam, of course, but she managed to ask around until she figured it out.

Okay, so the crazy person was going to be in his carriage. She hoped. If it was vice-versa, she was in big trouble. Like, pearly gates big trouble.

But, no, she was sure. She went over the details of the story she remembered and she was positive. The person who got wigged out on heights and jumped out came from the mayor's car. So which one was he? They all looked fairly normal on the ground.

Nick was wrong about one thing. It was remarkably easy to just stand with the others, even though they were mostly men, and walk right up into the car. Nobody noticed one extra woman, even if she was dressed like a "radical."

Her nerves jangled as the car rose, as the members of the party exchanged small talk and remarked on the wonders of the huge wheel. She kept eyeing her fellow passengers, trying to figure out who it would be. But nobody seemed strange or different. For men from 1893, of course.

But as the carriage shifted and lifted slightly off the ground, one man stood out. Was he really wild-eyed and sweaty, or was she projecting? He was fairly large, and he seemed to be a bodyguard of some kind. Well, if it was him, he wasn't going to be easy to subdue.

Uh-oh. She probably should've thought of a plan to do just that before she got on the Ferris wheel. *Damn it.* She was a planner! What was she thinking, freelancing on a matter of life and death?

She had to admit, she'd been so ready to prove to Nick that she really did know what would happen tomorrow, that she alone could save the day, that she'd barreled ahead without having a good idea of what to do.

Okay, so first step, she was pretty sure she'd identified the vertigo sufferer. He was definitely getting twitchy over there as the wheel turned and pulled them higher in the sky.

She tried to work her way through the crowd to get nearer, even though she still didn't have a clear idea what she was going to do. But she couldn't really get too close—he was right by the window, where people were more packed together to take in the view.

As she kept a vigilant eye on him, she noticed that the man next to him had apparently also noticed his companion's rising panic. He began to pat his neighbor's shoulder and murmur cheerful words. It didn't seem to help. Suddenly, the big man shouted something unintelligible and staggered sideways, shoving people out of the way as he lunged toward the door. Somebody fell down, somebody else screamed, and a terrified murmur caught the crowd, as several men combined to try to wrestle him to the ground.

"Noooo," the man shrieked, getting more and more frantic and out of control the higher they went. He was actually throwing himself at the iron door with its glass panes, trying to grab the handle and force the door open. Glass shattered, the car lurched and shook in a very scary way but he still couldn't get out.

Okay, you were right, you were right, and it's time to do something. Put up or shut up.

But what? Every time their car took a hit, she flinched. Not such a great idea to come up here, high off the ground, with a crazy guy. This was terrifying! Jordan glanced around. There was nothing there to bash him over the head with or a handy twentieth-century stun gun or anything. Adrenaline pumped through her veins. She'd never thought of herself as the hero type, but she had a brain, didn't she? There had to be something she could do.

Frantically, she looked down at herself. All she had was her clothes and the few dollars Nick had given her.

Her clothes.

Without thinking, Jordan unfastened her skirt and stripped it off. Striding over to the door, where her fellow passengers had cleared a space for the crazy guy, she whipped the skirt up over his head, going for a parakeet-in-a-cage kind of effect. So she was standing there in her petticoat for what seemed like ages. So what?

It was amazing. Immediately, all the fight seemed to go out of him. With the skirt over his head, he sank to the floor, whimpering like a baby.

The mayor and his friends were clapping Jordan on the back, congratulating her, practically weeping with relief. When one man complained about the scandal of a woman removing her skirt in public, three others immediately shushed him up. Maybe she had taught them all something after all.

A man near her chuckled something about a reward but Jordan just said politely that all she wanted was her skirt back. She wouldn't even tell them her name. As soon as the car hit the ground, as soon as somebody pulled her garment off the sobbing man with vertigo, she was out of there.

It didn't hit her until she was halfway down the midway that she didn't have anywhere to go.

All of a sudden, she stopped dead, almost colliding with two men carting a tourist in a sedan chair. What next? She'd been so set on saving the Ferris wheel that she hadn't even considered what to do next.

"Oh, my God," she whispered. "I expected Nick to be here, waiting for me, when I came down. I thought this would be the magic pill and now he would believe me and everything would be okay from here on. Presto change-o."

How ridiculous was that?

Yeah, she'd proved that she knew what would happen before it actually did, nipping one Ferris wheel accident in the bud. If Nick was paying attention, the logical conclusion would be that she wasn't a fake or a lunatic. But so what?

She still didn't know whether she was coming or going, whether Isabella was on a collision course with infamy, whether tomorrow was D-day, whether she was stranded here forever…

"Excuse me, Miss Albright?" a man in a blue Columbian Guard uniform asked off to her side. "Are you all right?"

She shook her head.

"But you performed a wonderful deed. You saved the lives of thirty people."

"But that's not what I was really here for, was it?" She turned to face the curator, that strange man at the center of this whole mess. "I feel like this whole thing with the Ferris wheel was just an accident. I only remembered at the last minute. What if I hadn't? And what about all the other terrible things? There could be so many other tragedies, happening every day, that I can't warn anybody about."

"Life doesn't work that way." A gentle smile curved his lips. "We each do what we can, that's all."

"I feel like I just used the lives of thirty people to prove a point to Nick," she argued. "That's crazy."

"But you did save them. When you remembered what would happen, you persevered at great personal risk," he said kindly. "And tomorrow, if you do your best before you go, that's good enough. Things may change or they may stay the same, but you will have left ripples in the sea of history."

Tomorrow… Before you go… Those words went straight to her heart.

"So you're saying that I have to go back tomorrow?"

She opened her mouth, then closed it again. Under the arch, no doubt, after everybody showed up in their assigned places and history took care of itself.

But what about Nick? She couldn't just leave him behind, could she?

"Yes, tomorrow," he echoed. "You seemed very sure that this time wasn't yours and you didn't belong here."

"I am sure," she said impatiently. "But why did you send me here in the first place if I don't belong?"

He peered at her, his blue eyes looking deep into her soul. "Haven't you figured that out yet?"

"Well, maybe. I mean, from the beginning, I guess I assumed I was supposed to save Isabella. But then Nick happened and I got sidetracked and…" She sighed. Everything was so complicated and murky. "I'm just not sure anymore."

"Whether or not you find a way to save Isabella, your time here is almost up." With a small shrug and one last thoughtful glance, the curator turned to leave her.

"That's it? No instructions? No guarantees?" She wasn't being flippant. She really wanted guidance.

But all he said as he ambled away was, "For you, Jordan, it's time to go home."

Which was really no help at all.

17

How to Be a Scandalous Woman, Rule 17:
Lust and love are two sides of the same
scandalous coin.

HOME. Where was that, exactly?

The apartment she'd left behind in 2006 Chicago was
nothing special. She could barely remember what it looked
like, and she'd been gone less than a week. Before that,
she'd occupied a series of equally temporary houses and
apartments. Even when she was little, her mother the poet
didn't like to stay anywhere too long. She got itchy.

So why did Jordan want to go home so badly? Because
she fit there? Because she loved teaching her class and she
had all kinds of wonderful new material for her dissertation
and she couldn't wait to dig in? Which was all dandy, except
for the hole in her heart where Nick should be.

She kept staring into space, thinking about how much fun
it would be to show him things like airplanes and convertibles
and television. Not to mention the thong. She wanted to show
him all the things she loved about her own time and place.

Home. It was a funny concept she couldn't quite wrap
her mind around. Almost time for her to go home? But
where was that?

Well, it wasn't the Tempest house, that was for sure. The

place was grand and imposing, with its turrets and trim, its drawing room dripping in gilt and delicate French furniture. But the house also felt empty.

Maybe that was because it was so quiet with the noisiest of its inhabitants elsewhere. She had no idea where they were, and she tried not to worry about that. Instead, she hunted up pencil and paper in the library, and then she sneaked back upstairs to her room, not really wanting to talk to any of them, anyway.

Her last talk with the curator, whose name she never had gotten, made it seem clear that she was expected to show up at the Women's Building first thing tomorrow morning and somehow avert disaster for Isabella. It wasn't going to be easy. What could she do? How could she make things come out a different way when she didn't know which one was the happy ending?

She'd been lying on her bed in her voluminous night-gown, staring at a blank sheet of paper, for hours. So much for being a planner.

There was a knock on her door. "Jordan?"

It was Nick. Of course it was Nick. Her heart beat faster just hearing his voice.

When she opened the door, he was standing there, his expression unreadable.

He said, "I heard about the Ferris wheel accident."

"That was hours ago," she pointed out. The implication was *If you wanted to come running to tell me you were sorry, you missed your chance.*

"I know but…" Edging back into the hall, he shoved a hand through his soft, dark hair. It was a familiar gesture, one that made her feel all warm and mushy. Just one simple, impatient gesture. How could he have tangled himself so inextricably around her heart in so short a time?

Jordan held herself very still, bracing herself against the doorframe, waiting to hear what would come next.

"I'm sorry," he said finally. "I'm sorry I was stubborn and it took me so long to come around."

Well, that wasn't what she expected. "Really?"

"It was just hard for me to accept. That you might actually be…"

A long pause hung between them.

"From 2006?" she said helpfully.

"I was looking for a word, a term. A time traveler, I suppose." Nick shook his head, speaking slowly, hazily, as he turned away. "It still doesn't seem real. But it has to be. Even from the beginning, there were just too many strange things about you." His head jerked back her direction. "Can you come into my room for a moment?"

"I'm in my nightgown…" She hesitated, but he didn't seem to care about her inappropriate attire. Impatient, he arched an eyebrow, waiting for her answer.

Well, why not? "Okay." Lifting the trailing hem of her gown, she followed him, curious to see what this was all about.

He led her to a small, polished desk set against the wall, and then he tucked a finger into his vest pocket, pulling out a silver coin. He slid open a cubbyhole in the desk, extracting another. Carefully, he set them on the edge of the desk, next to each other. Two coins, alike as peas in a pod.

"What's this?" She searched his face. "You said you didn't steal my Columbian half-dollar."

"I lied."

"But why are there two of them?"

"I don't know." Nick stared down at the twin half-dollars. "I bought mine last May, on my first visit to the exposition. And then, when you appeared, you had one exactly like mine. It was bizarre."

She took one coin in each hand, glancing back and forth between them. "I'll say."

"So I took yours," he admitted, "to compare the two. And they're identical. There is a small scratch across Columbus's eye on both of them. The eight in 1893 is darker than any of the other numbers on both of them. The word *United* is more worn, and in exactly the same way, on both of them."

"Do you think...?" Jordan set the coins down again, backing away. She expected *The Twilight Zone* music to start any time. "I have this weird idea that these are the same coin, that somehow you left it for me, and I found it and brought it back. Does that make any sense? I mean, if I brought the same coin back to 1893 that was already here, would there be two of them? Or just one?"

She began to pace back and forth, her thoughts running wildly. "And then there's the hand sculpture. Your hand. Right over there on your dresser. I found it in a gallery in Chicago a year ago. I don't know why—I didn't know why at the time—but I knew it was Isabella's work. Not just that, but it's *your* hand! How did I know that? Why was I drawn to it? I left it on my bedside table in 2006, came back here, and almost immediately found it again. The coin, your pictures on eBay, the hand... None of this makes sense."

"The mechanics of time travel are not my strong suit," Nick pointed out. "But it makes as much sense as you traveling here from 2006 in the first place."

And now for the $64,000 question, the one that had been driving her crazy ever since she'd arrived. "Why do you think I did?"

"That one's easy." Nick's crooked smile was enough to light up the bedroom. "You came for me."

She'd hadn't known that was the answer until he said it, and then it seemed so clear, so obvious.

Typical Jordan. To ignore what was right in front of her while obsessing over the details. A forest/tree problem. Her chest seemed to tighten. "You're right, Nick. That's exactly why I came."

She leaned in closer, put her arms around him, and simply laid her head on his shoulder. There wasn't the fierce pounding of desire between them this time, but something deeper and even more devastating. She could hear his heartbeat. It was the most beautiful sound she'd ever heard. It told her that for this moment, he was alive and real and standing next to her.

She couldn't ask for more than that.

She had so much to tell him, a lifetime of secrets to share, but she couldn't put that burden on this moment. So she just stood there in the circle of his arms, looking up at him.

His eyes held hers, soft and sure. "Jordan, with the coins, with that click of connection from the very beginning…I think we were meant to find each other, and…"

She waited.

"I think I love you. I think you're wrapped around my heart so tight I can't breathe without you."

She smiled, lifting her mouth to his. "I love you," she whispered right against his lips. "I think I always have. I've been waiting for you forever."

"Forever," he said, and then he slanted his mouth across hers, meeting her in a deep kiss that said everything that needed to be said between them. Passion, belonging, the perfect fit of two people lost in time without each other…

Perfection.

The temperature grew hotter, as it always did when they fanned the flames. Before she realized she was doing it, she was pulling him back to the high feather bed. They scrambled to push aside their clothes and the bed linens and anything in their way.

"I'm supposed to be coming up with a plan for tomorrow," she breathed into his mouth.

"For Bella, you mean?"

"No, it's more than that." Shaky, unhappy, she confessed, "Nick, I have to leave you tomorrow."

"You're sure?"

"I'm sure." Fear gripped her even to think about it.

"But right now, we have today," Nick reminded her. He propped himself up on one elbow, playing with her hair. "We can't think about tomorrow until it comes."

Blocking out the thoughts of leaving, she looped her arms around his neck, pulling him down to her. "Make love to me, Nick. Just you and me, the way it should always have been."

His wicked grin made her think of all kinds of naughty things she'd like to do with him. She smiled, too, willing to take this ride for as long as it lasted.

Purposely light and unconcerned, she announced, "We've only tried out two of the positions on the arch. Would you like to pick one to try next?"

"I'd like to pick all of them to try next," he whispered into her ear, biting down on her earlobe, pulling her on top of him. "What's the one where the lady rides astride the man?"

"I believe that's Artemis, the huntress," she said lazily, "after she's caught Orion and bent him to her will."

"Can you bend me to your will?"

Never one to turn down a challenge, Jordan set her mind to do just that.

There were no barriers, no distractions, no forces of nature conspiring to stop them from playing out their darkest, headiest fantasies as the night wore on, but there was something uneasy, almost frenzied, as they drove the heat higher and made each other beg for mercy. She'd never come so many times, she'd never roused her body for one more try when she was so exhausted, she'd never been this wild and wanton and demanding, but she kept pushing for one more time, one more memory, before tomorrow came.

As they took a brief respite, he lay alongside her, fitting his front to her back, his cock already rising again, ready for another tryst, as he nuzzled her neck. "Isn't there any way you can stay?" he asked.

She knew what he was asking. Her heart breaking, she murmured, "Even if I could, we both know I'm a disaster waiting to happen. I just threw my skirt over a guy's head on the Ferris wheel! I'm scandal personified. And you…" She smiled. "You're Nicholas Bonaventure Tempest."

"Nothing wrong with a bit of well-placed scandal, even for me."

"Not here. Not now. I just don't…fit. And besides, he came right out and told me I have to go home tomorrow. I don't know what would happen if I didn't. The world would end?" It was all too much, too deep to contemplate. She bit her lip, reaching a hand behind her to pull Nick closer. Trying to be brave, she asked, "But what about you coming with me?"

Nick slid her hair away to kiss her neck and shoulder. She couldn't bear to look at him as she made her case, but tried to sound positive. After all, she didn't know any of the rules. Maybe there was a way. There had to be a way.

Threads of full-on panic colored her words. "You would love it, Nick. Things move lightning fast and life is complicated, but wonderful, too. They've sent rockets to the moon, you can drive a car two hundred miles an hour, you can get to Paris or Rome in one night! Music, drama, art, right in your house any time you want it."

Rolling over to face him, she could read his doubt. But she persisted. "If I really did come all this way just to find you, then shouldn't I take you with me? Shouldn't we at least try?"

But Nick didn't answer, just brushed his lips against her shoulder, nudged her thigh with his hardening body, telegraphing his intentions to make love one more time. But instead of the relentless, take-no-prisoners pace of the last few times, he took it very slow. As if they had a lifetime.

She only wished she knew whether they had any chance at that lifetime at all.

This time, after they spent their last shreds of passion, Jordan nestled closer and closed her eyes. She just couldn't fight the exhaustion anymore, drifting into a dreamless sleep.

Dawn had already seeped in the windows when she lifted her head. *Uh-oh.* How late was it? They'd been up all night.

"Nick." She bumped his arm. "Nick, what time is it? We have to go head off Isabella and the whole Susan B. Anthony thing. Nick?"

He turned his sleepy face her way. All he said was something in the area of "mmmph."

"No, Nick, I'm serious, we have to get up."

There was a loud pounding on the door. "Nicholas! I need to speak with you."

"What the hell?" That woke him up. "That's my father. He never comes up here."

"Nicholas, it's an emergency. Isabella and your mother have both left. Nick, I need to speak with you immediately!"

And the door began to open.

"Why didn't you lock it?" Jordan asked as she ducked down under the covers.

Nick stood up, leaving the bed, wrapping himself in the coverlet as he strode toward the door to head off his father.

But it was too late. H. H. Tempest had already wrenched open the door, stomping into the bedroom, pointing at the bed, his face contorted and purple. "What? What? Our household is in shambles and you are too busy to deal with it because you're consorting with that vile young woman!"

Nick was already shepherding his father back out the door. "Yes, well, I can conduct my own private life, thank you. I don't need you in my bedroom at the crack of dawn."

"I don't think you understand me clearly," the older man interrupted, raising his voice even louder, shaking a fist. "We have a crisis. There's no time for you to be dallying with a lightskirt!"

"She is not a lightskirt," Nick shot back, picking up his own volume as he continued to try to maneuver his father. "Whatever this emergency is, I suggest you take yourself back down to the drawing room and I will meet you there after I dress. But there is simply no excuse for barging in on my personal affairs. None. We are going to have to talk about your inappropriate behavior. There are boundaries, sir, and you have crossed that line."

"You dare to reprimand me?"

"When you behave so disgracefully, I have no choice," Nick ground out.

"You call me a disgrace? Well, then," he declared, puffing up his chest, as a vein throbbed in his bright red forehead. "I may have no choice but to ask for your resignation at Tempest & Son. This impertinence cannot stand, boy!"

"I may have no choice but to quit," Nick returned. He was colder and more biting now. "In fact, I've wanted to quit for a very long time. Your store is choking the life out of me."

"How dare you!" At that, Mr. Tempest swallowed thickly, looked as if he had plenty more to say, but instead he suddenly clutched his chest, gasped, "No," and crumpled to the floor.

Nick was at his side immediately, flipping his father over, checking for a pulse.

Jordan bolted upright in the bed. "Is he okay?"

"He's breathing. I don't know." He loosened his father's collar and laid him out more comfortably. "He doesn't seem able to speak."

Oh, no. Jordan pulled on her nightgown, joining him on the floor where he was ministering to his father. "There was nothing about your dad having a heart attack. I swear! This didn't happen the first time, Nick. It's because of me. Because I changed history."

"It's not your fault," Nick assured her. Clearly rattled, he held his hair back with one hand and mumbled, "I'll get him a doctor and I'm sure he will be fine. Fine. I need to find my mother and a doctor."

She squeezed his arm. "I'm sure he'll be okay. He's very strong."

Spinning around, Nick took both of her arms, speaking very intently. "You need to get to the fair to get Isabella, okay? I'll stay here. But you need to go. Get one of the footmen to drive you."

"You really think…?"

"Yes," he said quickly. "Even if there is bad blood

between them at present, Bella will want to know. And if
the scandal still erupts, with her arrest, at the same time my
father is ill, it will only make things worse. Please, Jordan.
Do what you can."

"Well, okay. Are you sure?"

"Yes, quite." He'd grabbed a pillow to stick under his
father's head and he was pulling on his pants and hitting
the servant's buzzer, doing a million things at once.

Jordan backed away. Heart attacks, disappearances,
staying, going, leaving Nick, taking Nick… Crises at every
turn. Still, she didn't think she was helping here. On automatic pilot, she ran to her own room and threw on her
clothes. One more trip to the fair. One more up-close-and-
personal meeting with destiny.

The footman drove hell-bent for leather, bless his heart,
and she raced as fast as she could through the gates, down
the midway and up the stairs of the Women's Building. But
she knew as soon as she rounded the corner to the second-
floor gallery that she was too late.

Mrs. Stanhope and Susan B. Anthony were already
there, along with a cluster of other ladies who must be from
the Board of Lady Managers, and they had clearly already
seen the arch. Across from them stood Isabella, looking
angry and perturbed, her mother and Count Franco, who
had no business there whatsoever.

Who knew all those people would be here? *Oh, God.* It
was Susan B. Anthony. She looked like a sweet old woman
in a black dress with little blue flowers all over it. Susan
B. Anthony. Right there.

Jordan raised a shaky hand to her forehead. She needed
to somehow defuse this and get Mrs. Tempest and Isabella
aside, to tell them the bad news about H.H. But how, when
they were in the middle of a very nasty argument?

"Excuse me," she tried, but no one even looked her way. They were all talking over each other, gesticulating and pointing.

"This is disgraceful!" Mrs. Stanhope declared, pressing a handkerchief to her mouth. "Simply disgraceful!"

"I don't know," Mrs. Tempest said in a quavering voice. "I think you may be—"

"Maude, I don't know how you could have allowed your daughter—"

"I am an artist!"

"Shocking!"

"Indecent!"

"Disgraceful!"

If she lived the rest of her life without ever hearing the word disgraceful again, Jordan knew she would be a happy woman. She waved a hand to get Mrs. Tempest's attention, but it wasn't working.

"I completely agree with you, Mrs. Stanhope," Franco said in his oily tone. "This kind of thing should not be in your lovely Women's Building. If it pleases you, Mrs. Stanhope, I will be happy to go for the authorities myself, yes?"

"Franco! How could you?" Isabella cried.

So Franco was the one who got her arrested? Spurned lover taking revenge. It all made perfect sense.

"If I were you, young lady, I would watch my tone," Mrs. Stanhope sniffed. "You have embarrassed us in front of our distinguished visitor and we shall never live down this infamy!"

"That is enough, Portia!" Mrs. Tempest stepped right in front of the arch. She'd gone from anxious and tentative to a warrior in a split second. "You know as well as I do that this is a beautiful work of art. You will not speak to my daughter this way."

There was a stunned silence.

Hands on her hips, she continued, "I would like to ask our distinguished visitor what she thinks. So, Mrs. Anthony, are you as outraged as all the others? It seems to me that you have always admitted that women are passionate and sensual creatures. It seems to me that you might admire Isabella's work. Is that so?"

The dignified lady in the flowered dress chose her words carefully. "I think there is real talent here," she said finally. "I would rather see ten statues like this than one glorifying the manly virtues of violence and bloodshed. That is my opinion."

"Ha!" Maude Tempest snapped, "So you see, there will be no need for any authorities."

"Nicely done," Jordan said under her breath. The entire controversy had just been nipped in the bud. One protective mama pushing the right buttons in Susan B. Anthony, and it was all over.

Beaming, Isabella lifted her chin. "I'm so pleased that my mother saw fit to stand behind my efforts." She touched her heart. "So pleased."

Jordan was feeling a little choked up herself.

"I think," Isabella went on, "I shall stay in Chicago and create many more beautiful pieces, just for Chicago museums." She turned to Franco. "If you still want to purchase this one, I'll sell it to you. But be warned, it will not come cheap."

He wrinkled his lips as he considered her offer. "I accept. You name your price and I will meet it. My men will be here this afternoon to crate it up for me. And then everybody is happy, yes?"

Everybody except me, Jordan thought. *And Nick. And, of course, his father.*

Not sure how to broach it, how to turn the moment of triumph into one of possible tragedy, she moved up behind Nick's mother, tapping her gently on the sleeve. "I'm sorry, Mrs. Tempest," she ventured. "I need to speak with you."

"Jordan, my dear! I am so happy to see you," Mrs. Tempest said with a good deal of enthusiasm. "I must tell you, I felt emboldened by your influence, and you see the results. I have taken on Portia Stanhope and told her what's what. I must say, it feels wonderful!"

"You were amazing, Mrs. Tempest." She smiled. "But I'm not here because of that. I came to tell you... I'm afraid I have bad news."

The older woman composed her face quickly. "What is it? Not Nick? Nothing's happened to Nick?"

"No, no, Nick's fine." She paused. "This is about Mr. Tempest. He's..." What could she say? How to put it? "He's not well," she said delicately. "I'm not sure exactly what happened, but he fell ill suddenly this morning. Nick is with him and taking good care of him. But Nick wanted you and Isabella to know as soon as possible."

The two Tempests were running for the doors before she'd even finished. "Wait, I need to come with you," she tried. "I need to..."

Breaking off, unable to finish that thought, Jordan put her hand over her heart. Was it still beating? She felt as if she'd just plunged off the top of a high building without a safety net.

At times, this whole escapade had felt like just that, like fun and games, a chance to play Scarlet Woman in the White City, to be someone she'd never been before. But now, faced with leaving, she felt like curling up on the floor under the arch and weeping.

She took a deep breath, forcing herself to finish what

she hadn't wanted to say. She said again, "I need to come with you. I need to say goodbye."

Left unspoken was the most important part. *I need to say goodbye to the love of my life.*

18

How to Be a Scandalous Woman, Rule 18:
It's not whether you win or lose; it's who shares
your bed at the end of the day.

"IT'S THE BEST THING," Jordan said quietly.

Nick didn't say a word, but she took his hand. As they stood out on Prairie Avenue, in front of the grand Tempest mansion, she knew that the doctor was with his father, and his mother and Isabella had just gone up there, as well.

Biting her lip, trying not to cry or make things any worse, she told him, "I couldn't stay here, anyway, and we didn't know if you could come with me." She smiled weakly. "Face it, you're pretty attached to your family, and this way you can stay and run the store without your dad's interference. He'll be too busy recuperating to bother you. Maybe you'll even end up marrying Lydia and creating one awesome department store. I hope I told you how much I love your store."

That did it. Hot tears started to fall.

"Jordan, please," he whispered, brushing away a drop of moisture on her cheek with his thumb.

She squared her shoulders and tried to be sensible. She didn't want his last memory of her to be all sloppy and emotional. "I have to go back and finish Isabella's story. My mission is complete. Really."

"I don't want you to go."

"I don't have a choice. The arch will be leaving for Italy tonight." She licked her lip. "It has to be now."

"I know. I'm sorry."

They both knew what he was apologizing for. With his father's medical emergency, he'd been sucked back into the store, even more inextricably than before. If there was a chance for him to come to the future with her, he couldn't take it.

"But the good news is," she said, laughing through the tears, "that Isabella is saved, she wasn't arrested, your mother has acquired an amazing set of cojones, and all should be right with the world. And hey…" She laughed again, reaching inside her cloak to pat her pocket. "I've got my lucky coin. So I'm good."

"Jordan…" He reached for her, but she knew if she gave in, she would be lost.

Breaking away, she jumped into the waiting carriage, not bothering to wait for him to lift her in like a proper lady. In this world, she had arrived as a hoyden and an etiquette nightmare, so she might as well leave that way, too. "Promise me, Nick, whatever you do, don't get involved in car racing. Promise me," she called out as the carriage pulled her away. She twisted to watch his figure get smaller and smaller and then disappear from view.

Steeling herself, she turned back to the road. Back to her future. Even if at the moment, any future without Nick seemed grimmer and lonelier that she even wanted to contemplate. She'd never really thought about all those people in the world who kept going, kept putting one foot in front of the other, did what had to be done, even when their hearts were in pieces. Maybe her heart had never really been in play before.

But she couldn't think about that now, or she would order the footman to turn the carriage around and take her back to Prairie Avenue, back to her one shot at love.

"I could never live in that house, or with all those rules and restrictions. I would die," she murmured to herself. "But Nick would be so good in my world. He would fit, the way I don't in his. If only…"

But it was too late for that. The arch was going to disappear, and her ticket to 2006 had to be punched before that happened.

Once again, she went straight for the Women's Building as soon as she got to the fair. And as she knew he would be, the curator was already there, waiting.

"Well?" she asked him, peeling off Susan B. Anthony's purloined cloak to reveal her old denim miniskirt and silk camisole. She folded the coat over her arm, trying to be brave. Funny, she didn't feel brave at all. "I'm ready whenever you are."

"Take the leap of faith," he said with a smile, making a broad sweep with one arm of his Columbian blue uniform.

Taking a deep breath, Jordan closed her eyes, settled one hand on Apollo's fine butt, and threw herself headlong under the arch.

She felt herself falling through space, whirling and turning, just like before, but this time she didn't hit her head when she landed. There was a slight thump, she felt the floor hard underneath her, and she opened her eyes.

The curator was staring down at her, his mild blue eyes crinkling in the corners.

"Didn't it work?" she asked, sitting up. She was still carrying Susan B. Anthony's cloak.

He helped her to her feet, handing her the bright yellow messenger bag she'd left behind.

"Here you are, Miss Albright, good as new and back where you belong," he said cheerfully.

"So it is 2006?"

He nodded.

Why was that idea so disheartening? She'd been through so much, only to end up back where she started, no better off, no hero, no *anything*. Except alone.

Disoriented, she gazed around her. Isabella's arch was right back where she remembered, in the narrow, stuffy hallway crowded with statuary. But the glow was done, its erotic power dimmed.

"Why does it seem so different now?"

"History is a fluid concept," he said, patting her shoulder. "No time has elapsed since you left, and yet many things have changed. Interesting, isn't it?"

Maybe more frightening than interesting, but she was already going through her messenger bag to find her aspirin and her iPod and all the things she'd missed. And, of course, her pictures of Nick.

But they weren't there. "Damn it," she muttered, searching more frantically. "I need those pictures. I need to be able to see him. What am I going to do without the pictures?" She went back through everything in the bag. The photos just weren't there.

This was too much to bear. Not even a picture to remind her? Losing him seemed so final now.

She sank to the floor under the arch, clasping her bag to her chest. "I thought I made the right choice, the only choice. But what have I done? I wiped Nick out of my life?"

Maybe she should go through the messenger bag again, just to be sure. But when she did, she suddenly noticed that her key ring was different. She rifled through her wallet, checkbook, all of it. Good heavens, her driver's license had changed! She had a new address.

It was *The Twilight Zone* all over again. Everything around her seemed perfectly normal for a summer evening in the city and time she knew. And yet not normal at all.

Stumbling out of the Art Institute, Jordan couldn't help heading straight for Tempest & Trent. She'd know immediately if he'd married Lydia, because the Trent name would be on the store.

"Oh, my God." She stood on State Street, in the middle of the bustling crowd, looking up at an office building and bookstore. No Tempest & Trent. No Tempest department store at all. It just wasn't there. Grandma taking her to see Santa and the windows, all her memories of the store, were wiped out as if they'd never happened.

"How does a whole store disappear?" she whispered.

"Jordan?"

Hearing her name, she turned to the passerby standing next to her on the sidewalk. Oh, no. Daniel. Of all people to run into at this particular moment.

What did you say to the man you left behind, after you traveled through time and had the affair of a lifetime? *Well, I'm sorry I cheated on you, but then, I never really thought about you the whole time I was there, so that's not cheating, is it? Plus, you know, now I know what love really is, and it wasn't you, so let's let bygones be bygones, shall we?*

Ouch.

"Are you okay?" he asked.

She noticed for the first time that he looked different. It wasn't anything she could put her finger on, but his hair, or maybe his glasses…

"I thought that was you when I saw you there," he said awkwardly. "Do you remember meeting me at Professor McNulty's party? It's been some time, but… Well, we met. Exchanged pleasantries, you know. It is Jordan, isn't it? Jordan…Albert? No, wait. Albright. Like Madeleine. You're in the History department. I'm, uh, in Econ."

Her eyes widened as she tried to process the information. So she wasn't with Daniel anymore? That had changed, too?

"I'm sorry," he said suddenly, backing away as he took in her befuddled expression. "Clearly you don't remember me."

"No, no, I do," she assured him. "Of course I know you. Daniel."

"Right." He nodded. "You looked kind of, I don't know, upset or confused. I thought I could help. Seeing as how we met and talked at that party. But, you know, if it's nothing I can help with…"

"It's nothing you can help with," she told him slowly. She wasn't sure how to feel watching Daniel walk away. In this new incarnation of her life, he didn't even know her, and it didn't bother her all that much. How very strange.

"Excuse me," she said suddenly, turning to a lady carrying several shopping bags down State Street. "Did there used to be a store here? Tempest & Trent?"

"You're thinking of Marshall Field's," the lady volunteered. "Or Carson's. Just down the street. Both of them have been here forever."

"No, I want Tempest & Trent. Or Tempest & Son. It was right here," she insisted.

"Sorry, hon. No such animal in Chicago."

No such animal.

It was only the beginning of the craziness.

Her apartment? Wasn't hers anymore. When she left State Street and went to the address on her driver's license, she found a beautiful historic house in Hyde Park, small but exquisite, the kind of place she could never have afforded in her wildest dreams. And her key fit the door!

Feeling like a burglar, she sneaked quietly up the stairs, poking into three beautiful bedrooms. One of them had a carved mahogany four-poster that looked very much like what she'd left behind at the Tempest house, and when she opened the door of the closet, she jumped back. Her clothes were in the closets!

Stumbling to the next door, she discovered it wasn't a bedroom at all, but a studio, or maybe a gallery. It was full of white marble sculptures, displayed on pillars and shelves. The hand! Nick's hand was there. Thank God. She still had some piece of him.

But where did all this stuff come from?

Downstairs, she found a rolltop desk, full of financial papers and documents. Her bank account seemed to have multiplied itself while she was gone. She had stocks and bonds and a portfolio, not to mention the art collecction upstairs that was mostly Isabella's work, and incredibly valuable.

How did it happen? She had no idea. In a daze, she stumbled from room to room, cataloguing the contents of the house, the contents of her life. She almost jumped out of her skin when the phone rang.

"Hello?" she ventured, not sure who it might be in this alternate reality. A best friend she'd never met? Maybe her keeper from the loony bin, trying to figure out where she'd wandered off to?

"Hi, J. It's Mom."

"Mom?" She started to get teary. She'd never been close to her mother, but she realized now that she'd actually missed her. No matter what, her mother accepted her. Traditional, rebellious, scandalous, perfectly boring, her mom had always liked her just the way she was. Now that she'd been to 1893 and back, that was a very welcome quality. "It's so good to hear your voice."

"Aw, you, too. I just wanted to tell you that I'm going to be in Chicago for a few days next week. I'm reading some of my poems at an erotica conference. Want to get together?"

Before her trip through time, she would've made some excuse. Too busy, too focused, too whatever, to see her unconventional, embarrassing mother. But now… "I would love to. Can I come hear your poems?"

"Absolutely," her mother said happily. "And I would love to come to one of your classes. Your Scandalous Women class sounds so exciting. So perfect for you, Jordan. Did you find that piece you were looking for? The arch?"

"Yes, yes, I did." So she was still teaching her class at any rate. And the arch was still important to her. She breathed a small sigh of relief. What was stranger than that was that she had apparently shared some of that information with her mother. Not so estranged after all, it seemed.

It was weird to finally accept your place in the world this way, just when everything you knew about it was ripped out from under you.

After the conversation with her mom, she lay on the bed in her new bedroom for a good long time, looking up at the cupids painted on the ceiling. It was like some weird hybrid of *then* and *now,* except *now* wasn't the *now* she'd left behind.

With everything still mostly a blur, she got up, took a shower in her gorgeous new bathroom, dressed in clothes from her new closet, and found she had a car, a pretty little red roadster, in the garage attached to her house. And a key on her ring fit the ignition. So very strange....

Jordan drove right to campus, not at all sure her office would still be there. And yet it was. It still had her name on the door and everything.

But when she fired up her computer, she noticed immediately that her screensaver was gone.

Her dissertation, however, was right where she left it. Except, of course, there were no longer scanned clippings about Nick's wedding or engagement or his death. She hoped that meant he'd heeded the warning to stay away from the fateful car race.

"Please, Nick. I want to find out that you got away from the store, maybe climbed Mount Everest or helped the Wright brothers..."

But she didn't find anything like that.

As the days passed, she went through every scrap of paper meticulously, revising and reshaping the whole project, and she redid all her research on the Tempest family. It was painstaking work, and it took a lot of time to reconnect the threads of what had happened to them all.

Just yesterday, she'd found a small obituary for Henry Horatio Tempest, who'd quietly died in his bed in Venezuela in 1917. "American expatriate, former department store owner," it said. That was all.

So far, she had found no evidence that Isabella had married Tad or moved to Japan, but she did find records of several trips to Italy, accompanied by her mother, who was referred to as "a noted spokeswoman for women's suffrage." Well, that was different.

But she couldn't find even one mention of Nick anywhere. Nothing.

More days passed, and she didn't know what to do. She found herself visiting the "Sex Through the Ages" exhibit again and again, looking for her friendly curator. But he never seemed to be there. Finally, she had to stay away. Seeing the arch made her too sad, too needy, and it brought back way too many memories. Besides, a sign was posted at the entrance to the gallery now, warning museum-goers that the exhibit would be crated up to leave Chicago soon. That, too, made her sad, as if, when it was gone, the exhibit would take away any last hope that she had of ever recapturing her strange vacation in time at the White City.

She was already getting used to her new reality, the house, the car, the art collection, the money in the bank… Would there be a day when she forgot that it didn't used to be this way, that there was a time when she was plain old Jordan Albright, poor grad student desperate to finish her dissertation, the one who'd never heard of Nick Tempest?

So she buried herself in research, looking for more clues about what had happened to the Tempests. Staring at old microfilms was making her go blind, so she almost didn't believe her eyes when an ad from a June, 1894, edition of the *Chicago Tribune* suddenly popped up in front of her. She thought she saw her name.

"Huh. That's the day Nick was supposed to get married."

She scrolled back. It was a fairly large ad, bordered in black.

NOTICE. All parties desirous of making claims against

Messrs. Jordan & Albright, late of this city, should apply at the Arch Street address.

She read and reread the words. Her heart started to beat faster. Could it be a message from Nick? Jordan, Albright, arch… But what was he trying to tell her?

Did he want her to try to get back to him through the arch?

Whatever it meant, she'd better figure it out quickly, because the "Sex Through the Ages" exhibit was already being packed up to travel to the next city on its schedule.

Clutching a photocopy of the ad, she hopped on the train and raced back to the Art Institute, tracing the familiar path up to the Beckwith Gallery.

She saw a blue uniform, and she ran straight for him. "You need to unpack the arch," she said desperately, wasting no time on preliminaries. "I need to go back for Nick."

"But, my dear, your arch isn't packed yet." He beamed at her. "I was wondering if you would arrive in time."

Strangely, there was a small plaque next to the arch that she hadn't noticed before. It read "On loan from the Tempest & Albright Collection."

"Back in 1893, Nick and I are collecting art?" she asked, mystified.

"Not in 1893. Now," he said with a mysterious smile.

"Now?"

But there was no time to ponder the issue. As she stood there, clutching the mysterious ad, there was a rumble, a kind of a ripping sound, and a blast of white light. It was too bright—she had to look away—squeezing her eyes shut and stumbling back a step. Yeow. The noise got louder, the light got brighter and a wind suddenly whipped up, a warm, balmy breeze that ruffled her hair.

She forced her eyes open, just in time to see a black-clad body—a man's body—come tumbling through the arch from the other side.

Her jaw dropped to the floor. Nick was lying practically on top of her feet. Nick. *Her* Nick!

She scrambled down to pull him into her lap, kissing him and pelting him with questions. "How did you do this? Are you sure? All you all right?"

Running her hands all over him, she checked to make sure he was all there. She had visions of molecules stuck in 1893, bits and pieces in limbo… Nothing was missing, though. Nick! Her Nick! Dear, sweet, wonderful Nick. Here! She just couldn't believe it was real.

He was laughing and kissing her back and doing his best to fend off her searching hands. "I'm fine, I'm fine. I'm here. That's what's important."

"But how did you know when to come and how to get here? How did you find the arch? Did Franco take it?"

"Yes. The last time I saw it, it was in Milan. That was shortly before I leaped under it, of course. Your curator, the funny fellow in the uniform, told me to go after it," he told her. "I was still at Tempest & Son then, and he appeared as one of our security guards."

"Really?"

"Yes. I looked around one day, and there he was, giving me all sorts of instructions." Nick got to his feet, dusting himself off. "Strange way to travel, by arch."

"I know, but… What about the curator?" She looked around. The man seemed to have vanished from this time and place again. Who knew where he'd got off to this time. He was so unhelpful when it came right down to it. "What did he tell you?"

"He told me you were waiting. He told me it was high

time I stopped moping around and did something for my-self." He caught Jordan back in his arms, holding her tight. "Not so different from what you always told me. I was in a blue funk then—this was after we discovered that my father had faked the whole heart attack."

"He *what?*"

"Yes, I'm afraid so. The old reprobate. I guess he thought it was the only way he could continue to control us."

No wonder she couldn't find any information on his illness. "Nick, that's awful."

He shrugged.

"Once my mother discovered the charade, she took Isabella and Tadahito to Italy with her for an extended tour." He kissed her quickly, pulling her to him, before going on. "The family money was really hers, and she left him pretty much high and dry."

"But did that leave you high and dry, also?" Jordan asked. She was having trouble believing all of this, even if it did connect the dots. Mrs. Tempest turned into a major suffragette, Isabella creating more art, Mr. Tempest in exile... Ripples in history, indeed.

"I tried to resurrect the store. No," he told her, putting a finger across her lips, "not by going anywhere near Lydia. After I'd had you, I would never have resigned myself to that fate. I did, however, disregard your advice about the motor carriages."

"You did?"

He grinned as he dropped a kiss on the top of her head. "I invested in Mr. Mercedes and Mr. Benz, since you mentioned they were going to be fairly successful."

"Is that how all the money showed up in my accounts? You left me your Mercedes-Benz stock?"

His smile widened. "That and some other investments. I had to prepare for my journey, didn't I? I couldn't come empty-handed."

"Oh, Nick, you could've come stark naked, without a penny to your name, and I would've been ecstatic to see you." She closed her eyes and squeezed him tight, just for a moment, listening to his heart beat next to her ear. It meant he was real, he was here, and she could hold him again. Who could ask for more?

But when she opened her eyes, she saw that Nick's expression had grown cloudier. "Working at the store, I felt as if I were dying inside a little more every day. Isabella and Mother were both in Europe, you were gone... I knew I couldn't stay there. I had to find you. So I did."

"You did." She hugged him hard enough to imprint every contour of his body on her memory.

But Nick was looking around the exhibit over her head. "I can't believe I'm here."

"Me, either. I have missed you so much." Framing his wonderful face with her hands, she covered his mouth with hers, igniting all the passion and joy she'd been repressing since she last saw him.

"I'm anxious to see 2006," he said happily. "I want to see airplanes and TB."

"Tuberculosis? Oh, you mean *TV.* Television." She suddenly had a tinge of worry. "My dissertation is a mess and you don't have a career, a family, anything."

"But I have you." Nick grinned. "I don't know what we're going to do. Isn't that part of the fun? Wait, I brought you something."

He poked into his pocket, and she thought sure he would come out with his Columbian half-dollar. Instead, it was a huge ruby ring. The Burmese Red Devil, if she wasn't mistaken.

"I thought you might like it," he said simply.

"But…" She blinked. A priceless ruby. A priceless statue. No, he didn't arrive empty-handed.

He smiled, and she shook her head, wrapping her arms around Nick and holding on tight. She'd had to lose 113 years to find her heart, but it was worth every moment.

Now, in Nick's embrace where she knew she was meant to be, life felt great. In fact, it felt *perfect*.

"Are you ready to jump into 2006?" she asked him. "It may be scary."

"I'm counting on it," he said with a definite spark of mischief in his eye. "I can't wait."

He swooped down and kissed her again, hard and fast and indisputably *Nick*. Behind him, she could see the marble arch pulsing with life and sensual beauty. Her life had never had this much *life* in it. It was simply amazing.

Jordan clasped Nick's hand securely in her own, ready to take the leap. "What do you say we go find our future, Nick?"

"OH, NO!"

The reaction slipped out before Emma Valentine could stop it, for there stood the very man she most wanted to avoid seeing again.

He didn't look any happier to see her.

"Well, come on, get on board," he said gruffly. "I won't bite." One eyebrow rose. "Though I might nibble a little," he added, mostly to amuse himself.

But she wasn't paying any attention to what he was saying. She was staring at him, taking in the royal blue uniform he was wearing, with gold braid and glistening badges decorating the sleeves, epaulettes and an upright collar. Ribbons and medals covered the breast of the short, fitted jacket. A gold-encrusted sabre hung at his side. And suddenly it was clear to her who this man really was.

She gulped wordlessly. Reaching out, he took her elbow and pulled her aboard. The doors slid closed. And finally she found her tongue.

"You...you're the prince."

He nodded, barely glancing at her. "Yes. Of course."

She raised a hand and covered her mouth for a moment. "I should have known."

"Of course you should have. I don't know why you didn't." He punched the ground-floor button to get the elevator moving again, then turned to look down at her. "A relatively bright five-year-old child would have tumbled to the truth right away."

Her shock faded as her indignation at his tone asserted itself. He might be the prince, but he was still just as annoying as he had been earlier that day.

"A relatively bright five-year-old child without a bump on the head from a badly thrown water polo ball, maybe," she said defensively. She wasn't feeling woozy any longer and she wasn't about to let him bully her, no matter how royal he was. "I was unconscious half the time."

"And just clueless the other half, I guess," he said, looking bemused.

The arrogance of the man was really galling.

"I suppose you think your 'royalness' is so obvious it sort of shimmers around you for all to see?" she challenged. "Or better yet, oozes from your pores like…like sweat on a hot day?"

"Something like that," he acknowledged calmly. "Most people tumble to it pretty quickly. In fact, it's hard to hide even when I want to avoid dealing with it."

"Poor baby," she said, still resenting his manner. "I guess that works better with injured people who are half asleep." Looking at him, she felt a strange emotion she couldn't identify. It was as though she wanted to prove something to him, but she wasn't sure what. "And anyway, you know you did your best to fool me," she added.

His brows knit together as though he really didn't know what she was talking about. "I didn't do a thing."

"You told me your name was Monty."

"It is." He shrugged. "I have a lot of names. Some of them are too rude to be spoken to my face, I'm sure." He glanced at her sideways, his hand on the hilt of his sabre. "Perhaps you're contemplating one of those right now."

You bet I am.

That was what she would like to say. But it suddenly occurred to her that she was supposed to be working for this man. If she wanted to keep the job of coronation chef, maybe she'd better keep her opinions to herself. So she clamped her mouth shut, took a deep breath and looked away, trying hard to calm down.

The elevator ground to a halt and the doors slid open laboriously. She moved to step forward, hoping to make her escape, but his hand shot out again and caught her elbow.

"Wait a minute. *You're* a woman," he said, as though that thought had just presented itself to him.

"That's a rare ability for insight you have there, Your Highness," she snapped before she could stop herself. And then she winced. She was going to have to do better than that if she was going to keep this relationship on an even keel.

But he was ignoring her dig. Nodding, he stared at her with a speculative gleam in his golden eyes. "I've been looking for a woman, but you'll do."

She blanched, stiffening. "I'll do for what?"

He made a head gesture in a direction she knew was opposite of where she was going and his grip tightened on her elbow.

"Come with me," he said abruptly, making it an order.

She dug in her heels, thinking fast. She didn't much like orders. "Wait! I can't. I have to get to the kitchen."

"Not yet. I need you."

"You what?" Her breathless gasp of surprise was soft, but she knew he'd heard it.

"I need you," he said firmly. "Oh, don't look so shocked. I'm not planning to throw you into the hay and have my way with you. I need you for something a bit more mundane than that."

She felt color rushing into her cheeks and she silently begged it to stop. Here she was, formless and stodgy in her chef's whites. No makeup, no stiletto heels. Hardly the picture of the femmes fatales he was undoubtedly used to. The likelihood that he would have any carnal interest in her was remote at best. To have him think she was hysterically defending her virtue was humiliating.

"Well, what if I don't want to go with you?" she said in hopes of deflecting his attention from her blush.

"Too bad."

"What?"

Amusement sparkled in his eyes. He was certainly enjoying this. And that only made her more determined to resist him.

"I'm the prince, remember? And we're in the castle. My orders take precedence. It's that old pesky divine rights thing."

Her jaw jutted out. Despite her embarrassment, she couldn't let that pass.

"Over my free will? Never!"

Exasperation filled his face.

"Hey, call out the historians. Someone will write a book about you and your courageous principles." His eyes glittered sardonically. "But in the meantime, Emma Valentine, you're coming with me."

If you enjoyed what you just read,
then we've got an offer you can't resist!

Take 2 bestselling
love stories FREE!
Plus get a FREE surprise gift!

Silhouette® Desire®

**Introducing an exciting appearance
by legendary
New York Times bestselling author**

DIANA PALMER
HEARTBREAKER

He's the ultimate bachelor...
but he may have just met
the one woman to change his ways!

Join the drama in the story of a confirmed
bachelor, an amnesiac beauty and their
unexpected passionate romance.

"Diana Palmer is a mesmerizing storyteller
who captures the essence of what
a romance should be."—*Affaire de Coeur*

Heartbreaker *is available from Silhouette Desire
in September 2006.*

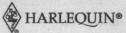

HARLEQUIN®

COMING NEXT MONTH

#273 MY ONLY VICE Elizabeth Bevarly

Rosie Bliss has a little thing for the police chief. Okay, it's more than a *little* thing. But when she propositions the guy, she gets a mixed message. His hands say yes, while his mouth says no. Lucky for her, she's a little hard of hearing....

#274 FEAR OF FALLING Cindi Myers
It Was a Dark And Sexy Night... Bk. 1

As erotic artist John Sartain's business manager, Natalie Brighton has no intention of falling for him...even though something about him fascinates her. But when mysterious things start happening to her, she has to wonder if that fascination is worth her life...

#275 INDULGE Nancy Warren
For a Good Time, Call... Bk. 2

What happens when you eat dessert...before dinner? Mercedes and J. D.'s relationship is only about sex—hot and plenty of it. Suddenly the conservative lawyer wants to change the rules and start over with a *date!* What gives?

#276 JUST TRUST ME... Jacquie D'Alessandro
Adrenaline Rush, Bk. 2

Kayla Watson used to like traveling on business. But that was before her boss insisted she spy on scientist Brett Thorne on his trek into the Andes mountains. Now she's tired, dirty...and seriously in lust with sexy Brett. Lucky for her, he's lusting after her, too. But will it last when he finds out why she's there?

#277 THE SPECIALIST Rhonda Nelson
Men Out of Uniform, Bk. 2

All's fair in love and war. That's Emma Langsford's motto. So when she's given the assignment of recovering a priceless military antique, nothing's going to stop her. And if sexy Brian Payne, aka The Specialist, gets in her way, she has ways of distracting him....

#278 ANYTHING FOR YOU Sarah Mayberry
It's All About Attitude

Delaney Michaels has loved Sam Kirk forever...but the man is too dense to notice! She wants more from life than this, so she's breaking free of Sam to start over. But just as she's making a clean getaway, he counters with a seductive suggestion she can't refuse!

www.eHarlequin.com

HBCNM0806